# POWERPLAY

PARINDA JOSHI

Published by
**FiNGERPRINT!**
An imprint of Prakash Books India Pvt. Ltd.

113/A, Darya Ganj, New Delhi-110 002,
Tel: (011) 2324 7062 – 65, Fax: (011) 2324 6975
Email: info@prakashbooks.com/sales@prakashbooks.com

facebook www.facebook.com/fingerprintpublishing
twitter www.twitter.com/FingerprintP, www.fingerprintpublishing.com
For manuscript submissions, e-mail: fingerprintsubmissions@gmail.com





ISBN: 978 81 7234 457 3

Processed & printed in India

To my mother
and her mother—with love

Watching his favourite IGL team in action always left Vivek feeling frustrated, enormously so. The team's fate had remained unchanged even after three years into the league, so much so that the media had unofficially conferred the title 'Official Losers of the League' on them. But, today, their game was touching an all-new low that was shocking even for them!

"Damn!" Vivek exploded, his face turning beetroot red. His eyes were following the star player of his chosen team, the faltering Ahmedabad Rangers. "Bloody incompetent son of a—" he growled, checking himself just in time.

Vivek was at Manny's, a trendy sports bar in Colaba. It was an ordinary Friday evening turned exciting or not—depending on the team one was rooting for—because of the match. The year's IGL, Indian Gamers' League, season had commenced and, today, the Southern Kings were crushing the Ahmedabad Rangers, one ball at a time. Literally and otherwise.

The captain and ace batsman of the Rangers, Janak Goyal, who went by the moniker Jango, was no ordinary piece of flesh and bones; he was the sole player the Rangers could count on when their worst loss was in sight. And tonight seemed well on its way to be qualified for that.

The tail end of the game was in progress, as was visible on the forty-odd high definition television screens in the bar. Adding to the woes of the Rangers, Jango missed another ball, eliciting a yelp from Vivek and a jubilant *'cheers!'* from others. "This is outrageous! He should quit the game and teach a *dandiya* class. Just look at his moves. Pathetic!" he fumed, thumping a solid fist on the mahogany bar table. Vivek let his gaze flick over the people in the bar. *Manny's can't boast of diversity tonight, its testosterone-charged atmosphere won't allow that*, he mused to himself. Amidst a flurry of official calls, e-mails, and text messages, which largely defined his evenings, he focused his attention back to the screen installed right across from him, murmuring, "Something's gotta give, baby."

Like a raging rhino, the bowler from the Kings zoomed towards Jango, hurling at him what appeared to be a full-toss. *Jango makes a living out of knocking these balls right over the boundary; this was going to be easy for him*, he thought to himself and smiled. But the pressure seemed to weigh too heavily on his shoulders. Jango mistimed the hit, and the ball, instead of soaring over the ground, ballooned up fifteen feet in the air and landed just a few feet from where the batsman stood. *Shit.* The bowler turned and pumped his fist. Though more than three overs remained, the smile on his face as he jogged towards his team's captain explained everything: *the Rangers were dead meat!*

"This team is going to the dogs. They are going to need a makeover to survive," a defeated Vivek vented at Omar, his young co-worker and company for the evening. Omar didn't look like someone who'd been chewing the insides of his cheeks or even bouncing his legs nervously, for that matter, while watching the game. In fact, the man had been happily sipping on his drink, marked tranquility reflecting off his face. *What an inordinately dispassionate joker*, Vivek thought to himself.

"Too bad. In their first year, they kicked some serious butt. Anyway, they have still got the sexiest cheerleaders. Some saving grace," Omar gave his two cents while playing with his smartphone.

An ardent lover of the sport, Vivek took cricket personally and the Rangers, even more so. It was a long-cherished dream of his to mix these two passions—cricket and work. He'd been persistently on the look out for an opportunity to work in sports, to drum up his business in this new domain—a domain his company, unfortunately, didn't specialise in. But he hadn't found a valid-enough reason to confess that to a roomful of men in his swanky Cuffe Parade office in South Mumbai. Not that it was necessary to bare his soul to them. So he played along, looking content with the industries they offered their services to. As it is he was deemed a shark—the youngest shark as colleagues unequivocally referred to him as—ever since he had been conferred the Vice President title at thirty-two, in his small but rather influential company of M&A named Cello Consulting. What made Cello unique was that it only hired from Indian Management Institute, Ahmedabad—the most coveted of B-schools in the country.

The Rangers were now trailing by seventy-eight runs with just two high-strung overs left to go. Jango, their only hope against an inglorious defeat, had departed for the pavilion, and with the six-foot tail-ender at the crease missing a ball, there wasn't even a bleak hope left for an abrupt change of luck. The Rangers were done for.

"If they lose, I'm out of here. Gone; before *you* lose it," Omar said, tongue firmly in cheek. Vivek recognised the dig for what it was; his emotional outbursts, the past few times the Rangers had lost, being played up by his underling. Or not? After all, he had cursed, yelled, and, forsaking everything else, done nothing but hurl the choicest abuses he could think of at the screen. It wasn't a night he was very proud of.

"Let's get out of here. I have a seven a.m. meeting to run tomorrow," he said, effectively bringing that part of the conversation to an end. Taking a few swigs of his fifth beer of the evening he rendered the mug empty and signalled the bartender to close the tab. An oblong grin appeared on Omar's face. He was the newest blood in consulting and invariably appeared delighted when someone offered to dole out the money.

A faint drizzle of the off-season rain greeted both men as they stepped out of the noisy, crowded bar. Vivek carelessly brushed off a few drops from his fine charcoal grey jacket and proceeded to signal his driver.

"Want to get some dinner? There's a great new Sushi joint nearby," Omar casually proposed as he waited for a cab to pull up.

"Nah, I'll head home and kick myself on the way for eating those chicken fingers. You check on the guys at the office; they might need an extra hand with the project plan. Just be sure to not entertain them like last time with the stripping act. *Yes, I heard,*" he warned sternly, his eyes following his driver as he took a U-turn from the other side of the street. Eighty-hour work weeks were the norm in his firm. More, if one was a newbie like Omar.

"I didn't strip. Is that what they told you? God! Such liars. They tricked me into this bet—"

"Omar, I don't need details. I just need to know that you don't treat office like a dorm room during after-hours. Yeah?"

"Yeah," he responded in a subdued tone.

Vivek checked into his car to head home. The location of his flat couldn't have been more suited to his lifestyle. Worli Sea Link, and all it afforded, beckoned from close proximity. Gourmet food markets, trendy shops, a charming variety of ritzy restaurants and conspicuous cafés, all were just a stone's throw away from where he stayed. As the driver swerved onto the vast street that led to the high-rise building he stayed in, Vivek looked at the countless palm trees that flanked the road: giant branches stretched out to blend with those on the adjoining trees, creating an illusion of continuum. He looked forward to these rides each night. It was the only duration in his immensely occupied life when he wasn't expected to be in the driver's seat. The neighbourhood usually offered him the comforting sound of the waves rolling in the sea. Tonight, just the faint cries of dogs fell on his tired ears. He drew in a breath and took in the distinct fragrance of the wet earth. But even that did not uplift him. He was bone-tired and agitated as hell. *Ahh Rangers . . .*

The car pulled up in front of his building and he made short work of collecting his stuff and entering the foyer. The building doorman, who had hastened to pull the enormous golden-plated door for Vivek, saluted him and extended routine courtesies.

He reciprocated in Marathi and made his way to the lift that would take him to his inviting fourteenth-floor pad. The foyer, with its specially commissioned art and sculpture work, effused the charm of a five-star hotel. It had a tall, cascading waterfall with midnight-blue granite gleaming through it in one corner and state-of-the-art lighting all over. The whole place bespoke class and sophistication. Vivek's friends and family often lauded his choice of digs.

As he entered his apartment, he chucked his shoes by the entrance, hurled his laptop on the rust leather couch, flung his jacket and shirt on the bed, and tossed his undershirt on the bedside chaise in quick succession. This had been his routine for over half a decade, ever since he had ventured into living independently. Roommates weren't for him, he'd realised early on in his life.

He entered the bathroom wearing his grey boxers but soon reverted to his earlier spot. There was something starkly different about his apartment. He walked back into the living room and glanced around carefully, scrutinising everything with squinted eyes. It looked perfect; not one object seemed out of place. The wall-mounted flat screen was still intact. The Blu-Ray DVD player, Wii Box, Digital TV receiver, and DVD storage, all were neatly stacked on each other, their edges aligned. Multimedia speakers still stood tall and elegant in certain corners of the room, and his personal MacBook sat serenely on the side table. The flat didn't appear 'broken into' from any angle. Everything he had spent a fortune on was still in sight, and the realisation brought back his breath. Then he began to look for clues.

The cordless phone was on its charging station and not next to the coffee maker where he often left it. The kitchen looked immaculate, unlike the muddled state he kept it in. The plush carpet was free of financial magazines and newspapers unlike its appearance that morning. And the adult DVD cover he had left on the couch the previous night had gone missing. His apartment unquestionably seemed to have had some activity. Perhaps the maid had come by, but that would have been odd considering she had requested leave until Saturday. The blinking on the phone base station, indicating there were three new voicemails, caught his eye amidst the stir.

Hey, Vivek, this is Jay. If you're down for a few rounds of squash, call me. I'll be at the squash court around eight this evening. See you. *Beep.*

It's almost nine, he noted. *Delete.*

Hello, Vivek. This is the building manager. I wanted to inform you that we will be conducting our annual termite inspection over the next three days. I will be coming over with a termite inspection team tomorrow between eleven and five. If you have any concerns, please feel free to call me. Thank you. *Beep.*

Sure. Whatever. *Delete.*

Hi, Bittu, this is mom—And this is dad—

The senior Mr Grewal had clearly contributed to the voicemail as well. Vivek began walking towards his bathroom, where the promise of a hot shower lured him, regally ignoring the message as it played on.

—*Beta, kaise ho?* We're here in your apartment, but can't find a piece of paper to write on, so calling and leaving a voicemail—

Vivek stopped dead in his tracks. His apartment? Did she say his *apartment*? The very words jolted him out of his inertia and he rushed back to the phone, his pulse rising. His parents lived in Pune, a good two hours away, and typically dropped by with at least a short notice—just enough for him to tidy up his place and hide all the conspicuous clues that gave his secrets away! *What was this 'we are in your apartment' crap, then?*

—Dad had to give a guest lecture at the Grant Medical College today and then had some free time, so I decided to join in, —his mother delineated in an animated tone— I have stocked up your refrigerator with a ton of freshly-cooked food. There are three types of chicken curries, and *lachchha parathas, rajma, kali daal, palak paneer,* and *gobi mattar*. Sadly, I didn't have time to make biryani this time. And, I've removed the fat properly from the chicken, so none of the dishes are too fatty. Eat well, okay? Don't waste it like the last time. And Bittu, your place is such a mess! Dad and I are cleaning it out so if you can't find anything, look patiently. And come by this weekend. It's been a while and—*Beep*. (Even the voicemail refused to take any more of that.)

Vivek, appalled and still standing in his boxers, visualised his parents stumbling on his used underwear and socks—two things that usually graced his bedroom carpet; things his mother would refer to as 'borderline decomposed'—and cringed. Then it struck him: his adult DVD cover! A vivid image of topless twins on that cover flashed in front of his eyes. He covered half of his face with his right hand, pressing his fingers against his forehead, and groaned inwardly. He wondered if his current age, three complete years over the big three O, meant squat to them. The night had officially gone from bad to worse.

Picking up the phone, he wasted no time in setting new rules. "Hi, mom. I am going to need my keys back. My building is changing locks for all the apartments." Being intruded on didn't go with his personality or alter ego one bit. Having told her off, he made way to his luxurious bathroom.

With hair still damp from the steamy shower, Vivek poured himself some rich Shiraz—a recent gift from a colleague who'd visited Dindori. The shower had cooled off some of his anger, if that was even possible, but he felt restless now. He had made a habit of consciously zoning out the rant and the noises which semi-defined his long days at work. His usual focus after a hard day's work was on bedtime reading and he decided to do that. *Financial Express* didn't seem to have anything engrossing that hadn't already been discussed at lunch hour that afternoon. *Outlook* and *India Today,* too, got tossed out after a quick scan.

With nothing exciting to indulge in, he decided to call it a night. Just as he was about to switch off the light on the night stand, he was drawn into picking up the latest issue of *Cricket Today*. "What's another hour," he said to himself and stretched against the beige and navy blue Ralph Lauren bedding to loosen his back muscles, and then sat up and began flipping through the pages. Cricket World Cup—which India had won . . . Formula One Grand Prix—to be held in the coming months . . . IGL—that was taking place now . . . *There is so much happening in the sports world*, he thought for the billionth time.

He finally settled on the IGL TICKETS Blog section in the magazine and scanned through the various articles in it till one caught his eye.

**FINANCIAL WOES CONTINUE FOR AHMEDABAD RANGERS**

> It has been an uphill battle for the Rangers right from the start. . . .

By the time he reached the closing paragraphs, the expression on his face had changed.

> . . . Ticket sales have steadily declined over the seasons. There has been a ceaseless drain of talent. And there is little clarity on the financial health of the team, which is buried under huge debt. If no drastic measures are taken, the team's future and existence in the League is anyone's guess.

Vivek picked up his Blackberry and began typing an e-mail.

*Get in touch with Harsh Desai's office and get me a meeting ASAP. It's in connection with the Ahmedabad Rangers.* He typed in one breath to his secretary, Alisha. Then he had another thought.

***

*Harsh, I have a brilliant proposal,*–he began–*you won't be able to turn this one down. It's better than the last two deals. If you're in Mumbai this week, let's meet. Else let's get on a call. Best, Vivek.*

He checked the time on his Blackberry: 12:58 a.m. It *had* to be! Every idea that had changed his life, and the fortune of the company he worked for, had somehow occurred between midnight and one. It was undeniably his lucky hour. The cricket zealot in him was convinced that the Rangers needed a makeover. And the opportunist in him knew without a doubt that they needed it *now*. All that the team required were crisp banknotes, and he had just the right billionaire in mind for the task.

Propped up against the pillow, he glanced at the Mumbai skyline through his bedroom window, which engulfed an entire wall of his room. He could never tire of seeing the shimmering lights against the silhouette of tall buildings that elegantly graced South Mumbai; it was the one constant thing about his nights. And it brought him immense comfort to think that the skyline would always be there for him. It was, in a way, the one non-negotiable aspect of his life. *Well, as long as I continue to pay a premium for it*, he thought wryly.

As the night progressed, he continued to e-mail his secretary, not worrying one bit about her Blackberry beeping yet another time. He wanted her to get him everything she could find on the topic, and more. He asked her to run complete statistics and do detailed research on Ahmedabad Rangers, mentioning that he would need the report by the end of the next business day. Once Vivek smelt blood, he didn't let anything come in his way. And to top it, this was the Rangers . . .

In a weathered sky-blue apartment in the middle-class neighbourhood of Ranip stood Keya, dressed in striped pyjamas and a short tank top, with both hands on her waist, warily looking out the window of her living room. Her long locks made their presence felt on her naturally toned arms and exposed lower back. The stud in her recently-pierced nose sent off a subtle hint about its existence as well.

It was yet another overcast morning in Ahmedabad and yet another mood-dampener for Keya. There was something about swirling dark clouds that had always upset her, and today was no exception. The murky sky heightened her sense of gloom and deepened her yearning for stability and contentment: two things she was sorely lacking in her life at the moment.

Lately, there had been an avalanche of melancholic news and her personal life had been on a downward spiral ever since. Professionally, too, she had been walking a tightrope. Ahmedabad Rangers, the IGL team she worked for, hadn't made it to the playoffs in three years; the consequences of which were rather unsettling for her and her colleagues. The threat of losing her team members or even her job, if things became *that* serious, kept her awake various nights. Being in the marketing team of the Rangers wasn't just a job for her. She had left her family, friends, and her life back in Chandigarh to relocate to a completely unknown city for this. She could still distinctly recall the excitement she had felt when she had moved here three years ago. It wasn't cricket that revved her up so much, but being able to use the best of her skills in such a charged environment that thrilled her.

But there was more to this unsettling feeling than just work. One of her biggest desires in life was to pen down a travelogue. A book on her travel experiences to South America. Her plan of vacationing in the great continent helped her keep her wits about herself on the saddest of days, but even that project, which had been in limbo for so long, had finally died a sudden death last evening.

Yesterday, while she was at Lit Lovers, her favourite book shop, to attend a book reading session, her mother had called from Chandigarh. Mama Singhal had told her in no uncertain terms that their vacation plan was going to be shelved since Keya's dad and elder brother were caught up with work. Keya had wailed into the phone, almost like a hurt gazelle. 'Noooo' she had screamed, stretching out the 'o's; her eyes widening, disappointment making her face pale. She had been looking forward to her family reunion for months, no doubt, but what she had been awaiting even more was wrapping up her travelogue. Two weeks to travel Brazil and Argentina, that's all she needed! She had been short of the final few chapters for the past couple of years now. Chile and Peru had happened eons ago with her family when she was fresh out of college.

Venezuela and Guyana had been a part of a spontaneous trip with a photographer friend a few years later. She'd spent hours sitting in quaint places under exotic, colourful trees and roadside cafés, indulging in the culture, breathing in the local air, and writing away, on both trips. All she needed was Brazil and Argentina to sum up her work.

Not having met her brother in over a year, she had thought this trip would be the perfect opportunity for some sibling-bonding. She'd made numerous trips back to Chandigarh and her family had made several to Ahmedabad just for this. She had wanted it to be special this time. There were too many occasions to celebrate: Her father's fifty-fifth birthday. Her parents' thirtieth anniversary. Her mother's coveted awards.

"I know. I'm sorry. A delegation is coming from China around that time and dad has to host them," her mother had offered.

Dad: that's from where she had imbibed so much love for the continent from. While growing up, she and her dad used to stay up late in his study and exchange notes from the books they read on the subject—he more on the history and economics of the countries and she mostly on the travel and culture—while sipping on some hot chocolate. Inspired, after reading several travelogues, she'd felt compelled to travel the continent and write down something of her own. Recently, she'd even signed up for the evening creative writing classes at the British Library in Ahmedabad to improve the craft her instructor claimed she was gifted with. She had stayed up nights working on it. Not that she always had publishing dreams, but writing made her happy. It made her feel content. And she needed something to offset a life that she often deemed mediocre.

"Keya, are you there?" her mother had asked after a

moment of silence had passed between them.

"Yes, yes. Ma, are there no other qualified, deserving IAS officers who know how to do their job and host foreign delegates?" she had asked, almost accusingly.

"It's not just him. Karan's play has been picked up by this organisation. He's performing in Delhi for Atelier's Youth Theatre Week." Karan was her older sibling who had hogged the best of his parents' genes, or so she felt. The man was brilliance, talent, and pure genius, all rolled into one.

"Nice! When does he make time for all of this?" She couldn't help but voice out her thoughts. Why her brother couldn't lead a normal life like other married men in their thirties was beyond her. Typically, he should have had his hands full—what with a gorgeous wife, an adorable child, and a demanding job that paid a fat salary and a bonus which was half that—but no, he still managed to squeeze more hours from the day than one should be morally allowed to!

"You know your brother. Always chasing his dreams."

"Just like you and dad. Did you adopt me by any chance?"

"Keya, don't be silly. You're doing so well."

"Ma, you have no idea," her voice had trailed off just as the book store erupted in an uproarious applause concluding the book reading session. She had disconnected the phone, as the blaring sound of claps had filled up the air. But, it wasn't just the phone line. Sometimes, Keya felt disconnected from her folks too. Especially since . . .

With a sigh, Keya reverted her gaze to the archaic window in her apartment she was looking out from. Usually, she pulled it all the way up and indulged in some fresh air to kick-start her morning. But today, she didn't want the raspy screams of the vegetable vendor or the playful honking of young boys off to college on their motorbikes or the furious yelling of one of her neighbours to invade her personal space. She pulled down the window sash and walked back into her 'yellow kitchen' to make some tea.

Naming of the rooms was something she had done solely to gratify herself. In reality, if she walked two steps from the kitchen she would be in her living room, and another two steps from the living room would land her in her bedroom. It was a studio apartment, barely six hundred square feet in size. She switched on the radio that was placed in the corner of her kitchen counter, auto set to her favourite channel, before flipping open a cabinet.

"*Today, we will discuss the moral implications of coercive female sterilization practices. With me, in the studio, are our guests—*" the peppy voice droned on, making Keya switch the channel promptly. She had a good appetite for worldly news but only a few topics made it to her eight a.m. slot. "Contraception talk before caffeine, ha!" she gibed. What I need is a good, upbeat track to snap me out of this unhappy state, she thought as she mechanically put all seven ingredients, à la the Gujarati masala tea-making recipe she had learnt from a neighbour, into the boiling water.

Masala Chai had turned into a life essential since the time she had shifted here; just as much as the other snack recipes she'd learnt to make: *undhiyu*, *thepla*, *muthiya,* and her favourite, *methi na gota.* As she impatiently waited for the tea to come to a boil, the radio programme broke into a peppy song, *O Meri Jaan* by Asha Bhonsle, instantly making her forget everything. Her eyes fell on a straw that was in the coffee cup she had picked up the previous evening as a takeaway on her way back from work.

She pulled it out, placed it in her mouth emulating a cigarette, and as one hand moved through her wavy raven hair, the other stretched out and her eyes half closed as a reflex. *O meri jaan maine kahaa.* She moved her body seductively, gyrating to the beats, an enticing expression playing on her face. *O meri jaan tune sunaa.* She was a closet burlesque dancer or so she liked to believe. *Dil ne dil se kya kahaa meri meri meri meri meri.* Her lips curled as she sang along, the straw staying put in her mouth.

Her sensuous dance was interrupted by the sizzle of the boiling tea as it hit the metal of the gas stove burner. *Crap*, she exclaimed, spitting out the straw while turning off the gas. Too late. Burnt, over-steeped layers of liquid was mostly all that was left of her tea. She didn't have the time to brew another cup. Irritably, she banged the radio shut and rushed towards the bathroom to take a quick bath. Along the way, she cast a mock scornful eye at the Radha-Krishna poster that hung in a golden frame on the side wall of her room, passing on the blame for her tea mishap. This was something she always did when things went wrong.

Already late for work, she speedily walked towards the local bus stop at the far end of her lane. Through the hazy layer of pollution, she spotted the local bus she usually took to office. The driver was honking non-stop. With still half a street to cross, she ran. Her heavy laptop bag bumped against her right thigh, making its presence felt rather uncomfortably, and her tote, which looked big enough to house a small dog, clanged cantankerously, indicating the collision of the million things she kept inside.

Two guys on the street stopped their talk mid-sentence as she passed them by. She could feel their gaze on her. She knew what they saw; people often praised her beauty, a little too much for her comfort. 'You have a striking body, a soft mouth, and deep, arresting eyes. And such oomph. That's why they all check you out,' a colleague had once told her.

Today, she was wearing skinny jeans, a ruffled white shirt, and hoop earrings along with uncomplicated flat shoes, which she referred to as '*dadima*' shoes for their lack of design and appeal. But even these weren't helping her. Just as she approached the bus stop, she saw the bus pass her by. The pristine morning was suddenly stained with expletives flying all around.

"Oh, there you are!" a gruff voice greeted her.

"Rosh! You didn't board that bus? You silly, silly boy!" *Granted, we take the same bus each morning but you didn't have to wait!*

Kourosh, leaning against the railing at the bus stop with legs crossed and a cigarette in hand, smiled an oblong smile at her reaction.

"I-I—no smoking on the bus, yes?"

"Yes." *He's such an inept liar.*

Kourosh, or Rosh as Keya called him, was her next-door neighbour. A young Harrison Ford look-alike, with rather pinkish lips that somewhat unsettled Keya, he seemed to have no qualms about displaying how enamored he was by her. He was born in Ahmedabad to a Parsi father and a Russian mother. Fascinated by Indian dance forms, his mother had moved to Ahmedabad to be trained in Kathak. His father maintained accounts for the dance academy where she was enrolled and they had fallen in love quickly. Too quickly. Soon after his birth, his mother left his father and moved back to Russia, where she raised him all alone. He had returned to Ahmedabad a year ago to take care of his ailing father and had stayed put after he had passed away.

Kourosh in a lot of ways seemed to be the perfect guy for her, if she were lonely and lovelorn, which she had reminded herself several times she was, to some extent at least. Between that and the cute-as-hell Russian twang in his speech, she had considered giving this a try but somehow hadn't been able to bite the bullet. There was something indiscernible about him that was a deal breaker. But her reluctance hadn't discouraged him one bit. She noticed that he had found a way to turn himself into somewhat of a support system for her. He accompanied her to the ice cream shop by the crossroad at midnight if she asked or helped haul in the furniture or home décor items she brought home. He had wangled a few dinner invitations out of it. But it would be a stretch calling it a date.

Keya, in return, was a support system for him, too. She helped him with the assignments he got in his spoken English class, which he was enrolled in at the nearby academy, and went shopping with him when he needed a second opinion. In a city where he didn't know many people, he told her he appreciated her company. A little too much if one were to ask Keya. There were times she wished he would stop being so smitten by her, so that they could actually be on the road to being good friends. *But, who would put that into his gorgeous Russian head?*

Kourosh came to stand next to her as she impatiently waited for the next bus to come along. Three blocks of walk awaited her upon getting off from the bus before she could reach her office at SB Stadium. Luckily, a bus came by soon and she found a vacant seat that was a good five rows away from where he found one. Keya thanked her stars for the little mercies in life.

The stately SB Stadium occupied prime real estate, all fifty acres of it, overlooking the Sabarmati river. Attached to the stadium was a majestic three-storeyed beige building, built just before the first IGL season. The stadium's entrance was entirely made up of glass and this was where the administrative offices of the Rangers were. Though the home team of this venue was the Rangers, the stadium was leased all-year-round, being a multi-event venue, for organizing several programs by the state government.

Just before entering her office building, Keya pulled out a snazzy pair of red high heels from her tote and effortlessly replaced her '*dadima*' shoes, limping into the building as she did it on the fly. The security guard, witnessing her daily ritual, gave her an all-knowing bright smile. She took a lift to the top floor where her cabin was at.

"Here is the post-game analysis you needed. The meeting starts in ten. Do you need anything else?" asked Sujata, one of the five people in her Strategic Marketing team, as she walked into the office right behind Keya, placing the report on her desk. "God, it's cold in here," she added, rubbing one of her arms with the other palm.

"Finished it? Good. I'm going to get some coffee and then check it. Running on empty this morning," Keya responded, putting away her handbag.

"If the thermostat in your office was set any lower, this office would be a refrigerator. And, we are fresh out of coffee."

"What? No!" The idea of getting through an intense hour-long marketing meeting with ten of her counterparts and superiors suddenly sounded dreary. Keya ran out, her high heels piercing the carpet, and returned right in time to the conference room holding a hot beverage in a thick paper cup from a nearby joint.

"How you can run in heels holding coffee and still look immaculate is beyond me," Sujata whispered to her, tilting her head, as Keya took an adjacent seat.

"Practice, honey. Over a decade of it," Keya leaned in to respond as she settled down.

The meeting agenda along with the printouts of the campaign report were neatly stacked infront of everyone. The Chief Marketing Officer soon walked in, wearing a soft pink shirt paired with steel grey pants, and assumed his position at the head of the table. He was fairly new to Ahmedabad and the Rangers, and had been brought in from a leading advertisement agency to improve the Rangers' marketing programs. An otherwise jovial man, his strict demeanor today raised Keya's antenna a notch.

"Let's kick off with the campaign effectiveness report. Keya," he decreed, his stern gaze aimed solely at her, "I'm told a massive amount of people have been unsubscribing lately from our e-mail campaigns. What are the stats?"

It was the first time he had directed such a pointed question at her, that too so early on in a weekly meeting. It disoriented her a bit. She tried attempting a confident response. "Well, it is a little more than the average rate of unsubscribes from our weekly newsletters but it is by no means massive. It is concerning though and we are looking into—"

"What is the current rate?" he brazenly interrupted.

"About one percent," she said, clearing her throat.

"And what is the average penetration per newsletter?"

"Approximately thirty-five thousand people per e-mail blast."

"Are you telling me we are losing three hundred and fifty people per e-mail blast? Is this not alarming to anyone else?" He threw this loaded question at everyone in the room. "Rangers is witnessing some of the most challenging times we've ever seen. Three weeks into the current season and we haven't sold half of the pavilion tickets yet, premium and platinum seats are suffering a great deal and don't even get me started on the corporate boxes, budgets have been squeezed, and no one knows how to pull their shit together. This is the time to smartly pick our target segments, to put some intelligence into it, to think out-of-the-box. Instead, we are just bombarding everyone and their mother," he verbally whiplashed everybody before zeroing down on Keya. "And you are telling me it's not massive? This is fucking *unbelievable*!" With the last statement he banged his Blackberry on the table. Keya recoiled into her chair as an involuntary reaction. No one had thrown the f-bomb so openly in a meeting before. Her toes curled, her hands clasped the chair handles, her stomach churned, her heart thumped louder than ever, and there was a trace of fear and embarrassment in her eyes.

"We cannot continue to operate like this. Do you guys understand? And this is only one of the dozen issues that have come to my attention this week," he relentlessly persevered with the rebukes.

An hour later, an enraged Keya, with a scowl pasted on her face, was at her desk, fuming.

"It's not a big deal." Sujata attempted to pacify her.

"Don't tell me that. Didn't you see how he insulted me? Like I didn't know my job. I hate public humiliation. And he isn't even my boss."

"Calm down. You're overreacting. He just said too many people unsubscribed in that last campaign."

"No, Sujata, you don't understand. So we lost a few people.

It's not such a big deal. Certainly not big enough for him to walk in yelling at me. Jerk," she defended herself without mincing words.

"It wasn't a direct attack on you."

"I knew it. This day was doomed. My tea was reduced to flakes this morning and I missed my daily bus because of the stupid dust. It couldn't have gotten off on a worse start."

Sujata burst into laughter hearing her reason. "Tea and dust! Those are the guiding forces of your life?" she mocked.

"Yes. And I have historical data to prove it. I have to get my life back on track."

With that Keya left the room.

As the morning sun hit Vivek full in the face, he woke up, his eyes crinkling against the unwelcome onslaught. From somewhere in his room, he heard the indistinctive beep of his Blackberry, indicating an unread mail, and instantly recalled the previous night's activities.

Vivek Grewal jumped out of the bed, adrenaline filling his body. He had work to take care of!

After packing five hours of work into mere two, Vivek was ready for a break. As he made his way to the office kitchen, he heard a distinctive voice from within. It was unmistakably Alisha's. He stopped by the unstable white board outside that outlined the staff's vacation schedules and harmlessly eavesdropped.

"I have to dab a ton of concealer to hide my dark circles for he wakes me up at ungodly hours. And *he* walks in looking flawless, without any make-up on. How is that even fair?" he overheard Alisha whine about him in one go to someone.

"Good genes," he replied from behind her, as he walked in with his frosted beer mug.

"Oh, h-hello, sir. I'm sorry, what?" she asked, clearly flabbergasted at being found out by her boss. The other person in the kitchen, an assistant, too, bore a stricken expression.

"I said good morning," he replied smoothly, briefly glancing at her blushing face as he poured some ice water in the beer mug. His boss had cautioned him in his last annual review that he was working his staff too hard and that they were strung too tight. This casual teasing, ribbing was how he made sure he brought in some levity and eased the pressure. If this didn't help, he didn't know what else would. He wasn't the 'let's be friends' or 'you have my shoulder to cry on' boss, and he had told his team that. This was work. Pure and simple. He was unabashedly ambitious and wildly driven when it came to his career.

"Shit, shit, shit," Alisha muttered behind his back, as he walked out from there. He was half-tempted to walk back into the kitchen and say something else, just to pull her leg some more, but then thought the better of it and kept walking ahead. There were better ways of bonding with his staff.

He knew Alisha would be stressing over her new assignment and struggling with it. After all, none of his tasks were ever similar to each other. What industry his new idea might touch, no one in the office could predict. In a genuine effort to be a more involved and a less demanding boss, he stopped by her desk several times after that to help her make sense of the challenge he had put forth her. At the end of the day, he got exactly what he wanted. He was pleased.

But, when by evening, he still hadn't heard from Harsh he decided that e-mail wasn't going to get the job done.

"Harsh Desai's office," a voice greeted from the other end.

"This is Vivek from Cello. Is Harsh in?" He spoke in a

crisp and cool voice; a voice that hinted at authority, a voice that couldn't be refused any wish, and a voice that belied the anxiety that was eating its speaker raw from inside. *Why hadn't Harsh gotten back to him until now?*

He had always thought very highly of Harsh who was a dapper, middle-aged billionaire based out of Bengaluru with impressive investments in a range of companies in India and overseas. He belonged to a working-class Gujarati family from Mehsana, who had changed their surname to Khumalo from Desai to blend in with the local crowd in Durban, South Africa, when decades ago his grandfather had landed on the port atop a flimsy boat. Harsh Desai's own father had made a reasonable living out of selling poor-quality towels and beachwear on the beaches of Durban. But it was his boyish charm and grey eyes that had help sell bikinis and sarongs to the ladies at the beach. And thus, Harsh had got introduced to the world of entrepreneurship at the tender age of ten. He had graduated with a degree in Economics from the University of Miami and seven failed businesses later, miraculously turned into a business tycoon, which was when he changed his surname back to Desai.

Harsh had a long, protruding nose that bent inwards at the tip. It made him look like a seagull, but it also made him appear approachable. Vivek had met him at a bar in Mumbai through an acquaintance and within two years of that evening had persuaded Harsh into buying two start-up firms to diversify his company portfolio. Harsh was one of his most trusted clients and Vivek liked to believe that he was one of Harsh's most trusted advisors. This was perhaps why Harsh never turned down his proposals. Not all proposals were brought to fruition but he invariably gave them a fair chance.

Vivek couldn't wait to embark upon this new adventure with Harsh by his side.

***

"I'm not feeling this one yet, Vivek," Harsh mentioned as they walked through the swanky lobby at The Landmark Oriental in Ahmedabad, minutes before their meeting with the owner and CEO of Ahmedabad Rangers. Vivek had made a dozen calls to the Rangers' office and had eventually managed a preliminary appointment. Given that such meetings were hard to come by, he was raring to go. The game wasn't the same with Harsh, unfortunately. He didn't really seem convinced about the new proposal. He was a retail tycoon and had not tested waters in the world of sports.

"Here's the plan," Vivek stated, bringing Harsh up to speed as they stepped out of the hotel. "Let's wait it out till lunch. If you still don't feel it, we'll call it a day and take the next flight back. Or better still, go to a Rangers' game later today and watch them get crushed." He let out a wicked smile as he concluded voicing out his thoughts.

A slick Mercedes-Benz S-Class awaited them right outside the hotel entrance. Vivek graciously opened the rear door for Harsh before the driver did, then briskly went around the car to get in. Warm city breeze seeped in between his unbuttoned blazer and shirt. He ignored it.

"SB Stadium, please," he directed the driver before turning to Harsh. "The Rangers have just picked up two promising young players this season. Not sure if you're quite in the know. They're zygotes; one's twenty and the other is twenty-one. Both are Ranji Trophy players, so I know the owner will try to play up that factor. I just know it. But let's not go above thirteen hundred regardless of their trump cards."

With that Vivek looked out the window, admiring the tall new buildings that had replaced the dreary landscape of the city that housed his alma mater. He had convinced Harsh to consider buying the Rangers from the current owner for a meagre thirteen hundred crores, when other teams were selling in the ballpark of seventeen. It was a number he'd zeroed in on after much analysis, industry reports, and meetings with Harsh's investors. He had spent the last two weeks—since that brilliant idea had hit him post midnight—digging up every detail about the Rangers, strategising and analysing numbers for all the million and one scenarios that had crossed his mind. He'd spent enough time convincing Harsh and couldn't wait another second to witness how it would all pan out. Nothing about this process was unusual for Vivek, though. It was standard operating procedure. If he came across the slightest possibility that interested him, he would leave no stone unturned until it reached a finale. Not that he always won. He often joked that he had had everyone's share of bad deals in Mumbai, including the beggars and the pimps. But those very losses had made him resilient and gradually turned him into a one-stop-shop on every M&A deal happening on Mumbai soil and some even in the rest of the country.

"Are you implying they have a trump card?" Harsh chaffed, his lips parting for the cigar smoke to escape.

"The stadium is next to a thirty-year-old dingy joint that serves the biggest meals. I'm talking about humongous Gujarati thalis with a truckload of sweets. There's a line of about a hundred people by noon every day. If nothing else, you could count on those people for buying season tickets. Is that enough of a trump card?" Vivek teased back.

"Nice homework."

"I studied in this city for two years. I can draw an accurate map of all the dingy joints in my sleep." The rush-hour traffic had turned their three-kilometre drive into a thirty-minute ordeal. "I can't drive here without breaking at least three different traffic rules," he added, as the car finally came to a stop.

Vivek breathed in the magnificence of the statuesque establishment as they entered through the revolving doors and spotted security personnel instead of secretaries. Getting to the administrative offices at SB Stadium was comparable to going through airport security—checking of IDs, sliding laptop bags through an x-ray machine, and walking through a metal detector.

"Is this all new? I came to this stadium about a decade ago, didn't seem so nice back then," Harsh enquired.

"Right after they got a home team, the stadium got renovated. This building with administrative offices is brand new," Vivek informed, pointing at the beige building. It was his first time at the stadium since his IMI-A years but he had all the information Harsh needed. "The rest of the stadium has been upgraded, too. New gymnasium, good indoor facilities, two more grounds in the vicinity, fifty thousand seating capacity."

"Do you have a seating chart and a hospitality map, too, genius?"

"Not yet. I can tell you how it is though," he replied, so intent on providing the complete background that he didn't realise Harsh was pulling his leg. "Seats are divided into four zones and each zone has two tiers, save one zone that has platinum and premium pavilions. Platinum pavilion has a private seating lounge with an exclusive food and beverage facility. Premium pavilion has the same layout without the exclusive eating lounge service. Of course, there are several food and beverage concession areas in the lower and upper stands throughout the stadium. And, I believe there are twenty corporate boxes in another zone, eight of which are brand-spanking-new. It's got a lot going for itself." Then, Vivek realised that Harsh had been messing with him with his question, and groaned inwardly.

"Fell right into that one, didn't I?"

Harsh smiled and remarked, "Good you did. You have always provided me with pertinent information. I like that. Now tell me this, what's the difference between premium and platinum seats?"

"More differentiation, more money. In theory, at least."

"Sounds promising."

"Yeah. The surrounding area got a facelift as well. Tons of food joints and little shops around. And some upcoming residential areas."

A suave front desk assistant guided both men to a conference room. The whole building was abuzz with activity. The Rangers were playing Delhi Champs that evening and the ground was definitely seeing some action. On his way in, Vivek had spotted the Champs' captain knocking in along with a few others of his team. From the distance he had been able to discern a couple of young players from his team but nobody else. *What were the Rangers up to?* he wondered.

As they entered the conference room, Vivek dropped his laptop and other belongings on the vast table and after discussing the last key points with Harsh, walked out in search of a restroom. For the first time that morning, he felt at a loss. To say that the Rangers' office was a maze wouldn't be an overstatement. There were too many little lanes going in all directions. He decided to retrace his steps back to where he had been escorted from. Once the deal goes through, I am going to ask Harsh to name these lanes and provide an office map to new employees and visitors, he made a mental note. Chancing his luck, he decided to take a left turn and found himself just a few feet away from a striking girl who happened to be walking in his direction.

He didn't believe he was going to do this, but he had no alternative. "Excuse me, do you know where the men's toilet is?" he asked, at the same time mentally lambasted himself severely. *Who says toilet to a pretty girl in the opening line?*

"Straight ahead this way. To your left," she responded, pointing in the opposite direction, with a slightly perplexed face. For a moment, he felt as if she was screening him. He was suddenly conscious of his crisp suit, power tie, and shiny shoes. They were a far cry from the quintessential Ahmedabadi dress code people here were used to.

The girl continued walking. He turned around and proceeded in her direction, finally finding what he was looking for.

Minutes later, a frantic Vivek scurried out of the men's toilet. He couldn't believe the nerve of the people here! What was wrong with this place? First, one had to deal with mazes, and as if that was not enough, a man couldn't take a tinkle in peace! No wonder they were going to the dogs, he concluded petulantly.

As he thought about ways for making the housekeeping more solicitous here, he spotted a woman's arched body in a room in front of him. Her face wasn't visible and the angle she was bent at drew his entire attention to her perfectly-contoured butt. "Sweet," he remarked, momentarily forgetting his distress. Before he could admire the rest of her tantalising body, her teeth-clenched face emerged. It was the same girl who had given him directions to the bathroom. *Great!* She was pulling out some really heavy-looking banners, almost dragging them in the process. The smallest of them was secured strongly between her teeth. It was a storage room from the sneak peek he got.

"Need a hand?" he offered to help, the gentleman that he was. Heels don't help much if you're pulling banners twice your size, he conveyed with one raised eyebrow.

"No, I got it. Thanks," she mechanically responded after pulling away the banner from her mouth.

"You didn't tell me women walk in on you in this bathroom. I wasn't prepared." Vivek was irked and wanted to blame it on someone.

"*What?*"

"The cleaning lady. She just walked in while I was . . . you know . . . in there." He didn't know why he was painting such a vivid picture for her, or for that matter even sharing this with her. It was way too much bathroom talk before introduction. What happened once was embarrassing enough.

"Oh," she simpered. When her smile turned into a laugh and bordered on being downright irreverent, she casually threw in an "I'm sorry. It's never happened to me."

"Even if it did, it'd be harmless. Aren't there stalls in there?" He ploughed on, successfully charting his way towards, what he thought, the most inane conversation he had ever had with a girl, that too such a pretty one.

"Right," she nodded, the mischievous smile still playing on her lips.

"I'm Vivek." She already knew his life-story, might as well know his name.

"Keya." She resumed dragging the banners out of the dungeon-like room.

***

Vivek took his seat across Harsh in the plush conference room. Cherry wood panelling ran from floor to walls, providing a very masculine, power-pronounced touch to the room. It reminded him of the winter cabin he often rented along with his friends at a ski resort in Manali.

A secretary swung by and after placing a few bottles of water along with glasses on the table, offered them coffee. They both declined. Harsh was a recovering caffeine addict and had just confessed to Vivek a minute back that he had already consumed eighty percent of his caffeine quota, assigned by his wife, of course, for the day and it was only early morning. Vivek poured himself some water and heard Harsh drone on about his problems with coffee. Or was it the wife? He stared at the glass of water, which happened to be lit up by a shaft of sunlight creeping in through the window blinds, as it created beautiful spherical patterns on the table, his mind drifting into thoughts.

"Sir will be in shortly." The same secretary who had offered them coffee popped in to relay the information about the owner and CEO of the Rangers, Srinivas Krishnan. She gave them a polite smile and walked away.

"Are you ready to kill it?" Harsh asked, checking his Blackberry.

"Yes, that prerogative is all mine," Vivek cheerfully responded.

Moments later, Srinivas Krishnan marched in. His presence filled the room; he had walked in like he owned the place, which Vivek couldn't help think was true. But just for now. Crisp white shirt, yellow tie, tall frame, broad shoulders, moustache, oiled black hair, and eye glasses; he appeared to be the quintessential jargon-throwing, thick-skinned, rigidly-conventional corporate type.

"Sorry to keep you waiting. I'm Srinivas. Srinivas Krishnan," the man said in a crisp voice, firmly shaking hands with Harsh and Vivek, and occupied the chair at the far end of the table. Ego fuel came in the form of business card exchanges. Vivek's read: *VP, M&A, Cello Consulting.* Harsh's, a bright blue in colour, read: *CEO, Desai Group of Companies.* Several pleasantries later, Vivek tactfully presented his case.

"Mr Krishnan, we really appreciate your taking out time to meet with us. We've come with a proposal. One that we hope you'll be excited about." He kicked off his usual waltz. Krishnan seemed unfazed. Vivek made a note of that expression.

"Much has been written about the financial state of the Rangers in the recent past. With the loss of two of the team's prominent players in this year's auctions and getting two unknown players in their place, the going might get bumpy. And the fact that the team hasn't made it to playoffs in the last three years can't help. Harsh is one of my favoured clients. I am sure you know his profile. Allow me to present the offer." He set the bait for his prey, careful about not being offensive, gesturing at Harsh.

"I'm curious to hear it," Krishnan replied, with an expression that hinted at anything but.

"My client's offer is fairly straightforward," Vivek began, conveying the details of his proposal and not sugar-coating it one bit. That wasn't his style. "He'd like to invest in the Rangers, bring in some cash, a new coaching team, and new management. He's proposing complete ownership of the team. And he's willing to make this worth your while. We're going with ten percent above the market price for thirteen hundred crores," he concluded, his eyes not leaving Krishnan's all this while.

Krishnan didn't react to that. There was nothing in his body language that would indicate whether he was mildly surprised or awfully shocked or anything in between. With a thoughtful look, he apparently mulled over that for a moment, and then responded, "I appreciate your offer. But honestly, I'm not sure we're ready to give up the ownership. The Rangers aren't just a team we own. We are very passionate about it. And while there might have been some financial troubles, we've made some major changes this season. The two new players we have signed on are Ranji Trophy players. They both are all-rounders."

Vivek smiled to himself. He had been positive Krishnan would bring up the junior players and their Ranji Trophy reference in the opening lines of his defence.

"I understand. Promising young players they seem to be. It'll be another season or two before they have established themselves in the team. And who is to say what happens till then," Vivek countered, taking a sip of chilled water.

"Perhaps your company is willing to sponsor? We work with some of the leading brands who are at various levels of sponsorship with the Rangers. Our Global Partnerships group will be happy to have a word with you on the subject."

That came as a complete shock to Vivek. What a ridiculously dumb counter offer, he thought. What does an acquisition offer have anything to do with sponsorships? Is this guy even cut out to be a CEO? Too many questions, no answers. *I'm just going to have to eat him alive*, he concluded in his head.

"Mr Krishnan, I'm not sure if that's a direction we are mentally prepared to explore at this time." Vivek clarified his bottom line.

There was an awkward momentary silence. Krishnan, Vivek suspected, had to be thrilled in some corner of his heart. Maybe not about the acquisition but about the fact that there was an interested party—for grapevine had it that he hadn't commenced scouting for potential stakeholders yet—and that they were ready to pump some much-needed cash into the team.

When the team's top two players had been traded that season for complete newbies, the last bit of hope had vanished. Three years of not making it to the playoffs was taking its toll, as was evident through a huge percentage of tickets not getting sold. Reduced profits had implied a leaner sales team. The undesirable process had left behind just a handful of people who had been assigned the mammoth task of selling tickets for a team with an apparently doomed future. Staff morale was at an all-time low and so were the profits, from what Vivek had heard. With a ten percent mark-up on the team's perceived market value, he was certain Krishnan wouldn't be able to throw away the offer.

An expected probe followed from Krishnan. Grilling, obvious questions. There was neither interest not excitement from where Vivek saw it. "I need some time to think about this," Krishnan dodged.

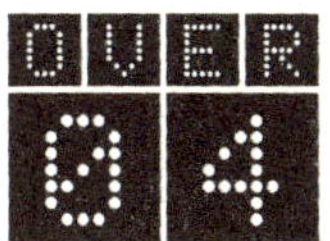


Keya reached her building entrance and lifted the top cover of the mailbox to collect her mails for the day. Kourosh was engaged in the same activity. Their bus times were synchronised and their mail pick up times were synchronised. *Great. Not much left for their lives to be synchronised about now, was there?*

Small talk was turning out to be their forte, which was quite remarkable considering she didn't speak Russian and he spoke broken English and Gujarati. Before she knew it, she had got herself a dinner invite to his place.

"This is *Lahmajoon.* You like it, I make more," he said rather sweetly, offering her what appeared to be a pizza knock off, wearing a black apron that read 'Kiss the Cook'.

"Make or bake? And what is this?" Keya's impertinence-laden voice enquired. She couldn't seem to help it.

"It's Armenian pizza. I buy pre-made from this Parsi lady in Kankaria. But I bake with feeling."

"I thought Russians didn't like Armenians." Keya ignored his sentiments, as always. The one thing she loved about their friendship was that she could say absolutely anything to him. Even insensible stuff.

He shrugged. "Not all. I'm nice guy. I don't dislike nobody. I like their Cognac too."

"That's baloney. Come on, no one's going to take you seriously when you say crap like that. I mean, how could you not dislike anyone?"

"But I-I—" An astounded Kourosh tried to reason but she tuned out. She knew it wasn't about him. It was about her.

"Rosh, listen, I'm sorry. I didn't mean to . . . it's just a bad day," she confessed to him, shaking her head in self-disappointment.

"It's okay, Keya. I know. You look sad. I make you some tea, yes? Russian teas are very—how do you say—condoling."

Keya laughed. "Consoling? That's a big word."

"I learn to impress you." Pure innocence glinted off his face.

"Aww Rosh. You're a nice guy. But I . . . look, you're very sweet. And I appreciate everything you do for me. Really. But—"

Before she could complete that sentence, he put a gentle hand on her face, covering her mouth. "Don't say. We talk about this later, yes?"

He was awfully close to her and his big eyes were doing this seductive dance as they met hers. Their breaths came out in unison. She felt the warmth of his hand all over her mouth. It made her brain swirl. His pink lips appeared to be an even deeper shade of pink, if that was possible. She felt a slight desire to embrace him but held back. He was so caring, she noted. So gentle. So honest. And so incredibly cute.

Then Kourosh withdrew his hand and leaned in to

kiss her, stopping short of a distance where only air could slither through. Her eyes closed as a reflex and her body felt like it was melting in the heat his proximity was generating. The unexpectedness of it took her by complete surprise. A flickering thought of whether this kiss would feel more sublime than any kiss in her recent past—which weren't many to speak of—crossed her mind. Then it hit her. There were no kisses whatsoever in the recent past, none since her fiancé . . .

She shuddered and pushed Rosh away, as that piercing thought rushed through her head, making her queasy. That feeling was further intensified by resentment.

"Don't be so imposing, you understand? Don't take so many liberties. You and I aren't—just go, Rosh. Leave me alone," she screamed at him in annoyance, wiping her forehead with her palm as if to wipe away those rusty, aching memories.

***

Between consummate yuppies focussed on chiselling their body to perfection and young mothers intent on getting back into shape, Vivek was relieved to find for himself the only available treadmill in his now-crammed but very well-equipped gym in Mumbai. He had been riding the treadmill hard for the past one hour and could continue to do so for a while. He allowed himself a little smile of satisfaction at that. Looking at the television screen in front of him, he lost himself to the news story that was being reported and reverted his gaze only when he felt his cell phone vibrate on the treadmill bottle holder. An unknown number flashed on the caller ID. He paused his workout as the walking belt came to a screeching halt.

"What's happening, handsome?" A sultry piercing voice enquired. It was unmistakably hers.

"At the gym, sweating away." He recognised the motive and cursed first himself, in all the three languages he knew, for answering the call, and then her for calling from an unknown number and fooling his caller ID.

"*And?*" she coaxed. It felt like a set-up. He knew what she wanted to hear.

"And watching an infomercial on how to improve prostate health."

"Very funny." Her tone had gone from sultry to derisive in a flash. She didn't seem thrilled. And that thrilled him.

"It's not, actually. I take prostate health very seriously. Did you know one in six men in the country is diagnosed with it?"

"What on earth are you talking about? I don't give a damn about prostate cancer."

*Cancer*? Clearly, she was annoyed! He was winning it. "That would be a very insensitive thing to say in certain groups."

"Cut it out, Vivek. It's really not funny."

"I don't claim it is." The verbal duel was in full swing, just as he had hoped.

"Whatever. You know what, you do this every time," she yelled. *Oh boy, she had had enough.* "Every single time I call, you go off on a tangent and say such absurdly irritating and irrelevant things. And none of it makes sense. It's like you don't want me to call you." She screamed so loudly that the tiny woman on the adjacent treadmill gave Vivek a scornful look.

Then there was silence. Offensive silence. He maintained his calm. She banged the phone hard. It wasn't the first time she did.

That was Natasha, a friend of a friend whom Vivek had briefly dated once. She had come across as a hot little number when they'd first met; he hadn't been able to resist her at all.

Her bee-stung lips, the vivacious curves, the tang of citrusy fragrance in her hair, the elaborate dinners she made him, the way she snuggled when they watched movies, all that had been great in the beginning. Now, her perpetual overly-sexy tone, the way she called him 'baby' with an emphasis on the first b, her everlasting pout, the lack of any depth, whatsoever, in their conversations, the dearth of goals in her life, the way he felt around her, none of this attracted Vivek. How she'd quickly gone from being desirable to being a pain, he still had no clue. So, he had let her go. Or so he had led himself to believe. Evidently, it would take more than that to just annoy her on the phone.

Vishal, his younger brother, constantly teased him about being a playboy. Vivek wasn't always inundated with such calls, but somehow, as luck would have it, he almost always received a few when he was with his family, thus leading them to believe that he was quite the Casanova. Being single in Mumbai, one rakes up a certain score of girlfriends who quickly turn into ex-girlfriends due to a variety of reasons, he would justify to them. He termed his behaviour as being 'careful' if not discerning. But his younger brother never bought into that crap. Clever kid, he.

The cell phone beeped again. It was Harsh Desai. Vivek's workout didn't seem to be working out. He would just have to swap the pizza he was thinking of ordering with something less stroke-inducing. He wiped his forehead with a towel, stopped the treadmill again, and answered.

"You're flying with me to Ahmedabad tomorrow." Harsh sounded excited. It was rare.

"Nice. What did they come back with?"

"No details yet. But we're invited."

Vivek picked up a thin-crust chicken tikka pizza on his way home for bribing Scarlett. Scarlett was his canine roommate, a female Golden Retriever named after Scarlett Johansson. "The only difference," he'd often joke to people he ran into while dog-walking, "is that I'm deeply fascinated by both Scarletts, but only one of them knows I exist and, incidentally, it's the same one who terrifies me."

He was sure she would be mighty upset with him when he'd go out of town the next morning. She wasn't particularly fond of the dog-sitter, a teenage girl who stopped by twice a day in his absence to walk and feed her. When time permitted, the sitter even took Scarlett to the nearby park and played games with her, but despite that the mighty Scarlett was not pleased. This was the third dog-sitter Vivek had called for in the past six months. He had frequently heard stories from his peers about their misbehaved kids who would often play pranks to scare away their nannies. He was ashamed to state that his precious Scarlett was even worse. She infamously acted up with the dog-sitters he painstakingly found for her. The past two had left on grounds of her not being trained and responsive, which really wasn't the case.

He was quick to infer that it was Scarlett's way of punishing him for leaving her behind while travelling. That or she didn't quite fancy female sitters. He'd even put in a request for a male dog-sitter at the local agency but had been waitlisted after being shot a strange look by the receptionist.

He had suffered through her periods of standoffish behaviour with him, until one evening, when he finally figured out what made her tick. On his way back home after a long trip, he'd picked up chicken tikka pizza from the airport cafeteria for himself. Before he could change into his night clothes, Scarlett had finished off the entire pizza and smacked her lips for a long time thereafter. She'd even nudged him, showering him with loads of love. That's when he'd figured out her weakness.

"I'm off to Ahmedabad tomorrow, sweetie," he told Scarlett later that evening, who didn't seem interested in anything that didn't look like a chicken tikka pizza. She had wolfed down hers in no time. "Is it going to rain there?" he asked. She barked in response. They often played the game where she would act like his psychic. Barking implied an affirmative response. It was his way of involving her in his life more. "What about the deal? You think I'll score?" he enquired, packing a few shirts into his carry-on bag that lay on his bed. She barked again. "That's my girl. Now tell me," he asked again, throwing in a couple of skinny ties, "will I meet a pretty girl on the flight?" She turned her face away and began to scratch herself. "No luck? Okay, let me be more specific. Will the person in the next seat be a girl?" Woof, she went. "Aah, sweet. Will she be a model?" He began to dig deeper as he packed two pairs of shoes and a few pairs of dark socks. Silence. "What about an economist? Will she be an economist? I like a girl who could talk something besides shoes and thongs." Silence again. All that remained to be packed were the phone, iPad, and laptop chargers. "Hmm, a nun?" Nothing. "I know. An actress, right?" He zipped up the bag and placed it by the main door. She gave him a loud woof followed by an attempt to climb on him, tongue hanging out, hyperventilating; her way of exhibiting excitement. "Really? That's perfect. Can't wait to meet an actress."

***

The gracious air hostess in his business class cabin reminded Vivek of his mother: their sole goal being to feed him the choicest of foods. 'Sparkling or still water?' was how she initiated the pampering process. First came roasted, skinned almonds and seasoned cashews with some Bloody Mary that the attendant made for him on the fly—mixing spicy tomato juice, Worcestershire sauce, a dash of lime, and a modest bit of vodka from a laughably small Smirnoff bottle. Then came a round of Swiss chocolates.

Just when the flight was about to take off, an attractive model-esque girl walked in airily and hurled her giant handbag on the seat next to his. An air hostess followed her in and helped her with her luggage. She looked oddly familiar from the sneak peek he got.

"Hi," she smiled, rubbing anti-bacterial solution on her hands after locking her seatbelt.

Wasting no time in speculation, he dived in. "Do I know you from somewhere?"

"Perhaps you've seen me on The Simple Life," she beamed. "It's my latest show on MTV. I've done a few ads, too." Her oversized sunglasses remained where they were as she dabbed some lip gloss and pouted seductively into the hand mirror.

He smiled to himself at the fluke. What were the odds that he'd run into an actress! Scarlett was clearly more gifted than he gave her credit for. "Aah yes, of course," he said.

A bit of small talk later, he began to read a magazine on his iPad. The first pill she popped during take-off made him suspect she had motion sickness. The pills continued to be popped during the duration of the flight, religiously so, every ten minutes on the clock. Curiosity consumed him as he tried to make trifling conversation after the fourth pill.

"I've been too stressed out. These help me relax," she admitted. She was on her way to attend a friend's high-end clothing store's opening in Ahmedabad after spending a week in Goa, she told him, and after that didn't spare him the details of why the tan she got from Goa was better quality as opposed to the ones from Phuket or Mauritius, her other two regular 'beach-time' spots. Vivek was intrigued by her interpretation of stress. He was even tempted to ask her for her physician or shrink's referral. His life seemed stress personified compared to hers, but he didn't want to open that can of worms in front of a stranger. He mentally switched off from the conversation.

"You know Mumbai is very superficial. I grew up in Delhi and people there know how to tough it out. They have warmth and personality that I miss in Mumbai. That's why I rush back to Delhi whenever I get a chance."

"Hmm." It was challenging to even feign interest.

"I'm sure you have seen the press about revival of Nishant Verma? Television has done wonders for his career which was like a car out of petrol—going nowhere. I always knew the small screen will ultimately rule the waves and so I switched to it after my first few films."

*First few B grade films where you were barely in three frames?* Vivek poured the rest of the vodka into his Bloody Mary and gulped it down in one shot as a physical reaction to her talk, hoping a chemical reaction would make his brain shut down. Vodka was all he could bank on to bail him out of the endless chatter.

The next thing he realised was that the flight had landed and the television actress had been whisked away by her entourage. He should have asked Scarlett an additional question of whether the chance meeting with the actress would be any fun.

He called Harsh on his way from the airport to the stadium.

"You beat my wife to this," Harsh scoffed, his voice lost behind the loud announcement an air hostess was making.

"She is the first one to call me the moment my flight lands."

"She must have a spy in the ATC tower," Vivek mocked.

"Yes, I'm *that* lucky."

"I'll be at the stadium in about twenty. Call me when you get there."

***

Vivek took in the magnificent view of the grounds in the stadium, as he sat waiting for everyone to assemble in the swanky conference room he had been ushered into a few minutes ago. Harsh sat beside him, shooting off mails to his Madrid office. Vivek could sense he was tense. For his own part, he felt a slight tingle of anxiety running in his veins. There had been no indication of anything, whatsoever, from Krishnan or anyone else from the team, but just a taciturn message asking them to meet. Up until then, he had had to field calls and follow-up on e-mails from their global partnerships group that was pushing him for sponsorship deals.

As Krishnan walked in with his array of C-level executives, Vivek noted that his demeanour was as austere as before. A quick introduction around the room was the only time spent in trivial formalities. "Tell me Harsh, why the sudden interest in sports? Your background shows anything but," he began without preamble. There was nothing like a planned interrogation to get the adrenalin pumping for Vivek. His mind sprung to complete attention.

"I have a number of retail ventures. I see a scenario where the sports market is ripe to take a cue from the retail industry," Harsh responded candidly, leaning into the plush chair; his attitude remarkably nonchalant. "Owning a sports team will allow me to diversify a bit and also push into the entertainment peripherals, which is a natural fit for my . . ." he carried on verbalising his justification as Vivek enthusiastically nodded in agreement. "And, frankly, I am a huge cricket buff. I've wanted to own a franchise for a long time. The timing is right. And I like the game of high risks."

"That's all very good, but, honestly, I fail to see the compelling reason." Krishnan furthered his grilling process.

"Allow me," Vivek interjected, the compulsive pitcher that he was. "Retail is all about segmentation, targeted marketing, statistics, analysis, and low margins. I see the cricket franchises all fat and happy with their star players and crowd frenzy, with no interest in doing more than the bare minimum to sell their tickets. No offense, gentlemen. I am certain that we could completely change the way sports teams are run by using our advanced analytics capabilities. It'll allow us to not only avoid overpaying for talent, but also to make sure we get the highest possible price for each ticket that we sell."

"But from beach towels to cricket, it's more than diversification." Krishnan didn't seem in a mood to yield. Or reveal, for that matter.

Harsh chuckled. Everyone in the room did, too. Vivek suspected the beach towel story would be with Harsh for as long as he shall live. It was how he had made his first dime, after all.

"Here's the problem," Krishnan argued. "That price tag isn't going down well with anyonc here. Thirteen hundred is far lower than what other teams are selling for. We could talk about a stake for you instead of complete ownership, if you're open to it."

*Far lower than other teams, yes, but, it's more than what your team is worth, buddy. Did no one tell you that the going rate for your team isn't a penny above twelve hundred?* Vivek mentally ticked him off, as Harsh responded to this. "In the interest of saving everyone's time and being completely transparent, let me just say that it's not something I'm interested in. It's all or nothing."

There was silence in the room. From behind the glass, while taking a sip of water, Vivek's gaze fixated firmly on Krishnan, assessing if he really needed any further convincing.

More heated-discussions later, Krishnan wound his way to the subject of sponsorships, again. Vivek knew without a doubt that Harsh was not even a bit interested in sponsoring players' underwears or shoes or socks or whatever the hell they were trying to get funding for. And he knew Krishnan had a fair idea of that. So then, why was he continuing this ridiculous streak of pushing them for sponsorships? Vivek studied him: his face was expressionless; his tone, tedious; and his frame, flaccid. But his eyes shone with trickery. *Gotcha!*

Vivek let the corporate poker kick-start. Things would get messy from now on; he knew that much from experience. But what he didn't count on was how ungentlemanly the discussion pertaining to the gentleman's game was going to get.

Krishnan put up bluff after bluff, unsuccessfully trying to get a firm footing on a deal he was fast losing grip of. Vivek watched him slip. Had he been on the other side of table he would have blown Harsh's case to smithereens. But, he wasn't, and that was the simple truth. So he let the Rangers' CEO humble himself as intense negotiations ensued. An hour passed in a blink.

"Let's call it a deal at thirteen fifty," Krishnan offered at one point, doing his best to grasp at straws.

"Mr Krishnan, we wanted to be fair right from the get-go," Vivek spoke on Harsh's behalf. "Obviously, this team is very close to your heart. We wanted to make it lucrative for you and get in at a price that would work for both of us. Which is why we're going with a ten percent mark-up on the market price. Believe me when I say, this is as high as we can go."

"That ten percent mark-up you keep referring to is purely your imagination," the CEO spoke curtly. Vivek couldn't believe what he was hearing. He wasn't about to take crap from this man. Right then he decided to call out his game. He was playing a stone-cold bluff, and Vivek was in no mood to indulge him further.

"I beg to differ, Mr Krishnan. I'll be happy to share appraiser reports and industry comparisons that clearly estimate the team's value at just *under* twelve hundred. It's eleven hundred and eighty, to be precise, as per Silverman Saks. GP Stanlay was not so generous. They pinned it at eleven hundred and change. What we're offering is a premium price."

"Look, this isn't as black and white as they'd like it to be. We have several great initiatives going on. No investment banks are going to factor that in. I'm afraid thirteen hundred will not cut it for me."

"Yes, I'm sure they haven't factored in initiatives like expanding the number of corporate boxes from twelve to twenty when even those twelve were going unsold." Vivek couldn't resist that snide remark, then immediately bit his tongue in self-realization. The discussion wasn't going anywhere. He needed to break the limbo, so that he could play him on multiple dimensions and find the best angle, not antagonise him further. "Let's take a ten-minute break and clear our heads?" he suggested.

"I need to smoke," Harsh muttered, signalling Vivek to walk out with him. Both men stepped out into the balcony to catch a breather from the long-drawn-out meeting. Vivek tapped his fingers on the waist-high railing, as if playing a piano, to release the slight anxiety impatience was causing him, while Harsh blew perfect smoke rings into the air. He began to think of other dimensions. Clearly, Krishan needed the money; so what was a deal-breaker here? Was it the control aspect? Was it the money versus power angle? Perhaps he needed to build in an exit pathway for Krishnan and cut him a side deal. There was no exchange of words between Vivek and Harsh until they headed back indoors. Such side deals that didn't impact the price were irrelevant to Harsh. The ball was in Vivek's court now and he was not only bending the rules but changing the game, sending the ball all the way for a six as he did.

"Mr Krishan, if we can agree upon a price, what are your thoughts about staying on in an executive role for a few more years?" Vivek dived in, using the epiphany he had just had, as a driving force. Krishan's eyes sparkled. It seemed to lead to a breakthrough for it was the first time that day Vivek saw him mellow down. Another hour of push and pull later, Krishan adjourned the meeting to have a private discussion with his board.

After countless rounds of the meet-break-meet cycle, they were all at that same table, yet another time.

"I have consulted with the board. And I'm happy to share that we've got ourselves a deal," announced Krishanan in an enthusiastic tone. A deal with the price Vivek had offered and a four-year term for Krishnan to continue as the CEO. All the suits in the room did the congratulatory hand shake. "We'll start the formalities with the authorities tomorrow. Goes without saying that we'll need to keep this under wraps until the nod comes through," he added. Everyone nodded in unison.

It was close to seven p.m. on a balmy May evening. A rush of relief mixed with ecstasy flooded Vivek's face. After a quick mental addition of all the deals he'd sold this year, he gave himself a thumbs-up under the table. It was a staggering number. He'd just earned himself some brownie points and a big fat bonus from his company.

"I almost forgot you like to celebrate in style," Vivek remarked later that night as he and Harsh entered Clay Oven, a markedly upscale rooftop restaurant in their hotel.

"I've heard the cannelloni sizzler and Thai chicken curry here are worth a kill."

"Courtesy *les* wife?" He knew Harsh liked to crack wife-jokes and he was happy to provide fodder.

"Of course. She is my very private restaurant guide," he nodded enthusiastically, falling for Vivek's friendly gibe as they made their way to a corner table. "She is also my TV guide. And my guide to my net worth. She knows the variance in my net worth on a daily basis. It is mainly to pre-calculate the settlement and alimony amount when she gives me the boot one day, if you ask me."

"That's funny."

"You don't read Sunday newspaper supplements? That's what billionaire wives do."

Nodding to that, Vivek said, "Nice place," hoping to change the topic. He enjoyed prattling only as much as the ex-girlfriend he was trying to get rid of!

Harsh picked up on the thought and beamed at the warmth and exuberance the place exuded. "Yes, not bad," he agreed. The restaurant had an inviting ambiance and offered scenic views of the city. Both men gazed around in silence, privately savouring much more than the interiors.

"Cheers to a new beginning. Let's get this baby up and running," Vivek toasted, after the waiter had placed their drinks on the table.

"Not so fast. Hang on. Let's celebrate with some real drinks," Harsh said as he signalled the maître d' to bring in some wine. The man returned with a good-looking bottle of a 2006 Stone Edge Cabernet.

"One of the finest wines from California," Harsh informed.

"In Gujarat?"

"You never had a real drink in IMI?"

"Sure I did; we bought indigenous brands from dark alleys in and around the campus. Not openly in restaurants, though."

"I've got a permit."

"I'm intrigued. How?"

"Well, I have an overseas citizenship of India. Did you forget I lived in *Amreeka* for years? That comes in handy, my boy. Cheers!" Harsh said gleefully, then creasing his brows after the first sip of red, enquired, "Do you taste mushrooms?"

"I taste some herbs, too."

"I don't understand Californian wines. They're pretentious."

"Just like the women in your town." Vivek made a little joke about Bengaluru. He'd been there twice and had had no luck with women there.

"I don't disagree. Anyway, I'm going to need some hand-holding from you as we kick off this project." Harsh steered the conversation back to business.

"Absolutely. I'll put my top guys on the team. You won't have to worry about a thing."

"I meant you."

"Well, I will spearhead it all through. I'll ensure—"

"Vivek," Harsh interrupted, "I need you to be here, in this city, until we're done with the integration. At least the first phase." The law seemed to have been laid down on Vivek. It was not how he functioned typically. His job was to get a deal signed and assign it to a project team while he went sniffing for a new one.

"What are your concerns?" he posed an open-ended question, gently.

"It's a new territory. It's not my turf. I need you to make me feel comfortable through the process." Vivek instantly realised what this was about. Harsh's vulnerability rang a bell. Grapevine had it that his last acquisition, a small precious-stones manufacturer, had gone awry, and the cost and time overruns had driven him into frenzied paranoia. He was probably just trying to avoid a repeat. Made sense.

"Okay. We'll work it out," he replied, imagining himself taking early Monday morning flights from Mumbai to Ahmedabad for weeks, possibly even months. It didn't make for a pretty picture. He sipped some more wine to take his mind off the bloodshot eyes early morning flights rewarded him with.

***

It had been an exceptionally hot last few days, with the mid-afternoon sun burning the edges of leaves of most plants in Keya's balcony. She had started leaving for work earlier than usual and returning late to avoid being out in the dry heat. One morning, while she was deeply engrossed in writing a review about an online retailer who had sent her a faulty product, Sujata, her subordinate, pinged her.

*Have you heard what I have heard?* Sujata IMed, with a string of sad emoticons.

*About?* Give me ambiguity or give me something else, she muttered.

*Rangers being sold!*

Keya stared at that sequence of words for a few moments, her face white and her eyes enlarged; the piece of information shook her up like a mini earthquake. If she could avoid the fast approaching panic attack, she would figure out where to begin her inquisition from.

*You haven't heard?* Sujata pinged again.

*No! What are you saying? Come by, please.*

Sujata gave her the low-down on what she had heard. Except she hadn't heard that much. Just a rumour from a friend of a colleague who told her at her birthday party the previous night that *kuch toh jhol hai.*

"Please keep this to yourself, Sujata. I'll find out what I can from LHF. There's no point spreading unsubstantiated rumours." Keya's mind was going through severe turbulence but she tried to sound calm. She had to get to the bottom of this with LHF immediately.

LHF was how she, and all the girls in her team, addressed Aman, her boss. It was short for low-hanging fruit, a term Aman conveniently threw around in meetings and general conversations at least half a dozen times a day. After the first few times, one of the girls in the team had commented on how gross it sounded, associating it with Aman's anatomy. From that day, each time Aman wielded that term, the girls would give each other a mischievous look and titter.

Keya rushed to LHF's cabin down the hallway, but it was locked. Panic had officially struck her, in fact taken a good hold of her. She returned to her desk. Her face appeared frozen. Chills ran through her body but her palms turned sweaty and so did the back of her neck. Her mind went blank. It was as if different parts of her body weren't in communication with each other, but they all sensed danger.

There was a new e-mail: *Urgent senior management meeting in the third floor main conference room at ten a.m. Attendance is not optional.* It was from Mr Krishnan's assistant on his behalf. She glanced at the time on her screen. It was fifteen minutes to ten. Her heart began to thump loudly. A million and one scenarios whizzed past her mind. She ran her hands through her hair, and bunching them up in her fingers, put her head down on the desk. *Oh God, oh God, what was he going to say? Maybe: Rangers have been sold, and effective immediately, everyone is terminated.* Just the thought of this terrified her. She instantly realised she had a team of five to protect. The newest member in her team had just relocated from Delhi. It hadn't even been three months. The rest had been with her and the company for less than a year. It was a brand new team she had been given the sole responsibility of building. She'd gone through hundreds of resumes to scout for ideal candidates and spent hours conducting phone and personal interviews. After careful evaluation, she'd handpicked the five people whom she called her 'favourite five'. She'd stayed back day after day to train them and bring them up to speed. She'd invested a significant amount of time and effort motivating them, individually and collectively. They'd all made their mark on her in one way or the other. She couldn't bear the thought of seeing them go. She could perhaps deal with her own termination but not theirs.

*Too many thoughts, too little time*, she said to herself. Pretending to appear strong, she walked by the cubicles of her team members and informed them that she would be in the main conference room for a meeting. The room wasn't big enough to accommodate everyone who was invited. Keya caught a glimpse of the senior leadership, dressed in dark suits, at the other end of the room, their faces gravely serious. Employees who couldn't find seats were requested to line up against the walls and make way for others. The flurry and murmur continued as everyone squeezed into the confined space.

Keya's gaze travelled the length and breadth of the room, trying to decipher what was happening. The undercurrents hinted at the news Sujata had shared with her a while ago. But despite that there was something else she could not put her finger on. She continued to look around and spotted the lost guy she'd run into in the lobby, a few days back. He was casually talking to the senior management. Then something bizarre happened. The lost guy from the lobby—that's what she would call him from now on—emerged from behind Krishnan and picked up the cordless microphone. It had never happened in the history of her time at this company that an outsider had opened a meeting, especially when Krishnan was around. He was known to open with a joke, and a funny one at that.

"Good morning. Sorry about the short notice. I'm Vivek. Vivek Grewal. Vice-president, Cello Consulting, an M&A consulting firm based out of Mumbai. We've just been brought on-board to help out with some new projects." *Vivek Grewal* . . . she made a mental note of the name. She continued to look at him, baffled. *What is this clown doing here?*

"Most of you are probably wondering what I'm doing here. We have an exciting announcement to make this morning. I urge all of you to be calm and patient, and not panic." The second those words were out of his mouth, fear swept over most people's unsuspecting faces. A few more words and he made it sound like a nuclear threat was imminent. *That fancy VP title and not enough tact,* Keya thought.

"It's no news that for a while now the Rangers have been struggling. Especially after losing two skilled batsmen in auction this year, it has left us in a weak spot. I have no doubt about the bright future of this team, though. I see that you all are just as passionate about it as you probably were when the team was first formed."

*Us?* Did he just say *us?* She craned her neck to look at Krishnan and saw a beat-but-trying-to-look-upbeat face. *What was happening?*

"This is an entirely new direction for the company. One we've never had to venture into in the past," the Vivek fellow added.

*We? What was with the 'us' and the 'we' he was throwing around? How was he a part of the Rangers already?* She tried to get past all this and reflect on what he was really saying. She had never heard of a company mass-firing all its employees. Then she began to think through it rationally. It wasn't like Krishnan to put them all on a boat and send that to the Niagara Falls where it was destined to sink. No, he had more heart than that. It wasn't going to be a massacre. That would be absurd. She tried to think of possibilities before that Vivek Grewal verbalised them. That way she would be prepared. Even the worst nightmare, if predicted, had some balancing effect, after all.

"We've been fortunate enough to get two of the top Ranji Trophy picks this season. Both the young boys are promising athletes and it's a commitment we've made to ourselves and to our fans that this team will emerge stronger," the man continued. She had to hand it to him for masterfully assessing the fears and hopes of those collected and playing to them.

Having thought that, she caught a breather. He was still raving about the team and they'd all already heard this a million times before. So, if the cricket team wasn't going anywhere, the employees wouldn't be, too. They couldn't all be fired. Who'd do their marketing? And handle their sales and advertising? And run their charity foundations? And hospitality? And customer support? There was no way, right?

"But we've had our share of challenges too, this year. Particularly with losing our top best players who pulled in the crowd."

*God, why is he still talking?* Here came the ugly part on a rollerblade. Her eyes closed forcefully, as an involuntary response to the announcement she was sure he would make.

"Sales have been very weak. Half of the tickets for our home games have been going unsold and there's a huge inventory of pavilion, premium, and platinum tickets to fill up. The corporate boxes are deserted, too."

Her hands wanted to cover her ears in a theatrical gesture but she kept them pinned to her thighs. She was overreacting, she knew it. Her mother didn't call her a drama queen for nothing. "I know I'm speaking on Mr Krishnan's behalf here,"—Krishnan nodded—"given the grim outlook, we feel lucky that we've had some interest from a reputed investor." His 'we's' seemed to be working. Keya was beyond the acceptance stage. "I'd like to take this opportunity to introduce Harsh

Desai. He's the owner at Desai Group of Companies. Harsh is based out of Bengaluru and has a wide array of successful businesses."

Harsh waved at the crowd. *God bless your heart, Harsh Desai*, she wanted to scream. This wasn't as bad as she had speculated. She carefully looked at Vivek again. Were those honey eyes? If she'd seen him on TV, she'd have gasped, perhaps looked him up on Google thereafter. He was *that* gorgeous.

"Harsh has stepped forward to acquire the Rangers. He will bring in the much needed cash to support several sales and marketing initiatives that have been curbed due to lack of funds."

HOLY CRAP! Sujata was right. Rangers *was* being sold to some stranger!

Then Krishnan added his two cents with a jarring aftereffect. "The downside is, eventually, Harsh will bring in some of his own staff, which unfortunately is the dark side of every acquisition."

She knew it; she wanted to jump on the table and say that angrily. She had a sense that he was going to talk about staff reduction. She felt deceived; just because he took the detour of hinting at an 'investor'. Harsh wasn't an 'investor', he was the buyer. Her passion, her team, her job—they'd all just been reduced to a commodity.

"But I urge you all to not panic or think of the worst-case scenario. I'm not going to lie and say it's going to be the exact same headcount a year down the line. It may not be. One of the side effects would be that we'll make every department as lean as possible. Some departments, on the other hand, that don't have enough manpower, will get augmented. It'll all be about striking the right balance," Krishnan added.

Suddenly, she was unsure of how she felt. Reduction on one hand, augmentation on the other. *Contradictory messages do nothing for me*, she wanted to tell Krishnan.

"We will be analysing our structure closely over the next few weeks, possibly months. We've engaged Cello Consulting, which specialises in mergers and acquisitions, to help us through the process. Once Cello presents their findings to us, we'll go through several rounds of discussions with every department head to determine if Cello's analysis is accurate and whether they agree with its recommendations. So you see, this will be a process we'll all undergo together as a team."

She wished he hadn't shared this information. What was the point of knowing about the commotion to come if you didn't know which way it was going? *Stupid stress-inducing acquisition*, she cursed under her breath.

Then Vivek took over again. "Needless to say, it'll be futile to worry about something we don't know yet. So let's all go about life as usual with a positive outlook."

*Yeah. Whatever.*

"I like to think of this as a self-correcting exercise. We'll learn about our strengths and weaknesses. It's not desirable, but sometimes it's essential."

*Wow, this Vivek guy is going to go all Dalai Lama on us.* She craved some of her self-made tea. It was the only thing guaranteed to give her momentary relief in dicey and undesirable situations.

"I request you all to fully cooperate with Cello Consulting as they try to work through resource analysis," Krishnan appealed to the crowd.

*Right. Sleep with the enemy.* That's what he was asking, wasn't he?

"I just want to conclude by thanking you all for being such

integral parts of this team. For making this company reach the heights it had during good times. For believing in it despite the challenges. For giving it your love, dedication, and passion. I thank you from the bottom of my heart. Together, we'll reach new heights, again. I promise you that. But it's going to be an emotional journey, one that will require us to support those around us. Have a good rest of the day," Krishnan concluded with trite, empty words.

She wanted to be the first one to walk out of the conference room. Constraints blocked her. It felt like having a seat half way down in an aircraft. One had got to wait until half the people deplaned. She wanted to avoid looking at Mr Sad eyes, Ms Forced smile, Mr Stoic, Ms Poker face, Ms Anxiety attack, Mr Sweaty palms, Ms Tears hiding-under-shades, and the rest, but they were all right there, in dangerous proximity to her.

This meeting had given her a bad taste in the mouth but she was no longer afraid. Whatever was destined would happen. Can't stop it, so why even try? It was all about the journey, not the destination anyway. She felt a tad better with that last thought.

*Vivek, bring it on*, she mouthed defiantly.

"All right team, you know the drill. Let's get on with it," Vivek firmly instructed his team of three, comprising of Omar, Akshay, and Satyen, as he took off his jacket in the conference room at the Rangers' office. Blown-up action shots of several star players of the Rangers, in thick golden frames, were the claim to fame of the conference room his team was assigned. It was, officially, the first week of the engagement and the conference room was to be their companion through many days and late nights now. Akshay and Satyen had executed several M&A deals with him and operated like clockwork. The beginning of a transaction was always the most exciting part for Vivek. Like blank walls waiting to be painted. He especially enjoyed the chaos and confusion the initial stages promised.

"Omar, you take org charts. Take a stab at formulating the target organisation model. Roles, responsibilities, reporting lines, workforce transition, headcount reduction; the works." Omar made notes with a hyperactive body language. His elbow inadvertently pushed the over-filled coffee mug that caused some of the coffee to spill on his sheet. Hired through campus placements, Omar had been with the firm as a consultant for three months now and had been nudging Vivek to get him on a project that he was overseeing. This was his lucky break.

"And will you stop playing with yourself?" Vivek added as an after-thought. The rest of his team instantly cracked up without even being filled-in on what had transpired.

"God, I'm not," Omar blatantly defied charges.

"Either I'm crazy or I just saw you do it again," Vivek accused, referring to Omar fiddling with his crotch through his pants. He had been caught in the act several times by everyone on the team.

"Do you wear speedos underneath? That could get really uncomfortable," Akshay, the senior consultant on the team, teased, making Omar's face turn red further.

"I might know what it is. You get bikini waxes done, don't you? I hear it could get scratchy once the hair grows back," Satyen, the project manager, laughed, not wanting to miss out on the fun.

"Fuck off, you guys. It's a medical condition." The same lame excuse by Omar, as he lashed out at Akshay and Satyen.

"All right, that's enough, guys. Let's calm down and get to work," Vivek imposed, reminding them that they were not at a bar where smack talk was welcome. "But seriously, speedos? Man, you need to go shopping," he teased one last time with an extended drawl. Omar exhaled loudly, shaking his head in disbelief, embarrassed. Being the junior-most consultant around, it had been made known to him, in jest, that he had got to pay his dues by being on the receiving end of the jokes. And, boy, they were aplenty.

"Anyway, they're looking to take some significant costs out on this one," Vivek instructed Akshay, who was slightly more senior than Omar and had been around for a year. Being on back-to-back projects, he'd picked up the basics rather well. "We need to come up with our initial cut on synergies. I need headcount, every facility they engage, all contracts with vendors, suppliers, etc, and a detailed outline of their technology. Also, I'm assigning customers to you. We'll need to ensure there is ample communication and this comes through as a seamless transition. No disruption." Akshay made notes in shorthand. The speed at which his team made notes made Vivek realise he was probably talking at the speed of light. But that's exactly how he preferred to talk while laying down the law.

"Satyen, you know the deal, buddy. Front office, back office, ticketing; let's include everything we can find." Being the senior-most guy on the project, Satyen was one of the lucky few who were in Vivek's innermost circle of dependable people. If Vivek signed a deal, Satyen was on it regardless of how many other projects he was involved in. Satyen nodded.

After he was done briefing his team, Vivek looked outside the glass walls, towards the city skyline, planning on what to handle next. His eyes fell on a tall, futuristic-looking, beige-coloured building that stood elegantly next to an equally high, medieval-looking, green-coloured one. His viewing angle made the futuristic one peek from behind the medieval one and the juxtaposition of two starkly different structures plugged his interest. He stared at it a bit longer. It was the first time since his IMI-A days that he had felt drawn to the city in some strange way. It wasn't just about the building; Ahmedabad was somehow attracting him much more the second time around.

The calmness in his head was rudely interrupted by a sharp noise of collision. He looked in the direction of it and noticed an accident. An auto-rickshaw had rear-ended another one and the driver of the latter rickshaw was half hanging out of his rickshaw, yelling at a girl. He narrowed his eyes to catch a glimpse of the girl, who was now taking off her slippers on the side walk, and putting on bright orange heels, which she had just pulled out from her handbag, all this while giving a royal ignore to the screaming driver. It was the girl who'd given him directions to the bathroom on the day of his first meeting. He tried to recall her name, but couldn't go beyond the letter k. *Keisha? Kripa? Or was it Keya?* She looked beautiful from afar, he casually noted.

The driver in the frontward rickshaw was yelling at the driver who had rear-ended him, who in turn was yelling at the girl. But the girl appeared to be blissfully oblivious to any of this. It didn't take long for him to figure out that she must have run across through the intersection on a blinking red light, leading to the collision. He chuckled while shaking his head in astonishment.

He diverted his attention back to work. It had been a while since he'd gotten involved post kick-off meetings. The life cycle of a typical project for him began at identifying opportunities and ended with sealing the deal. Execution of the transaction was something he monitored from distance. This case was different from the rest in three ways, he'd reminded himself as a self-convincing exercise. One, Harsh was a special client; comparatively easier to convince and guaranteed to pump in a huge amount of money. Two, his affinity for cricket had been going steady for years. And three, it was his first sports project; a project that would be his foot-in-the-door in the exhilarating world of cricket.

"Three months is too aggressive, Vivek. Just look at these deliverables. Realistically, I don't think it's doable." Satyen shared his take on the timeline for integration, drawing Vivek's full attention.

"That's all we have." He had done this countless times. It invariably started off looking 'aggressive' then gradually turned into 'impossible' with cost and time overruns, until it all got wrapped up 'successfully' with successive sleepless nights for the entire team. Actuals almost never ended up being the same as estimates, but that's why they were called actuals. He shrugged; it didn't bother him for it wasn't a reflection of his team's efficiency. It was just the nature of the business. The unknowns and assumptions that they often started their new projects with usually turned out to be ambitious and humbled them in the process.

"The key to being successful in M&A, in case you've forgotten, is to be able to flow with the tide, to be prepared for the twists and turns that are inevitable, and to adjust accordingly. Adaptability is the mantra," he educated them, as they nodded in agreement.

There was a faint knock on the door. Omar opened it. It was the secretary.

"There's someone outside to meet you," she said, looking at Vivek uncertainly. It didn't seem like she remembered Vivek's name.

"Who is it?"

"A Shailendra Tekwani."

He couldn't recall that name, so he curiously walked out behind the secretary. By the reception desk, he saw a tall man clad in a green *khadi* kurta wearing horn-rimmed retro glasses, seated on a comfortable chair. She pointed Vivek towards him and took off.

"Hi, I'm Vivek." He extended a hand towards the visitor, his brows raised in anticipation.

"Shailendra," the visitor said with a loose handshake. "Thanks for your time."

"I'm sorry, but have we met?"

"I'm a senior sports reporter with Ahmedabad Chronicle. I wanted some details on the Rangers' sale. Do you have a few minutes?"

*Holy crap*. It had barely been hours and the news had already leaked! Discomfited, he gingerly attempted escape. "I'm sorry. We'll have to do this another time. I'm late for a meeting."

"Just a few questions?"

"I really have to go. Sorry."

"No problem. Here's my card. Call me when you have a few minutes?"

***

Keya had just received an e-mail from LHF, demanding to see the budget sheet. The previous two weeks hadn't been easy on her. Department assessment, much like self-contemplation, wasn't a fun exercise, especially when thrusted upon, she had concluded. She had been assigned the task of putting together all minor and major expenses for the department. It felt like documenting one's life to the detail of every small purchase. Worse still, providing justifications behind those actions. If she had to justify buying products like ear buds and deos in her personal life, she would die of anger. Why one must *rationalise* the need to buy things, she wondered. The bobble-head doll on her desk, of the most celebrated player of the Rangers, Jango, seemed to be staring at her. She stared back in oblivion, until the doll answered: "Because Rangers are paying for it, baby. They need to know where their money is going. Just how it works." The doll winked at her. She snapped herself back to reality with a grin.

The budget sheet was now complete and accurate. It was nothing too extravagant, not to her anyway; just money spent on resources, overheads, training, administration, and operations.

LHF gently knocked on the door, then raised his eyebrows from above his rimless glasses in lieu of a question.

"It's ready," she responded to the non-verbal question, moving her swivelling chair towards him. "I've accounted for everything in the last fiscal year, from stapler pins and summer interns to the virgin pinacoladas at that one team lunch we had."

"Great. What's it looking like?" He was sporting new worry lines on the forehead.

"There's no fat to trim, sir. I don't see how they could make this group any leaner."

That was the hard truth. Keya and her team of five weren't enough to keep up with the daily load of work. She'd often tell LHF that her team was her oxygen tank. If one went on vacation, she stopped breathing. They frequently ended up hiring 'temps' to keep up with projects that surfaced sporadically.

LHF, being a golf enthusiast, religiously played with his friends at the cantonment. He had recently torn a ligament when his caddy had accidentally tripped on him while chatting up the golfer behind him. He had to undergo ankle surgery shortly after. With his intermittent absence on account of surgery, Keya had been struggling to keep it all together. *Manning the fort is not as much fun as it sounds*, she'd frequently say to herself. She had been thrilled initially at the additional responsibility but over time it had added up significantly, wearing her down.

"I wouldn't worry too much, Keya." LHF was optimistic as ever. "There is no indication, whatsoever, about all departments being asked to trim down. I'd call it a mere formality at this point," he intoned in his signature style, pausing after every few words. Something about the manner in which his speech was rendered gave him an intellectual touch. She nodded thoughtfully, although not entirely convinced, and handed over a printout of the budget.

"I hope you're right, sir. I just can't bear to see anyone from the team go."

"If you don't believe me, see this." He pulled out something from his pocket and extended a hand towards her. She grabbed it from him and gave it a closer look. It was a ticket for the corporate box at the stadium for that evening's game. Ahmedabad Rangers vs Mumbai Mavericks. "It's a Meet 'n Greet with Desai and Cello. Harsh Desai is the name. And the chap from Cello is Vivek, I believe. I have a follow-up appointment with my orthopaedic today. Can you go?"

"We're entertaining them?" Her question had a screeching after-effect.

"It's a partnership, Keya. They're not the enemy." He smiled. "So, what do you think?"

"Yeah, I'll go."

She didn't know what to pray for: a victory or a defeat. What would ensure her position in the company?

Keya dabbed some gloss on her lips, looking into the tiny handbag mirror. One quick layer of mascara and brush through her hair and off she went to the game. She took the lift to level three. Level one had pavilion, premium and platinum seats, level two general admission seats that led up to the stands which comprised of the upper tiers, and level three, with its corporate boxes, was where the action really heated up, at times much more than that on the field.

One of the twenty corporate boxes on the third level was the 'home suite' and co-workers, especially sales staff and senior executives often used it game after game. Keya had been invited on several occasions to be a part of this elite company, and it was always stimulating but today nothing permeated through the cold reality of staff reduction.

'SUITE E 20' read the golden plate on the glossy cherry door. She slid her ticket into the electronic lock; it beeped, matching in frequency to her heartbeat. She opened the door to her immediate future that was filled with uncertainties.

Small talk. Restrained, plastic smiles. Handshaking. Business card exchanges. Beer in coloured plastic cups (meant to be overlooked by those who adhered to the concept of a dry state). French fries, paneer and chicken tikkas, and a whole assortment of finger foods neatly lined up on the side tables. The box was an incessant chatter of power-hungry people and, if one was to take a guess from the spread, food-hungry as well.

Down on the field below, the pre-match interviews of both team's captains had just concluded and they were now getting together for the coin toss. Crowds—the stadium was not really sold out—cheered. The NRF blimp was hard to miss just as much as the flashing ads of luxury cars and electronics companies on the ground ad spaces. Then it struck her. This was a crucial match for the Rangers. They desperately needed to win this.

The double round-robin had exhausted a majority of teams but the Rangers had been faring the worst. If they didn't clinch tonight's win, they were out of the series. For good. The pressure on the team was palpable, not that that did anything to satiate its blood-thirsty fans who were waiting, just waiting, to either indulge in exultant celebration, should the team win, or draw blood and exact their pound of flesh should the mere mortals they had elevated to the status of demigods prove their total impotency.

Mumbai Mavericks won the toss and elected to bat. The opening batsmen walked towards the pitch to the sounds of boos and cheers in equal measure; putting on their gloves, adjusting their headgear. The Chief Minister had just walked in with his Z-level security and was now seated comfortably in a corporate box diagonally across from Keya's. She could always tell by the piercing sirens of a fleet of cars if the Chief Minister was in the stadium. She spotted a few yesteryear-actors-turned-politicians in pristine white kurtas and matching white beards hobnobbing with him. Then there was the owner of Mumbai Mavericks adding the glamour quotient in her team's jersey and jeans, oversized designer shades, and handbag firmly in place, accompanied by her son and the British-accented playboy kid of another team's owner. She and the playboy discussed serious business from the looks of it, while her son looking terribly bored, resorted to his phone and cola.

The cheerleaders had lined up by the side, prettified with false lashes and thick layers of foundation that wouldn't even allow a smile, ready to entertain at the sound of a whistle. Much as she tried, she couldn't find a red flag. The atmosphere was so electrifying and the excitement so thrilling that she could only sum it up with the iconic line: I almost peed my pants. This was how she had always sensed it to be; even a person as disinterested in the game as her was revved up by it. But today there was something else to it. Something lethal. The Rangers had to sweat it out tonight or else . . . She shuddered at that thought.

A known face from another department spotted Keya. A few more joined. She looked around, searching for the foes who weren't really foes according to her boss.

"Where are they?" Curious, craning her neck, she asked one of her colleagues.

"They were here a second ago. I just spoke to Harsh. Nice guy."

"I'm sure he is." She craned her neck some more. The suite, technically for a crowd of about twenty, had at least fifty people around this evening. Not the easiest set-up to spot one's target.

When she was done talking to her willing and available colleagues, she looked around for a beer can. Anything that could relax her was welcome. Not spotting any on the side table, she went around the podium that filled in for a bar. She crouched to open the mini refrigerator that was safely hidden away like a giant cask filled with precious jewels. As she made a move to get up after grabbing a pint of Haywards, she heard a voice.

"I'll have a beer," the voice demanded.

"Excuse me?" she questioned, straightening up. Her eyebrows were raised and there was more than a hint of indignation in her voice.

"Do you have Kingfisher?" the voice without a face asked impatiently.

He finally turned around. She looked at him, defiantly. His face appeared familiar. She blinked and almost immediately it hit her. It was him—the lost guy from the lobby. The one with the fancy spiel on the acquisition the other day. *Vivek, was it?* And why was he always asking her for something when they met? Directions to the toilet. Beer. Her job. Okay the last one wasn't quite true but that's where it was all headed!

Keya casually placed her Haywards on the podium but before she could clarify that she wasn't a bartender, he picked it up with a faint 'thanks' and walked away. Enraged, she followed him.

She contemplated catching him by his shirt collar and giving him a dramatic sermon, but one of the VPs she had been chatting with earlier, arrived on the spot and turned him to her.

"Keya, have you met Vivek? He's from Cello Consulting," Mr VP said with a tie so tight around his neck, it looked more like a strangling device than an accent. *I could use that. To throttle 'Vivek from Cello Consulting'.* And, of course, she had met him. She remembered every unkind word he had uttered, distinctly, from his acquisition speech.

"Yes. Just did." Her voice dripped sarcasm and her unyielding gaze awaited an apology. But Vivek just looked at her instead. Not a word from him. *Asshole*, she concluded.

"Vivek, Keya heads marketing for Rangers." Mr VP introduced her albeit with a bit of incorrect information. He might as well have called her the Goddess of fertility.

"Oh. Good," 'Vivek from Cello Consulting' responded, very obviously disengaged. *Oh? Good?* Definitely an asshole.

"Actually that would be my boss . . ." *LHF . . . not LHF . . . low-hanging fruit . . . not that either . . . ugghh, what's his real name?*

"uhh, Aman, who heads Marketing." Not one to live in lies, she confessed.

"Right, when golf permits. Haven't seen Aman in a while now. Did he undergo surgery recently? All well I hope?" Mr VP asked. Before she could answer his question, he joined the rest in the mission that seemed to unite everyone that night. "Where's the beer?"

"It's in that hidden refrigerator behind the bar." She was slowly turning into a beer guide. This couldn't have ended well.

"Let's just move the buried refrigerator out of that hidden spot, shall we?" Mr VP said while moving the mini refrigerator into the spotlight. Vivek, evidently agreeing with the seriousness of the issue, gave him a helping hand.

Minutes later, the crowd had dispersed and it was just the two of them in a corner with a looming, awkward silence. She pushed a few strands of hair away from her face. Vivek leaned against a walnut-coloured wall, staring at the big screen in the suite where the game from the stadium was being broadcasted. He still hadn't apologised or said a single word or anything else for that matter.

*I wonder who is he rooting for: Mavericks or Rangers?* Keya was still miffed, but something about Vivek captured her interest. She tried not to think about it but couldn't help noticing the enormous sex appeal his chin cleft exuded. It made her heart skip a beat. His chic haircut looked deliberately tamed for a corporate setting. His two-toned blazer, with a tie that could have been too skinny on anyone else, spelled refined charm. It was as if he couldn't go wrong, no matter what he wore. She was even able to spot a hole in his left earlobe sans earring. It gave her a feeling that he must have been a wild child while growing up. In the dim, recessed lights she grasped how handsome he was. Tall, broad-shouldered, honey eyes, great sense of style. Swoon. Before her right hemisphere could complete that thought, her left interjected with a 'Here's the catch. Dreamboat is a jerk.' Sigh. *Maybe, just maybe, he hadn't recognised me because of the dim lights while asking for beer*, she tried to reason with herself. But it was futile.

"Keya, is it?" His brusqueness broke the silence.

"Yes." She wanted to quip instead of giving a straightforward affirmative answer but nothing occurred.

"Haven't heard that name before. Is that a local favourite?"

She had been asked several times if she were a Bong. Her long dark tresses, bronze skin, big eyes, all good fodder for the guessing game in a city where not many were from a varied background. But, *local favourite*? What was her name, a fruit?

"That would be North Indian," she replied.

"You're a Punju." Was that a question, she wondered. Or comprehension? Smugness?

"Yes." One word answers again. She could do so much better.

"Nice. Likewise. Guess my folks weren't all that creative. What does Keya mean?"

"It's a rain-flower. White. Pristine. Looks like a toy windmill."

"I'm intrigued."

"It's used to make perfumes. Actually I believe it's also used as a stimulant and an antispasmodic." Uh oh. Awkward.

"I haven't been defeated in the name game like that before. Mine just means wisdom. Plain and easy. No layered meanings." He hadn't said one strange thing in the last thirty seconds. Something was wrong!

"Well, at least there isn't a dark side to yours." Sweet. She was finally able to quip. Wait, that wasn't quipping at all, she realised. Just something silly and vastly unimpactful!

"Now you're making it up."

"I wish. I believe Keya has been mentioned in Hindu mythology as a cursed flower," she candidly confessed.

He took yet another sip of beer with a thinking face. "I'm no expert but I think a lot of things in the Hindu mythology were cursed. I wouldn't take it personally. But then again, your folks must have thought this through."

This time, she was done with him.

"I'll see you around," she said as curtly as she could manage before merging into the crowd. *Dog!*

A few weeks of studying the organisation structure and reporting lines had given way to some clarity for Vivek. It was time to discuss redundancies with department heads and pick the chosen ones who would soon be ex-employees.

Vivek walked up to Aman, the Director of Strategic Marketing Services, and knocked on his office door. Keya opened it from within. It startled him slightly.

"Hi, Vivek, come in. I'm just wrapping up with Keya," Aman called out to him from within.

"I can wait."

"*Arre aa jao bhai.* No problem. Keya, you need anything else?"

"No, sir."

All Vivek could manage was a forced half-smile at Keya when they crossed each other. She did the same, acknowledging his presence, then walking out. Vivek made himself comfortable across from Aman after Keya closed the door shut.

"I have run some numbers and done some preliminary analysis," Vivek said to Aman, kicking it off. "In order to get the synergies we are looking for from the deal, we will need to make some cuts. But you know that already, don't you?" He didn't wait for Aman to respond. The question was more rhetorical than anything else, and was solely aimed at giving Aman the time to orient himself to the upcoming discussion. His answer wasn't important. Getting him focused was.

"Yes, I'm aware," he responded without any deliberation.

"So who is redundant in your team? My initial take is Keya Singhal at the mid-level and these three at the level below her?" Vivek asked, circling Keya's name and the names of three of her subordinates on an organisation chart with his Montblanc rollerblade pen. The pen had been very close to his heart. He had earned it as recognition of his contribution to the firm when he became the youngest VP at the age of thirty-two. He considered it his lucky mascot, something he needed to bring out when the stakes were high. He knew if he were to orchestrate this acquisition successfully, he would find his entry point to the lucrative Media & Entertainment market that had been eluding him for the longest time. This would be the first significant ladder he would need to climb before the market started recognising him as a strong player in the cut-throat M&A world. Well, that's for later. *Focus*, he instructed himself.

Vivek stayed in Aman's office for over two hours, sipping on some Red Bull, asking questions, making notes, contemplating, and understanding the core strengths of Aman's team, their operations and the implications on the rest of the organisation.

It was time to make some decisions.

"It's never that easy, is it?" Aman's tone had taken on a glum tone.

"This is what I have cut my teeth on. If there's one thing I've learnt, it's that people are indispensable," Vivek said, then paused for effect and added, "unless a merger happens."

"Hmm," Aman mulled over that, then asked, "have you met Keya?"

"Briefly."

"She's a bright girl."

"Not important, is it?" Vivek spoke with a straight face.

"Listen, I can make this easy for you," a thoughtful looking Aman offered, raising Vivek's curiosity a notch. "And I presume you'll keep this confidential?"

"I'm curious to hear it."

"Okay, here goes. I have been on the verge of quitting for some time now. I have to undergo another surgery for my ankle and need some time off to recover." His voice dropped down several notches.

Vivek studied his face, looking for signs that would raise his internal radar. This was something he had honed over the multiple deals he had run.

"Quit for that? What about sick leave or leave without pay?" Vivek questioned. Why was Aman backing out so quickly? What was behind his interest in keeping Keya around?

"It's not just the surgery. Got some unfinished personal business to take care of. I have some family property in Munnar. A farm house with some cows and horses. There's even a small tea estate. Part of it is disputed. It's going to take me some time to sort out the mess."

"You just made that up, didn't you?" Vivek said with half a smile. He would have to do some research of his own to figure out the truth.

"I wish. My old man refused to move away from his horses and tea."

"Horses and tea! True life treasures."

"Indeed," Aman agreed. Then he added, "Coming back to business, let's do this. Let's uncircle Keya. She can handle the team easily. This team needs her. Count me out. Leave the rest of the team as it is."

"Two issues with that," Vivek inferred instantly. "One, if you leave, that would leave a void at the director level and the team won't be considered stable. Two, the total team size—"

"Let's promote Keya to the director level in that case," Aman interrupted.

"You think she's ready?" Aman was making it too easy for Keya, baffling Vivek.

"Yes. She's been ready for a while."

"Let me think about that. In such volatile environments, we usually don't recommend first time promotions. At best, she could continue at her level and still handle her team. What about the five employees under her? Anyone redundant there? Seems like a pretty big team for the job function."

"It's not. We actually barely get by with the workload, but I'll discuss with Keya and get back to you."

The two men talked for another half hour before heading out to lunch. On the way out, Aman stopped Vivek mid-stride and said, "In reference to Keya, I understand your concern about recommending someone for a promotion at such a time. See if you could include that as a suggestion from me. She is deserving of it. The way she takes her team forward, I doubt anyone else can. The team will thrive under her leadership."

There hadn't been many times when Vivek had heard

a boss speak so highly of a team member. *You must be quite something, Keya Singhal.*

Later that afternoon Vivek was at his desk in the conference room—a stack of organisation charts from every department spread out in front of him—counting the total number of names circled in red. The names he'd circled with much discussion and deliberation with the heads of these departments. The names he'd be presenting to the C-level execs at the Rangers for a first look. The names of those who'll soon have the distinctive misfortune of being ex-employees.

There was a gentle knock on the conference room door. The room was usually locked when the team worked with confidential documents. It was Omar, the joker of his team.

"Here are Aman's HR records." He handed over the documents to Vivek, closing the door behind him. "He's been with Krishnan for a long time. Fifteen years to be exact. Been with the Rangers for three as Director. Before that he worked for Krishnan in one of his other companies. His promotion to VP level fell through twice. The first time, they got someone from outside, instead. The second time around, there was a mega project failure in that department, which got negative publicity within the organisation." Omar spoke in one breath with the seriousness of an investigating officer in a homicide case.

"Is there a pension plan in the company?"

"No."

"What's the severance package policy?"

"One month's pay if you've spent at least six months with the firm. Over three years, it's three months."

"Bingo!" Vivek exclaimed, solving the puzzle effortlessly. Aman wasn't likely to be promoted anytime soon; perhaps never. He'd been on high-burn projects, some of which had hurt his reputation. He needed time off for surgery, his tea estate was disputed, and he would get three months worth of free pay if he could pass off his resignation as lay-off.

"Keya," Vivek muttered to himself looking at her circled name on one of the sheets, "You are one lucky doll!"

He then looked up at Omar and said, "Good work, buddy."

Omar beamed. "Do you still need Aman's records?"

"No. You may return them."

Just as Omar was half out of the door, Vivek saw Keya enter the conference room, much to his shock. As a reflex, he swept his desk in one quick motion, gathering all the organisation chart printouts and turning them upside down.

When he looked up, Omar was holding the door since Keya's hands were carrying a plate full of what appeared to be cake pieces dripping with molten chocolate.

"Hi," she said cheerfully to everyone in the room. Vivek's face was static but his eyes conveyed that it wasn't a good time to barge in. The papers he'd just turned around were pink slips-in-progress. It certainly wasn't the occasion to rejoice with cake. He mentally cursed Omar for leaving the door open for too long.

Uninvited, she walked in confidently. The smile on her relaxed face immediately got erased when her gaze met Vivek's. She took a few steps forward and put down the plate she was holding on his desk, next to his paperwork, making Vivek a little flustered. He noticed one stray sheet of paper, face up, right between the pile he'd managed to turn over and the cake. STRATEGIC MARKETING SERVICES, the heading read in bold. Sure enough, Keya's department. Murphy was either God or the devil, he reckoned. In one quick motion, Vivek threw himself on the enormous conference table to catch that paper and turn it upside down with the rest of the pile, almost shocking Keya in the process as she retracted with a puzzled face.

"Whoa! What was that?" Omar, the emperor of inappropriateness butted in.

"I hope I'm not intruding," Keya stated, her question masked as a statement.

*Yes, you are indeed,* Vivek wanted to snap but resisted the urge. She looked lovely, he noticed, in her bright orange, fitted dress. The lights in the room bounced off her dress giving her skin a sun-kissed look.

"We just had a mini celebration in the department and had a ton of cake left. Thought I'd share."

Before he could respond with a 'no, thank you', Omar had begun devouring it. A thick drop of rich chocolate rolled down the side of his face, disgusting Vivek.

"Someone's birthday?" Omar asked with his mouth full.

"No. Actually, my colleague's younger brother just got selected to IMI-A." Each word broken out, expressing her pleasure.

"No way!" Omar exclaimed, then looked at Vivek and pointing a piece of half-eaten cake at him, remarked, "Another smart kid, just like you, Vivek. Can the world handle so much intelligence?"

"You went to IMI-A?" she stared at him, blinking her eyes in what appeared to be disbelief.

"Um—"

"Yes, of course he did." Omar seemed delighted at an opportunity to fill in the gaps. "Bachelors from NM College. Internship at a prestigious investment bank—GP Stanlay—in Mumbai. MBA from IMI-A. Youngest VP at Cello. He's a stud boy and my role model." He spoke with unrestrained excitement and in one breath, as usual.

"Easy, buddy. You don't have to sell me so hard. She isn't here to buy," Vivek admonished.

"Can't help it," Omar defended with a shrug.

"Enjoy the cake," Keya breezily responded and walked out.

Vivek locked the door from within instantly and turned to face Omar, hands in both pockets. "Let's go down the checklist again. No unlocked doors. No verbal diarrhoea in the client's presence. Are we clear?"

"But I was just—"

"Omar, are we clear?" he asked, more severely this time.

Omar nodded, his eyes staring at the granite tiles.

Vivek resumed his work: highlighting Aman's name in the Excel sheet, un-highlighting Keya's, and then saved the sheet.

***

With a pen horizontally clenched between her teeth and a pencil holding her locks in an arty bun, Keya sat in her office, rerunning a report for the third time—carefully yet hurriedly verifying the numbers on her screen with the printout she held in her hand. It was something LHF had asked for an hour ago, but the numbers seemed to be playing mind games with her. Her face was set in a puzzled and thoughtful look, wondering where she was going wrong. Just then a gentle knock on her door made her look up beyond the monitor, breaking her concentration.

"Can you come to conference room F please?" It was the HR manager, standing in her signature cotton sari: starched and neatly draped.

"Right now?"

"Yes."

Keya instantly suspected, and somewhat concluded, what it was all about. Conference room F was towards the corner on the topmost floor, the least glamorous compared to its counterparts all through the stadium, and was seldom used. Over the years the room had gained the reputation of being the bearer of bad news. It was out of the way for most departments and strategically placed where no one could hear your screams or cries for help, if they were to tie you up and forcefully inject tiny traceable devices under your skin. Not that anything that dramatic had happened, yet.

The two times she had been in there were both mildly unpleasant experiences. The first time, there had been a security breach with the data servers and someone from the IT department was ultimately deemed responsible. All employees who worked with data were given an hour-long lecture on security and protection of data. None of it was new information, so Keya had sat through it, trying to count the fine lines on her palms. The employee responsible was immediately let go.

The second time, a year back, the announcement was about the company's decision to discontinue contributing to employee retirement account due to lack of funds. The tallying-of-fine-lines-on-her-palms game had become old so she had resorted to sketching cartoons on the information sheet. She'd grown up trying to replicate RK Laxman cartoons from newspapers, and had developed a knack for it over the years. She sketched the HR lady, with a creepy face, big round hips, a giant bindi, and crooked teeth, barking at employees. Up until that point, the company matched employee contributions a hundred percent up to a certain limit. Keya had no interest in saving for her retirement if it didn't involve her company's contribution. She was too young for that, and moreover, she had a long list of things to save for. One international trip a year—although her father insisted on paying if they went together, a pricey Satya Paul sari she had been feasting her eyes on for a couple of years now, new stereo speakers, Diwali gifts for her family, a car—although she could never drive one in Ahmedabad, a house if she ended up single by thirty, and books. Lots of books. She had once calculated her monthly expenditure on books, magazines, and newspapers and found it to be around four grand.

Today, she knew there would be no such news that would only remotely affect her. Her churning stomach told her it was going to be more personal than that. It had been a few weeks since the acquisition of the Rangers had been in effect. Now must be the time to merge employees. Reduce 'redundant' staff members. Send them home with humiliated faces hanging low, as they carried their belongings in sad little brown boxes. Or whatever the hell they called it in diplomatic HR terms. As far as Keya was concerned, it was cutting off the umbilical cord. Relationships she had nurtured and cherished at work turning into a memory of the past in a heartbeat.

Though she had no reason to suspect, she couldn't help feeling that it was going to be at least three necks from her team who would have to go on the chopping board. Her department was big enough in size to get all the prying eyes wiggle their eyebrows with suspicion. LHF was the backbone and the face of her department to the rest of the company, but her favourite five were the actual doers—the worker bees—in this hierarchy. The fate of worker bees would always be the same. Ejected, after they were no longer needed.

She stepped out of her office and took a few steps towards Sujata's cubicle. She wasn't at her desk. None of her team members were. Keya walked to the conference room with the awful image of a few of her team members walking out with a brown box, running on auto play in her head. She cringed, her steps were devoid of energy. She bumped into the HR manager again, right outside the conference room, who informed her that they would 'get started shortly'.

Get started? On mass execution? Sigh.

Keya hesitantly entered the dreary room, the stale air from within making her uneasy. She scanned the room and noticed people from several departments. A gang of three from her team didn't go unnoticed. Where were the other two? And where was LHF? She briskly walked up to them, found a spot adjacent to them and got seated. All three threw a look at her that told her that as their boss, they were expecting her to know the details. She looked away, embarrassed.

Her stream of what-should-have-been thoughts was interrupted by the head of HR. She walked in, took a seat in the middle of the room, and set the tone of the announcement by saying, "I'm sorry to break this news to you."

Keya cupped her mouth with both her hands, her eyes widening.

"All employees who are in this room will no longer be with the company."

Everyone looked around frantically. Keya did too. There it was. The stark naked truth. She and three of her team mates. Gone. Done and over with. History. Just like that. In a heartbeat. Her heart began to ache. There was no recognition of their work. No words of explanation or solace. No goodbyes.

"The good news is that this isn't like firing. Your positions are just being temporarily put on hold. Which means, should there be a need for your skill set again, you will be contacted," the HR head assured diplomatically.

Keya covered her face with her hands, ignoring the lump in her throat, tears rapidly forming in her eyes. Was this all it took? Three years of her work life, over in a few crumbling moments. She needed to see LHF immediately. *Where on earth was he?* From the day he had hired her, and endlessly praised her, mind you, to this dark day of disappointment, he ought to have been here. To see her off one last time. To look into her eyes and acknowledge her effort, her potential, her dedication. To appear remorseful while facing her for she deserved better.

Dazed, shamed, she stormed out.

"Everyone please stay back for the exit interviews."

Laying off a third of the staff, easy as it may sound for consultants, was anything but for Vivek. Most of the remaining two-thirds had modified job functions, a misleading term for 'picking up responsibilities of those who were let go'. It hadn't been easy consolidating skill sets and job functions, creating new offer-letters and executing it in conjunction with the HR department, especially a sluggish HR department as Vivek had discovered. The head of HR was a middle-aged woman who paused for an abnormally long time, each time, after saying a few words, and then went off on a tangent. So much so that he'd started referring to her as Atal Bihari Vajpayee in his head. Vivek would have to patiently bring her back to the topic on hand, but he was slowly losing it with her. She left him with an uncontrollable urge to thump a fist on the table and yell, 'Will you bloody just finish?' He'd started sending Satyen to meet her, after suffering the first few times. But he had his eyes firmly on the silver lining. It would all be over in a few weeks' time.

"Here's a final list of all the employees who were let go. Their exit interviews have been wrapped up." Omar handed over a printout to Vivek. "And the HR slow mover said she has the exit interview transcripts if you need them."

"Nice. Could you do a cross-verification on the lay-off list I'd turned in? I want to make sure it matches."

He and his team had been in a dead spot—working eighty hours a week, quickly burning out as was visible on their stressed faces, and dropping out successively like dead flies. They often blamed it on the weather or food but the reality of it was obvious. Vivek often missed things he'd taken for granted half his life. Like hanging out with his buddies, watching cricket and other sports, bar hopping, crashing at a pal's house, watching movies all night long. He mostly hung out with people from work now. He missed his gym regimen. He had been a karate kid while growing up and always had unfailingly toiled to create an athlete's muscle tone. When he'd hesitantly checked his body definition after a shower a few days ago, he had been mighty disappointed in himself. *Your triceps look like a pre-teen girl's*, he'd told himself in the mirror.

He'd also missed out on countless family events in the past few months. For his father's birthday the previous week, the cardiology unit in the hospital, where his father was the senior-most doctor, had thrown a surprise party, putting together a video montage of several of his patient's emotional testimonials. His father had received several customised presents including flight vouchers to Bali. All Vivek had been able to make time for was assigning his secretary the task of sending flowers back home. It was a career choice he'd consciously made and often felt that he had no right to complain.

"Matches for the most part," Omar declared, looking up

from his desk. "Except for this one person who wasn't on your list. Keya Singhal."

"Huh?"

"Keya! Wait, isn't it the same girl who brought in cake the other day? Guess they let her go, too."

He rushed towards Omar in one swift motion, grabbing the list from him. "What? Let me see that." There it was. In alphabetical order on the list of 'Employees laid-off as part of Desai acquisition', highlighted by Omar in fluorescent yellow, was the name Keya Singhal.

"How did this happen? Aman was supposed to go instead of her. This . . . this can't be right."

"Must be some internal politics." Omar added his two cents.

Vivek stormed out of the room, hotfooting to the office of the HR head. He didn't know why it bothered him so much. He barely knew the girl. It must be just the mystery of it, he reasoned. But whatever it was, it had hit home. His mind could conjure a scenario where he saw Keya being handed the pink slip and it made him cringe. And *that* was especially odd for that was a first for him. Thirty minutes later, the mystery became clear.

"Please treat this as confidential information. It was conveyed to us from Mr Krishnan himself to not let Aman go. Mr Krishnan asked us to relieve the employee directly under him in place of him. He picked Keya himself." A lucid explanation from the HR head.

Aman had been with Krishnan for the last fifteen years. Obviously, he was in Krishnan's inner circle. Keya was perhaps just another girl in his firm, slogging away. She was possibly a nobody to him. It was useless thinking about it now. It was already history. And he was no one to judge Krishnan. He'd picked Keya himself initially.

Vivek knew Aman wasn't going to be around with his impending surgery and the personal issues he needed to tend to. With eighty percent of Aman's department gone, they were going to have an immensely tough time with marketing. *Morons*, he exclaimed.

***

Hours had passed, possibly days, since that ill-fated moment when she'd walked out of her office wearing humiliation instead of her usual scepticism. She'd taken an auto rickshaw home, cursing HR, LHF, Harsh Desai, and more than anyone, Vivek, with every breath she took. As the auto had come to a halt, she'd rushed towards her door, forgetting the brown boxes in the auto.

"*Arre ben, tamara khokha rahi gaya. Leta jao,*" the driver had called out to her.

She'd yanked out those boxes, sobbing, feeling breathless. They hadn't allowed laid-off employees to extract a backup from their laptops. All her personal data, her travelogue, her photographs was in HR's trash now.

As she had reached her home, she had indulged herself in a good crying fit. She couldn't remember the last time she had vented out her fury and pain like this . . . oh wait! she did. But, she didn't want to get into that now. Once she had cried herself dry, she had sat in the balcony for hours, sipping on some tea, opening up her sorrow to the world. The disgrace of being laid-off, the helplessness of not being able to save her employment or that of her team's, the darkness of a future largely undefined, her shattered life that had seemed perfect not too long ago, devastated her. There wasn't a soul around to console her. A bunch of kids continued playing cricket in the open ground by the building entrance. A lady in her neighbourhood and her maid were mid-way through a verbal duel. A retired man, who lived above her, was arguing with a postman over not delivering his daily mail early enough. A couple of young men were zooming on a bike, back and forth, in the lane; honking, to draw attention to their boisterous machines. The noises registered, knocking on her bubble of sorrow, but couldn't seep through. Every burdened tear brought back memories of a challenging but hopeful past.

One afternoon, just a few weeks ago, Keya had dropped by at the desks of her team members, asking them to pack up for the day and gather at the reception in fifteen minutes. She had treated them to a picnic at the Gamdi-Eco Adventure Resort that was an hour's drive away.

Once they were done with the adventure sports and had begun gorging on snacks, Keya had said, "I certainly don't want to turn a fun day gloomy, so forgive me if any of you get that sense. But I'm here because I value each of you, individually and collectively. I cannot thank you enough for your contributions. Your dedication, your work ethic, your passion, I see it all." She'd looked each one in the eye. They'd all sported baffled expressions. "Hard as I try, I just can't ignore the elephant in the room. I have no visibility into the future of our team. I don't know if we'll all stay or some of us will go. It's the rabbit's hole. Unless I jump in, I won't get a sense of what's coming. But," she'd said, taking a deep breath, "regardless of what happens, know that I will always cherish our time together. This is not to say that I'll accept status quo. I will fight with all my might to make them see why each of us is crucial. But ultimately it may not be in my hands." She'd noticed tears forming in their eyes. One of them had broken down, her face wet as a waterfall.

Each of them had taken turns to voice their concerns, the fears that had been hovering in their minds ever since the acquisition news. They'd all told her how much they appreciated her. It had made her heart swell with pride. Her five fingers were intact. When she formed a fist, she could feel the strength it was capable of. "We'll fight this one out, guys."

Between that day and today, her world had tumbled. The IGL season had come and gone. Chennai Powers had won the championship for the second consecutive year by beating the Royal Raptors. The Rangers, meanwhile, shared their luck with other teams that hadn't even qualified for semi-finals, like the Delhi Champs. They were left in the bottom heap, their fate unchanged. Their identity was still intact thought. Keya's on the other hand . . .

She had continued outpouring her grief onto the balcony floor, throwing silent questions at the universe. There would be no answers.

It was terribly unfair that Vivek, while doing his job, had made her lose hers. Maybe she wasn't justified in feeling this way, but a part of her wished him the same pain . . .

***

A neat stack of documents, demanding Vivek's prompt attention, peeked out at him from atop his grey Formica desk at his office back in Mumbai. Statement of work documents, expense reports, benefit of pay documents, invoices; the list was unending. He suspected that Alisha added a pile of general printouts to the stack in his absence, just to play pranks with him. There was no other explanation for the stack to increase this substantially in size every day, especially when he signed off at least half of those before leaving office each night.

Taking a break, he stretched out, his gaze taking in the cricket match that was running on mute on his wall-mounted, fifty-inch LED television screen. He glanced away from it, took a big bite of his cold chicken sandwich, and focused back on the project plan for the Desai-Rangers acquisition. The phone rang. It was Alisha.

"Mr The Schmuck is on the call for you."

"Who?"

"I don't know. Perhaps I'm saying it all wrong. It's an odd name." He always detected a hint of nervousness in her voice, each time she was unsure.

"It's not a real name, Ali. What is it about?" he questioned calmly, wiping the mayonnaise off his lips. Instead of the foreign accent she used, crediting it to her local convent education, of course, he wished she would put her mental faculties to use, just a tad more.

"He said it's a personal call. I honestly think someone is playing a prank." Maybe she knew who it was and was playing a mental game, again, he thought to himself.

"Put him through."

Seconds later, he was connected to a feminine voice.

"Is that Vivek?"

"Yes."

"Oh, hello Vivek. This is Deshmukh speaking. Sanjay Deshmukh." *Mr The Schmuck?* He mentally thanked Alisha for infusing some unintended laughter in to an otherwise dreary day. But, he couldn't place him. Before he could probe, the voice spoke again.

"I got your number from your mother." Crap. *No, no, no.*

"She must have informed you that the Independence Day celebration is this coming Saturday at the Andheri Sports Complex. I'm sure you're aware of how grand a scale we do it on each year and how many activities we organise to celebrate the fifteenth of August." No, she hadn't. And, no, I haven't gone since I stopped sucking my thumb, he wanted to proclaim. He silenced his mind and diverted his attention back to the call. There was a looming silence on the line. Mr Deshmukh was probably waiting for a response. Why was his office number being passed around so liberally? He wanted to call his mother and set the rules straight right that second.

"Your mother has been generous enough to make a huge donation. She has also signed you up for volunteer services this whole week including the weekend. Basically, we need volunteers every evening on weekdays, you see," the wily man explained laughingly. "And on site all day Saturday for the mega event. I just wanted to confirm whether you would be able to make it this evening and if so, then at what time. Our office is in Andheri."

Vivek's jaw almost dropped to the floor! Only his mother had the power to give him such moments. Not his boss, not the biggest of his clients, not the Mumbai police department, not one girl he'd dated, not his college-going brother's sexual escapades; no one.

"Sorry, I wasn't aware, Mr Deshmukh. Can I please take down your number and call you back?" The chant of 'respect all elders' he had heard while growing up was ingrained way too strongly in his mind.

"Please call me Sanjay. No need to be formal." *Well, how about The Schmuck, then?* Vivek cracked up again and then realised how silly he was being.

A meeting reminder popped up on his screen. It was time but he couldn't possibly go without settling this. In a fury, he dialled away.

"Hello, Bittu. Calling me from work?" Futile questions. She was a master of them.

"No, Ma, from Andheri, where I'm volunteering for the Independence Day event. You might, perhaps, be aware."

"Really? They told me it's only on evenings in the weekdays."

"Ma," he yelled. It was rare for Vivek to raise his voice with his family. "Why did you do this?" Exasperation laced his tone.

"The donation? We donate every year." She was avoiding the burning issue. Sly.

"Why did you sign me up for the entire week without asking me? I barely have time for a shower every day."

"Bittu, you're single. A thirty-three-year-old single man" She said it as if it sounded disgusting. "You should go to some social events. And who knows, you might find a nice Punjabi girl." Two-headed snake. Community service and a proven platform for bride hunting. Both sure-fire ways of raising his mother's stock in the Punjabi community.

His mother was somewhat of a case study in his family. Family reunions, back in their Pune mansion, usually meant all three boys—he, his brother, and his father—ganging up against her. His parents lived in a Colonial-style home that sat on almost a whole acre of land in the affluent suburb of Aundh, located in the north-west part of Pune. The house featured a beautiful foyer, grand archways, winding staircases, hardwood floors, six bedrooms, five and a half bathrooms, a family room, a library, a formal dining room, several fireplaces, an attic, a four-car garage, a greenhouse, and a fish pond. Back in the day, his father had bought it for peanuts. Now it would probably easily sell for over a couple of crores. Just a walk to the artistic mailbox on the boundary of his home qualified as a morning walk.

During family reunions, Vishal, his younger brother, would invariably play the role of a troublemaker. He'd initiate action and their father would be quick to follow suit. Vivek always promised himself that he'd abstain from troubling her, just so she could have someone on her team, but the three-men clique was too much fun for him to keep that promise. His mother almost always ended up being annoyed, creating drama, storming out of the living room, and slamming her bedroom door shut. Once that happened, his father would pour himself some of the strongest whiskey and tell both boys about their 'cookie-cutter Punjabi mom' over a game of billiards. Vishal, himself a little tipsy, would egg on his dad to explain what the epithet meant. Being the younger child, and being around at home long after Vivek left for Mumbai, Vishal had been pampered and spoilt by his mother, and thus took all sorts of liberties with her. And as it was, both boys knew it was their dad's favourite part of the reunions.

"She is as sweet as *gajar ka halwa* but she can burn my system like *vindaloo,*" their father would kick off. Then he'd pretend that he was thinking his way through this and come up with, "She is as fair as a white lily but, unfortunately, she is also round like a pumpkin."

Vivek, not wanting to hear the routine yet another time, would attempt to bring his dad to a halt and focus on the game instead, but he'd get outvoted.

"She is as calm as a cow but when she is angry, she could be as dangerous as a charged rhino," Daddy Grewal would continue. Vishal would burst out laughing, encouraging his dad fervently while shooting some winning shots. If his father could pocket a ball on the billiards table, he would add, "She is my lucky charm, my Goddess Laxmi, but when furious, she could destroy me like Kali."

"That's enough, Dad," Vivek would have to put his foot down to end the chain reaction.

"Last one. Last one. She can cook single-handedly for the entire nation but when I ask for *paneer pakoras*, it brings out her dark side."

"Dad, you're a cardiologist! *Paneer pakoras*? Some perspective, please." Vivek wouldn't be able to see his mother being roasted any further. "One day you'll need to send out a written apology to all the Punjabi moms."

His father would laugh as if Vivek had proposed something preposterous. "They know I say it with love, mama's boy. They don't call me a 'jolly good fellow' for nothing." A 'cookie-cutter Punjabi mom' for a mother and a 'jolly good fellow' for a father; Vivek couldn't have asked for better lineage.

"Bittu, are you still there?" His mother's voice brought him back to the present. He had to get himself out of the Independence Day event.

"Ma, I can't juggle it with work. Seriously. Plus my weekly trips to Ahmedabad start again next week. Too much to be done before that."

"Work will go on, Bittu. Community service is also important." Why did she always pull that card? And why did it hold such power over him?

"I'll go on Saturday. Okay?"

"Saturday and Sunday." Such a negotiator. All the new employees in his company should get trained under her, instead of the pricey training they were sent for.

"But Ma, the event is on Saturday."

"Yes, I know. I've signed you up for the cleaning crew as well the following day."

Despite his commitment, Vivek reached at what could only be passed off as offensively late, the following Saturday. Andheri Sports Complex looked like one big block party. People, food stalls, gift stalls, a massive stage with seating area, large speakers, and countless volunteers running around like ants to get everything in order. Amidst the furore, he located Mr 'The Schmuck' who was too busy to notice his late arrival. The man was quick to assign Vivek as a helper to a college kid with rabbit teeth and thick glasses. The kid was scuttling around, working on an array of random tasks diligently, as if his life depended upon it. Vivek was suitably impressed.

Finally the event began, and it was a reprieve for him to learn that it wasn't just he who had been tardy. The emcee, a beat-looking man with an inappropriately worn event sash—which made him seem more like an unfortunate looking beauty queen than anything else—initiated his welcome speech almost an hour late, using his stuttering, stammering voice to its full potential. 'Proud to host the event again', 'proud of numerous achievements', 'proud of all of you who've come to cheer', and countless more 'proud's was all Vivek could grasp from his speech. After the twelfth 'proud', Vivek's interest level swayed and his eyes fell on the beauties in the front row.

"Buddy, quick question, who are those girls?" he asked Rabbit Teeth who was watching the emcee intently.

"They're both upcoming Bollywood actresses—Shriya Sen and Sarah Sen. And twins. Gorgeous, right?" the kid responded, his eyes sparkling.

Seconds later, the camera panned on them, catching the eye candies in the act of giggling and gossiping. Their mother, along with a French-bearded man, began to march towards the stage slowly. The beauties followed suit. "Please welcome Namita Sen, actress and daughter of renowned Tamil actress Chitra Sen," the emcee introduced the mother.

Rabbit Teeth cracked up as if he was at a stand-up show. "That is Namita Sen, a popular yesteryear's actress. And her mother is a *Bengali* actress, not Tamilian! And guess what? Her name is Pavitra, not Chitra. This emcee dude is completely clueless." Clearly, Rabbit Teeth was having a grand time.

Vivek shrugged and looked away. Not being much of a Bollywood fan, this wasn't his scene at all. Then the emcee committed a non-bailable crime and forgot the name of one of the daughters. Not that he looked even remotely embarrassed about it. "She is here with her two daughters, Mrs Sarah Sen and the other one."

Rabbit Teeth held his gut, laughing hysterically, alternately crunching and falling on his back. "Oops. B-lun-der," he said in a sing-song manner. "Both girls are single. Very, very single. God save the emcee after the event. He's going to be bashed up mercilessly."

Can the night become anymore annoying? Vivek wondered.

After the debacle of the much-hyped show, it was time to stand in queue for dinner. I can't believe what all I put up with for Ma's sake, the thought crossed Vivek's mind for the nth time that evening. Taking what he could in the name of food, he hastily made way to a corner table, where an elderly man sat.

"Amit Gupta," the man introduced himself, once he had had a few bites of his food. Vivek inwardly groaned. *I am never again falling for ma's traps*, he vowed to himself.

"Vivek Grewal."

"So what do you do, young man?"

KBC had officially begun.

"I work in M&A."

"Nice. Consulting?"

"Yes."

"You should keep in touch with me. My company—Gupta Financial Investments—works with consultants extensively. Here's my card. Call me sometime."

"Sure." You and everybody else works with consultants, Mr Gupta. What's the big deal?

"Are you single?" Didn't even need a stopwatch for that. It had taken this fellow under a minute to jump to that question. This was precisely why Vivek avoided gatherings recommended by his mother. They all had a deceptive exterior; political, social, cultural, charitable but right beneath that falsified exterior, it was nothing short of a glorified marriage market!

Mr Gupta took his silence as an affirmative response and was quick to propose a solid plan of action.

"Between you and me," he whispered, leaning in closer, "Mrs Sen is looking for grooms, in Mumbai itself, for both her daughters. Such beautiful girls, right? They're models as well as actresses. Pure Bengalis. Well-read, well-cultured. Come by after this event. We're throwing a pool party. You could borrow my swimming trunk," he wrapped up with a rather pimp-like expression.

That unambiguous and very ludicrous image of him in Mr Gupta's swimming trunks made Vivek almost puke out the artificially-coloured mango lassi he'd just taken a few swigs of. He coughed.

"Are you all right?"

"Yeah. I'm already in your pool with the girls," Vivek answered with a wink, and got up to leave. He had done his bit of community service.

Just as he reached home, his cell buzzed. MA CALLING . . . the screen flashed. His mother couldn't even wait for the day to end!

"Bittu, did you meet any girls?"

"Yes."

"Thank Krishna. I knew it. I knew it would work. I'm so excited. God is great."

"Ma, wait till you hear it all."

"Tell me she is tall, fair, and lovely. And not too skinny. Bittu, Bittu, is she in consulting as well?"

"It's not she. It's they. I met twins. My ultimate fantasy. Ma, I am so psyched!"

"What?" Her scream had an instant deafening effect.

"And you won't believe the icing on the cake. They're both actresses and stunning." He imagined a wedding invite with his name and a single blank spot with the bride's name falling from her hands, as she fainted from an artificial stroke. "Unfortunately, non-Punjabis, so I didn't chase it."

It had been a while since he'd played a good prank on her.

***

Mindlessly flicking the television channels, surviving on tea and double chocolate ice-cream, cutting off communication with friends and family, worrying about money troubles, and basically being incapable of yanking herself out of this phase of mild depression was becoming all too overwhelming for Keya. It had been over a couple of days since she had run a comb through her hair and even more since she had taken a bath. There had been instances when she had forgotten to lather with soap while taking a bath, and remembered only hours later.

The stillness of her life had eventually brought about restlessness. It affected her mind in strange ways. Sometimes, she didn't want to do anything about any of it. Other times, she was overpowered with an urge to voice her opinion on how unfair it had all been to her and her teammates. She owed it to herself to fight it out, right? Three years of dedication met with such severity was insulting and unacceptable. It felt like a conspiracy.

She'd been receiving several calls from other laid-off team members. It had been three weeks since the lay-off, and yet not one had received their severance package. They were all entitled to a month's salary as severance as part of their employment contract and she was entitled to three months' pay. Keya was in no mood to let this one slide.

She'd left several messages for the HR head but hadn't heard back. She'd even left a message for Vivek. After all, the HR department now worked for Harsh Desai, and Vivek was her only connection to him. If she had to get anything done, she had to work the new channel. She was certain nothing was going to fall in her lap. She had to be a fighter, not a loser. And most certainly not a victim! She had to act like she was made of steel. But if she were to bring about a change, she had to first go about life as usual.

So, she had pushed herself to get out of bed, take a bath, this time not forgetting to lather herself with soap, and get dressed after countless persuasive phone calls from Radhika, her closest pal.

"Where are we going?" She spoke to the mirror while dabbing some gloss, then pursed and pouted her shimmering lips alternately to ensure perfect coverage. Her phone receiver was on speaker and lay tucked between an array of cosmetics on the bathroom vanity shelf.

"Don't worry about that, love. I'll pick you up in twenty," Radhika assured. Radhika almost always showered Keya with endearments like muffin and cupcake. Keya, on the other hand, could never get herself to reciprocate this way, despite caring a lot for Radhika. It just wasn't how she was built.

Radhika was a trained fashion designer who had moved to Ahmedabad from Mumbai a few years back to set up a store and build clientele for a renowned fashion designer. Keya had bumped into her at an organic food store where they'd both tried to pick up the last bottle of chilli garlic sauce. Keya had been courteous enough to let her have it. Minutes later, when they'd bumped again, this time in the restaurant section of the same market, they'd gotten talking and taken a break from shopping organic produce to try out some spinach and feta cheese frankies. To spice up the rather bland frankies, Radhika had cracked open her new purchase of chilli sauce that had marked as a prelude to them exchanging notes on each other's recently bought possessions. They'd pitted their passion for organic ingredients and exotic recipes against each other's and decided that they both were equally obsessed. Three years, and several other common obsessions, had turned them into the best of friends.

When Radhika came by to pick her up, Keya noticed how stunning she looked in her flawless make-up and her risqué dress that left very little to imagination. She even had a long scarf wrapped around her face and her head, presumably to protect her salon hair from the windy rickshaw ride. Radhika always looked stunning, but if there was a possibility of running into men, she pulled out all the stops. The 'three-o-and-still-single' phenomenon had rendered her somewhat desperate and frustrated as was often visible in her attitude and behaviour. Strangely, there had never been a dearth of men. She'd dated a huge variety with the underlying aspiration of finding a rare cerebral type who was drop dead gorgeous and had qualities of hundreds of leading men of romance novels combined. Sadly, none of the real men had made the cut and it was largely attributed to her delusions than the merit of the potential grooms. The pool of eligible and available men on dating sites and via enterprising relatives and friends had started shrinking in stark contrast to her anxiety on the subject. Despite that or maybe because of that, she put in a great deal of effort in her appearance and took every opportunity to go out and meet new people.

"Where are we going, Rads?"

"You'll see in about twenty minutes," Radhika replied, dodging her question about their evening plans.

About twenty minutes later, on the outskirts of the city, in an area known for immaculate farm-houses, their rickshaw pulled up in front of a sprawling mansion.

"We're visiting someone at their home?" Keya enquired, somewhat startled.

"There's a popular artist in Ahmedabad, Kamini Lakhiya. This is her house. She has a grand theatre as well as an art gallery all in there," Radhika informed, pointing at the mansion as the girls stepped out of the rickshaw. "Each time she travels abroad, she comes back with some rare movies and showcases them here. They all usually have a social impact or message or theme. Oh and her movies are the best kept secret in Ahmedabad. No one talks about them. If you're in that elite circle, you get to be a part of it. Else you'll never know. Unbelievable, right?"

"That's odd. What are we doing here in that case? I don't know about you, Rads, but I can assure you that I'm not the elite of Ahmedabad," Keya confessed sheepishly.

"I know the photographer who works for her. He got me two invites." Radhika pulled out a tiny mirror from her purse and coated her eyelashes with another layer of mascara before stepping in.

Behind a line-up of fancy cars, Keya got her first glimpse of the sharply-dressed elite of the city, which had been her home for the past three years. The girls showed their passes to the guards at the entrance and were guided inside. The cool, modern foyer with high ceilings, open stairways, and marble tiles led into a plush theatre. Radhika smiled and nodded her head in acknowledgement as they passed by the privileged few. The show was yet to begin and Keya noticed the crowd lingering around in the lobby.

"Shouldn't we walk up to the host and say hello?" Keya considered courtesy despite the awkward feeling.

"We should, ideally, except, I don't know who she is."

"What?!"

"Anyway, are we ready for this?" Radhika posed an open-ended question.

"I guess so. What movie is it though?" There were no banners or brochures or any other clues that would give it away.

"It's an exciting one." Radhika continued her dodging mode as she signalled Keya in the direction of theatre. Keya stiffened and was noticeably appalled when she came across a rather tiny banner outside the theatre that read:

THREE-WAY: A TRILOGY OF VINTAGE EROTICA

"Wait. A. Minute." Shock didn't begin to cover it for her. "Rads, you dragged me here to see *porn*?"

"Shh . . . don't scream, cupcake. And correction. It's vintage erotica. We don't call that porn."

"Shut up, Rads! What the hell is wrong with you? Vintage erotica? That too, a trilogy?"

"Yes! An epic trilogy."

"Okay I'm leaving," she threatened. "I'm so not in the mood to watch three porn films back-to-back in some stranger's house, so if you're done with the shock treatment, let's leave."

It wasn't particularly the subject that Keya was opposed to. She had never seen movies that broadly fell into this category in a theatre and especially a home theatre at that. The surprise element of the evening served as somewhat of a blow to her. Radhika was known to be particularly wonky and outlandish in her ideas but this topped all the eccentric moments she had ever had.

"Relax. It's not back to back. It's one film a night. And it isn't just for entertainment. These are aimed at investigating the fantasies and realities of sexual representation."

"You're doing their PR now? Seriously Rads, what *are* we doing here?"

"Baby, you needed to get out, I had a great event to attend. Two birds, one stone. You understand, right? Somewhat?"

Radhika was holding their tickets, she was dressed for the show, and she looked thrilled. That didn't leave Keya with much of an option. She glanced around to quickly gauge the crowd and noticed quite a few 'arty' couples; senior citizens with giant bindis or statement necklaces paired with traditional saris or scarves around the neck; all sporting at least one element which would qualify them as 'creative'. A few young men and women indulged in gossip and loud laughs, holding a champagne glass. Subdued and somewhat mortified, she followed Radhika who was happily sticking out her chest and looking for their seats. The movie of the night was *The Wild Pussycat*, a bizarre portrayal of art that combined erotic scenes with sadism. The naïve, beautiful lead actress was miserably in love with her gorgeous boyfriend, who pimped her out to ugly old men to pay his rent. Later, when she became pregnant with his child, he tortured her by tying her to a chair and gagging her while he shagged other women, making her watch it forcibly.

"Such a misleading name," Keya whispered to Radhika as the movie turned into an intense, grossly-depicted dark comedy instead of just another sexploitation drama that she was assuming it to be.

"Yeah, it's not what I thought. Want to get out or stay?"

Radhika was sporting a huge frown on her face. She looked obviously displeased at what had transpired on the screen.

Clearly, she had given it no thought and true to her reputation, was unable to make up her mind about watching the rest of it.

"You owe me an elaborate Gujarati thali and half your wardrobe," Keya said authoritatively as soon as they quit the film halfway through, her face revealing how she'd have to suffer through successive sleepless nights after watching it.

"I seriously had no—"

"I don't want excuses. I want dinner and your wardrobe."

At a village-themed restaurant, Maharani, that night, over steaming hot *undhiyu*, *puri,* and *jalebis*, among several other stories, Keya narrated her pain point. "I can't get over this guy. I feel such rage against him."

"Can't get over, you say?" Radhika asked.

"Yes. He gets on my nerves so, so much, it's not even funny anymore. You have known me for so long now. Have I ever reacted this way?" Without waiting for Radhika's response to that, Keya continued with her tirade. "You know, our first encounter was downright weird. His asking me for the directions to the loo and following it up with all that random talk afterwards. Despite that I somehow thought he was okay. But then came his sugar-coated talk on lay-offs. I mean, he was leading every single person in that room to believe that he was some kind of a saviour. But dammit, he is not, Rads!"

Keya's eyes talked more than her tongue did. Radhika looked like her heart was going out to her and Keya felt comforted seeing that expression on her best friend's face. Then she continued with her outrage.

"Is he a potential romantic interest kinda guy?" Radhika asked, raising her eyebrows as far north as they would go, once Keya had stopped.

"*What*? she asked, disgusted. "The guy who got me laid off? Vivek? No. He's a jerk!"

"No harm in asking, Keya."

"Are you even listening to me, Rads?" Keya wondered out loud. "I hate him."

"Hatred . . . That's precisely where all love stories begin. Don't they?"

"Sometimes, I don't even know how to talk to you."

"Okay, okay. I'll keep my theories to myself."

Not convinced that Radhika empathised with her totally, Keya narrated each episode leading up to the lay-off debacle with microscopic details, once again. "And," she added, "to make things worse, he made me feel inferior. We were just having a regular conversation about our names and he insulted me. To my face. And I couldn't even retort. I don't want to be this dumb cow when people say nasty things to me, you know? I want to be like a Woody Allen heroine. Say something intelligent, right back to them. *Ugh*."

"Pardon my naïve take on this but what exactly are you so mad about, sugar? That you couldn't come across as this glib-slash-witty girl with clever rejoinders or that your job was taken away from you, by him, as you insist on saying?"

"I am jobless. Can you be a little more sensitive than that? And he's responsible for it."

"Be that as it may, but you know what? I haven't seen your eyes sparkle this way in years when talking about a man. It's finally time to get over Raj," she winked.

The Monday-to-Friday routine to Ahmedabad had unfortunately been rather steady for Vivek. The acquisition, which was supposed to be quick, had suffered one roadblock after another leading to time and cost overruns. Dealing with that hadn't been easy. On top of that, Harsh was being considerably more difficult than Vivek could account for; each goal becoming a moving target for him. It had led to a few clashes between the two.

As Vivek sat in the conference room, which had become his office now, replying to some e-mails, he received a call. The screen flashed a number that seemed local. His eyebrows went up a notch.

"Morning. This is Vivek." The call had taken him by surprise given that he hardly knew local folks here anymore.

"Hi, Vivek. This is Keya." *Oh shoot. Keya!* He'd received a message from her via a secretary a couple of days ago, requesting a call back.

"Hi, Keya." It was awkward as hell. "I got your message. Sorry I missed out on calling back."

"No worries. Got a few minutes?" She sounded

confident for someone who'd gone through what she had had. He was the one fumbling, and he didn't like that one bit.

"Yes, certainly." Then he realised why he was ballsing-up. He'd never had to speak to an ex-employee while involved in the lay-off process. She'd come prepared with ammunition and caught him off-guard. He closed his eyes and imagined her petite form braced for a fight. He could tell she was spoiling for it.

"I was a part of Strategic Marketing Services department. Three of my direct reports were let go a few weeks back, in addition to me. Not sure if you are aware." She knew how to hit where it hurt, he had to grant her that. It made him feel barbaric. But that voice of hers, it was doing a number on him. He couldn't find it in himself to strum up anger in response to that voice. It inspired something primal in him, something he couldn't name. Yet.

Vivek shifted uncomfortably in his seat. "Yes, I'm aware of the unfortunate measure."

"The thing is, they haven't received their severance packages yet." *Phew*. There was no need to break into a sweat, he admonished himself.

"Well, HR handles that—"

"Yes, I know," she interrupted him sternly. "But I've had no luck getting through HR. My reports were told during the exit interviews that the cheques would be mailed within a week. It's been quite a few weeks, Vivek."

"Umm . . . I don't really—it's an HR function, frankly, so I'm not sure I—"

"I know all that. But since you work for the new owner, I'm hoping you could expedite it." Whoa. This woman had balls. And a voice that elicited the damndest of reactions from him. If it had been anyone else, he would have cut him or her to size. Within seconds. With her, strangely enough, he found himself doing the opposite.

"I'll see what I can do. I'll speak with the HR today. Should have an update for you by end of the day tomorrow. Do you want to call me then?" He promised earnestly. *Update*? For an ex-employee? *I'm such a moron.*

"Appreciate it." She hung up. He loosened his tie to ease the unsettling feeling. There was something about the girl that had piqued his interest . . .

Vivek sat back in his office, sipping a cup of steaming coffee.

Much as he had tried to think in the past hour since her phone call about what had happened that had resulted in her getting pink-slipped, he couldn't exactly pinpoint. On his way out to grab a coffee, he had walked past Aman. On a whim, and defying all professional sense, he had about-turned and walked back to him, intent on getting to the bottom of it. Before he could have asked him anything, Aman had enquired, "Got a few minutes, buddy? Need to discuss something important."

"Sure. Just need some coffee. Be right back."

Vivek had been meaning to speak to Aman ever since the lay-off to get to the bottom of the story but one thing or the other had kept him from it. Keya's call had put it right on top of his to-do list. What had really transpired that Aman, despite having a strong desire to quit, was made to stay back? How was the team functioning with Keya and three others gone? Aman was the big boss. The delegator, not the doer. It must have been far from smooth, he contemplated.

Aman entered with: "I'm putting in my papers today."

Surprise flitted across Vivek's face, an imperceptible moment of amazement that was squelched before Aman could notice. He continued sipping his coffee, raising his left eye in question.

"Same story. I have an ankle surgery coming up and need some personal time off. I might be moving to Munnar for a bit. Can't deal with work for now. I was hoping to slide through with the lay-offs but no such luck."

"Yeah, what happened with that?"

"Nothing good," Aman responded, pulling out a cigarette from his shirt pocket and lighting it in one swift motion. Clenching it between his lips, he took a deep drag of the cigarette and then added with a thoughtful look, "The team is struggling. Hanging by a thread. I know it's probably not news to you. After me, there'll be two junior marketing analysts left. No strategists. No planners. It's really sad where this is all headed."

"I gathered. What happened during the lay-off exactly? I'd put in your name—"

"Krishnan. I've worked for him for years. He wasn't ready to let me go."

"And now?"

He blew a smoke ring into the air. "Tough luck. I'm giving him no option. Call me if you need to talk. And Vivek, find a way to save my department. It's falling apart."

***

Radhika and Kourosh left no stone unturned in bringing Keya back to normalcy. Or what was their definition of it. Radhika would drag her to odd events or places that invariably turned out to be bad judgment calls. Kourosh had resorted to doing what he did best—cooking. He made her *baghali polo*, the only Parsi recipe his mother had learnt from his father before she left him. When Keya devoured it after days of not eating well, he'd made several other Russian dishes for her over the days, trying to cheer her up. As far as Keya was concerned, in spite of herself, this was turning out to be her new normal self.

One morning, the rackety phone ring interrupted her peaceful state of being curled up in bed with her copy of *What the Buddha Taught*. She offered the phone a petulant scowl, befitting a toddler. As she flippantly glanced at the caller ID, her mock scowl turned into a look of surprise. It was from the Rangers' office.

"May I speak with Keya, please?" HR's voice had taken on a strong manly tone. *Weird.*

"This is she."

"Keya, Vivek here." Her cell phone slightly slipped from her hand. She positioned it back properly.

"Oh. Hello."

"I was wondering if you could drop by the office sometime today or tomorrow." Great. He'd finally heard back from HR on a dozen reasons why they hadn't been able to mail out the severance cheques. And why they had planned on caning the idea, right?

"Yes, I can make it tomorrow."

"Good. See you then." With that Vivek hung up.

The next morning Keya was back to the all too familiar setting. She tried hard to fight the embarrassment that was seeping in. Avoiding eye contact with the security personnel, she took the lift to the top floor. Once outside the lift, she took a deep breath and raised her chin a bit, trying her best to give an appearance of being in control, upbeat, and self-assured; not defeated. With a pounding heart, she knocked gently on Vivek's door.

"Come in."

"Hi." She peeped in to find Vivek and his team seated; papers and coffee mugs scattered all around as if she'd walked into a dorm room.

"Keya! Thanks for coming. Let's talk in the other room." He grabbed his phone from the desk and walked towards her. He led her to one of the empty offices, which were several, given how many employees no longer worked at Rangers. Once inside, he shut the door behind him and signalled her to assume the chair right across from him.

"I know I owe you an answer on the severance cheques but let's save that for later." That startled her, her head jerking slightly backwards as a reaction. She maintained her silence. Vivek took that as a cue to proceed. "I'll jump straight to the point. How would you feel about working here again?"

"Huh?" She leaned in, stupefied. Her mouth parted slightly and her eyes dilated a little. Her heart started cart wheeling inside, chanting: *They want me back!*

"Bit of a shocker, I can imagine. Basically, Aman just quit and the department needs someone to hold the reins. What do you think?"

*Easy, easy, Keya,* she cautioned herself. Before she could come up with a suitable response, Vivek added, "It'll be the same position. Same job description. It's your kingdom and you get to rule it."

The cart wheeling stopped. There was silence for a moment. Keya mentally kicked herself for her gullibility and foolhardiness. A wry smile formed on her lips. She looked him in the eyes and saw an insensitive salesman. The man who'd ruthlessly cut off her life support just a few weeks ago was now offering it back without any trace of guilt or any other emotion. Nothing had changed. She was a headcount back then and she was being offered to be a headcount again. He'd proposed replacing herself with herself. *Heartless, aren't you, Vivek from Cello Consulting?*

He looked at her with expectant eyes, eyebrows slightly raised, and asked smugly, "You'll take it, right?"

Vivek needed to learn a new word. It was *please.* She felt like taking off a shoe and flinging it at him for playing with her feelings. Instead, she just curled her toes and held back the anger.

"I need a few days to think about it." *You're making a big mistake if you think I am going to join back just like that*, she let her eyes warn him.

***

It had been a few days since Vivek had offered Keya her old job back. When he didn't hear from her by the end of the week, he left her a voicemail. And another one. And then a third one. No response. It annoyed him slightly. The CMO had raised the issue of a collapsing department and stalled marketing activities to Harsh, who in turn had mounted pressure on Vivek. *You do stupid things, you pay for it,* he'd conveyed to the CMO non-verbally. But he'd still have to fix it. And for that he needed Keya.

Then one morning, Keya was kind enough to return Vivek's call. If it was attitude, it was definitely not working on him.

"Can I drop by tomorrow to discuss this?" A nonchalant question was all he got from her.

"So, you are taking it?"

"Let's talk in person tomorrow."

*Wow*, he thought, *she is playing hard to get. Fine. Play your game, lady. They don't call me a veteran for nothing.*

Next morning, Keya was at his door as promised. In a sleeveless, lavender salwar kameez she looked radiant, composed, and confident. She greeted him with the tone reserved for meeting someone for a casual dinner; no sense of anxiety or urgency to discuss official matters, whatsoever. It threw him off a bit.

All the time they bided in inconsequential chatting, he took in her striking beauty. Till now he hadn't really appreciated her full form, but today he perused over her every curve. Discreetly. Having had his fill, he itched to get down to the matter at hand. Keya had effortlessly turned the meeting into a game of who would jump in first. Knowingly, unable to resist, he did.

"So?" No articulation necessary, he reckoned.

"I can't function without my team." She didn't beat about the bush much.

"What are you implying?"

"Any chance you can hire them back?"

"Keya, I don't—"

"They were willing to keep Aman who was probably paid more than my entire team put together. It's the same logic. Right?" She was invincible. He wasn't prepared to discuss this one bit.

"It's not that straightforward. I can't justify the headcount."

"People."

"Huh?" he asked, baffled.

"They're people, Vivek. Not just headcount," she pointed out with a sweet smile. A saccharine sweet smile. A sickeningly over-sweet smile meant to cut him to size. She was beating him up effortlessly and with such charm! That was a first! "Anyway, I'm sure you've heard from Aman how impossible it is to run that team with two people. And I'm sure you could try and squeeze in a few if not all three." She had jumped from one thing to the other so quickly that Vivek didn't know what to say.

"I could . . . umm . . . try and perhaps squeeze in one more," he finally relented, but stayed clear from promising anything.

"Let me ask you this. Don't you think this was a big mistake?"

He was not going to fall for that one. "Bygones," came his curt reply.

They were both waltzing this perfect corporate dance. He knew the steps, he knew the tempo, hell, he did this for a living, but she couldn't have had much experience. *Any* experience. Still she was outfoxing him, that too with such élan that he was left amazed. And impressed. That was a first, yet again. Vivek Grewal who was as glib as anyone could ever be, was beginning to feel apprehensive. Keya Singhal intimidated him, intrigued him, interested him . . .

Choosing to end the charade without losing much blood, he looked directly into her eyes; wordlessly threatening her to not take this any forward. *Say yes, woman. Quick. I have a hundred other battles to fight.*

"I want a pay raise with a fifteen percent increase." This kept getting more interesting by the minute. It was even beating those hundreds of acquisition negotiations he had been a part of.

"Keya, I am not authorised to—"

"Let me finish," she rudely interrupted. "I was up for promotion this year. It was right around the corner. It's only fair after what I've gone through."

"I understand, but I can't justify such a huge increase for the same position."

"Then hire me as a consultant."

It was rare when someone out-manipulated him. Twice in a day!

"I-I'll have to look into that."

"Look, I don't mean to be difficult. But I haven't even received my three-month severance yet. I loved this job more than my life." Her hands were on her upper chest area, as if to establish a physical connection to her heart. "I considered the team my family. I nurtured these relationships. The eventuality has left me shaken. Something must change if I have to come back."

He looked into those unyielding eyes. It was not arrogance he saw. It was hurt and pride, swirled with defiance. He'd perhaps ignored seeing the truth about the dark side of lay-offs. It was a world he never had to step in to. Until Keya came along.

"I guess you are justified in your claim, but I can't promise anything."

"Don't promise. I know you work closely with Harsh. If you can get this approved, I'll be happy to be back."

He sighed. "Okay."

"I'll look forward to your call." With that she slid her slender hand into his warm, big one, and turned, blinking at him once as she did, for once not looking composed.

Lunch with his team was turning out to be far from elaborate for Vivek. All that his packed schedule could allow was a quick stop at a cafeteria near the stadium that offered gross versions of local cuisine in flimsy take-out paper containers. A quick bite, a few jokes about Omar's constantly beeping phone—courtesy his girlfriend from Mumbai, and regular office banter was how he and his team spent their lunch hour today. As they walked back to the stadium, Vivek spotted a familiar face sitting in the coffee shop they were passing by. Keya. It had been weeks since she had joined back—as a consultant, on her terms, with her desired pay raise, and with one of her teammates in tow. She had played it so well, he had had no option but to give in.

She was seated on a table in the patio, alone, preoccupied with twisting the straw in her coffee. He narrowed his eyes to take a closer look. A white kurta paired with a contrasting lime green dupatta, tiny sparkling stuff all over it, a red bindi, and thick kohl applied artfully with no other purpose but to leave men weak in their knees. He grinned.

The infamous Sabarmati breeze blew a cluster of hair off her face, showcasing her daintiness to him. Just then it struck him who she reminded him of—Indira Varma, from the only Hindi movie he'd watched without any persuasion from anyone, *Kama Sutra*. Similar fragile face. Narrow jaw line. Slender frame. Expectant body language. Innocence blended with raw sultriness. Long wavy hair. She had never looked more beautiful. He had never felt more drawn.

He and his teammates continued walking in the direction of the stadium when a man who had just walked past them abruptly turned around and called out to Vivek.

"Vivek, right?" he asked, with a delighted look on his face and sparkle in his eyes.

"Hello."

"I'm Shailendra with Ahmedabad Chronicle. Shailendra Tekwani. We've met before. Not sure if you recall. At your office? I'm a sports journalist."

"Look, I'm late—"

"Don't worry. I won't stop you this time. The Rangers' spokesperson has been very cooperative with me. I've been getting all my details firsthand," he replied with a firm, self-assured smile.

"That's great." Vivek waited for him to be done with his small talk and leave.

"If you ever have interesting news, I'll be all ears," the man said, finally coming to the point. He handed out his card again.

Vivek grabbed it and quickly slid it in his wallet. As he turned to leave, the sun glinted in his eyes, automatically making his hand go to the front of his shirt, where he hung his aviators. He narrowed his eyes in comprehension as his hand came back empty.

"Guys, go ahead, I'll join you back at the office." He hurriedly walked back to the joint his team had lunched at. Not finding his prized possession on the table and surrounding chairs, he bent to look under the table. *There!* His aviators hadn't gone missing; for once, they hadn't. He had had a terrible streak of luck of leaving souvenirs at every place he visited. An oblong smile flickered on his face as he began to walk back to the stadium.

Spotting Keya at the same location doing the same activity with the same lack of expression, he didn't resist the urge to stop by and say hello. When he greeted her, she appeared startled. *Women are so oblivious to their surroundings*, he hastily inferred.

"Oh, hi." Compliant response from her and not a hint of smile . . . odd.

"How is it going?"

"It's . . . good. I'm good," she replied meekly. It wasn't that hard a question. His forehead creased a bit.

"Good to know. I was just walking back to the office. Saw you, so stopped to say hi." Forced, tedious explanations. He wasn't a fan of those.

"Right. I was just waiting for my frankie."

"Do you usually eat alone?" Hands in pockets, back erect, enough distance between both feet, he knew he was coming across as creepy with the array of questions he was bombarding her with.

"Yeah. Kind of. Gives me some time to reflect."

"May I?"

He didn't wait for a response. Vivek usually wasn't game for making friends, that too at a client site. Hence, his own action took him by surprise. He'd never before cornered an isolated client employee to spend a few minutes. Business lunches and dinners were the norm with members of the client team he was directly involved with. Keya didn't fit the bill. It wasn't about her being attractive either. He'd met as pretty, if not prettier, clients. The thought hadn't even so much as crossed his mind ever with anyone else. Then again, he had never had a Keya for a client. He blamed it on his intrinsic ability to be pulled by girls who held their ground.

"So, do you—" They both uttered the same words at the same time, then paused to laugh.

"Go ahead," Vivek prompted.

"Nothing. I was just asking if most of your projects are in Ahmedabad."

"No. Actually it's my first project in the city."

"Ahh. How do you like it here?"

"Haven't been about town too much. But I'll tell you this. I feel drawn to it like I have never been before. There is something that adds the mystique factor," he confessed, an expression of sheer incredulousness marked clear on his face.

"It's the food. It has kept me drawn for the past three years." Her face went from expressionless to happy as she spoke. She looked content.

"Ha, that's funny."

"I kid you not. You know, when I moved here from Chandigarh, *gujju* food used to make me throw up in my mouth. I couldn't get used to the *meetha*-in-dal-and-veggies ordeal. Can't live without it now."

The server from the café appeared with a bulging, crispy frankie and placed it on Keya's side of the table. The contentment on her face went up a notch and her eyes lit up as she glanced at the food.

"That is a heavily pregnant frankie," he remarked, eyeing her food as she unwrapped the silver foil. It was bigger than the biggest one he had ever had. He was convinced she would need to borrow a belly to finish it. She laughed at his absurd joke. He noticed slightly inward teeth behind thin coral-coloured lips. They were white and glossy with a slight gap between the two front ones. The minuscule black speck on her lower lip caught his eye. It looked so inviting that he felt an overwhelming desire to a run a finger over her bottom lip to check if the lip and the speck were a package deal. Before he could drift further, he realised she had caught him gaping at her. He hadn't meant to stare, so looked away as a reaction, then tried to get back on the track of safe conversations.

"What were you saying about the food?"

"I think it represents the extremes in my life. A bit sour. A bit sweet. And a teeny bit spicy." She ventured on the path of food and philosophy, neither of which he had an appetite for at the moment. Life's philosophies had eluded him all throughout; neither was he good at it nor comfortable. He wondered why he was sitting here listening to her.

"Shall we?" She signalled to him as she picked up her paper plate along with the soiled tissues and began to walk in the direction of a nearby trash can. Her lean frame hadn't given the impression that she could finish the enormous frankie but she had. He was pleasantly surprised.

"I'll get the cup for you," he responded, picking up the used paper cup she had left behind on the table. "You're too pretty to carry trash in any case," he added in an undertone. As he got up, his mind still on that thought, he almost collided into her. Apparently, she hadn't moved.

"Excuse me?" she snapped.

Evidently, he had spoken out a little too loud. Her reaction startled him slightly. Her eyebrows were still raised in lieu of a question. He had to put a spin on it. Quickly.

"I mean, it's a part of the M&A services we offer our special clients." Nice save, he told himself, discreetly biting on his tongue.

"I'm presuming by special you mean clients who can't get their act together? I am perfectly capable of managing things, even picking up after me, you know." Embarrassment and slight confusion were splashed across her face, which was turning red by the moment.

*And you thought you were having a good run. Such a goof up is inexcusable. What are you, fourteen?* "I was just messing." Watching her not get convinced by his explanation, he continued, "Seriously, I did not mean to be sarcastic. Apologies. Let's go. It's almost two p.m."

"What did you just say?"

"I said I was playing. Let's go."

"No, what did you say after that?"

"Apologies."

He noticed, what he thought was anger, melting away as she continued to look at him with what could only be classified as blushing. He wasn't good at recognising emotions so ignored his take on it. He could have sworn it was blushing though. He just struggled with why that'd be the case. There was no exchange of words between them on the way back. The awkwardness grew exponentially with each passing minute. When they almost reached the stadium, he tossed a few words to ease the tension.

"So what do you do on weekends or after work?"

That lit up her face. Bingo. "I like to read. Hang out with

my friends. And I'm working on a travelogue as well." She finally let her guard down.

It must have gone really well from that point on, for Vivek never realised when the discussion turned to more pleasurable topics. His love for books, her incomplete manuscript, his travel schedule, her desire to travel, his Punjabi parents, her Punjabi parents, his favourite sport, the sport she called work. They had more in common than he would have imagined.

***

"He went down on his knee and apologised. It was all too dramatic," Keya, hardly able to contain her excitement, zoomed towards Radhika who was stepping out of her car, yapping nineteen to the dozen. The girls were meeting up for an eight-kilometre hike surrounding Thol Lake.

The morning was fresh with the sun's warmth just enough to nourish their faces and not burn their skin. Heaps of dewdrops lay nestled on tall weeds that beautifully lined up both sides of the trail. The path was narrow and etched unswervingly for miles. It was the closest one could come to perpetuity in an urban landscape. Though it was a little too early for 'guy talk' even by Radhika's standards, Vivek was all Keya could talk about, and Radhika indulged her.

"No way. I don't buy that," she replied, adjusting the cap on her head.

"Believe you me, girl. He apologised."

"On his knee?"

"There is no God in details." Then with a smug smile, she added, "Okay, I'm stretching it a little but he did come around. Fancy that. Honestly, I never thought he had a decent bone in him. Know what I mean?"

"Oh yes. Keya, honeybun, you have no idea how well I am getting this. Do you think he's out to get you?" Radhika enquired after a beat. That caught Keya's attention but before she could let her thoughts drift further along those lines, Radhika quickly retracted, saying "But, he's a jerk, and, more importantly, he's no—"

"Kourosh," Keya concluded.

"Precisely." Radhika had always been an advocate of Keya dating Kourosh, for reasons best known to her.

"I know," Keya persevered, "but he isn't all that I thought he was. I mean, honestly, I guess I have been unfair. He seems like a nice guy, Rads. I haven't felt like this about someone in ages."

"Here's my two cents on it. I think he's the wrong guy for you. He's a total prick," Radhika declared blatantly with a thoughtful face, her body picking up pace as they began to advance on their hike. "But since you're so very enamoured, let's move it forward. What say? You know you need somebody to put you on the path of love. All I want is to find out whether this has any potential. Let's make you two fall for each other. Then, hopefully, either *he* gets his act together or *you* realise what a massive blunder this is and we could go back to the theory of why Keya and Kourosh should be together."

Keya spit out the lemonade she was sipping from her bottle. "Did you just hear yourself? That is preposterous!"

"Keya, my love, it's going to hurt but I'll say it. If you don't initiate action and just wait for a guy to show up with a dazzling wedding ring at the fag end of this trail, it may not happen in the next twenty years."

"It's too soon. I've barely talked to him once after I joined back."

"Oh please. There was that time at the game where he thought you were a bartender. Oh and the time before that in the bathroom."

"You should rename yourself *Agony Aunt*."

"No, I'm serious. Stop waiting for it to happen. Make it happen instead."

"Breathe, Rads. I can't push this. And he fired me, remember?"

"No, all I remember was that you got yourself re-hired on your terms. It is all so sexy. First he fired you and then he was smitten with you. I can see it all clearly in my crystal ball. It's the perfect plan. Though I am rooting for him to turn out to be a total prick, but for your sake, I hope he is anything but that."

"Err—"

"And you have to push this. Else the loneliness in your life will be . . . will be like this l-lake, Keya. Vast. Sprawling. And with no end in sight. No matter how hard you try, things won't change. Get it?" Radhika's voice had become sombre with every spoken word, her words dark, desperate, and ominous.

That threat felt like a thwack to Keya. She couldn't fathom when the discussion had turned so intense and reasonably insulting. "Easy, girl. You're attacking me. If it were that simple, you'd have taken action and found someone yourself. And we wouldn't have to do the rounds at every damn event in the city in search of a potential groom. So there. My two cents," she responded, the pitch of her tone a strong indication of disappointment and miff.

Radhika stiffened visibly, staring at Keya in disbelief with her mouth open, her jaw dropping to the ground. Dense tears began to form in her eyes and before long one rolled down through the side of her left cheek. She shook her head sideways and with somewhat trembling lips, softly proclaimed, "I can't . . . I can't believe you said—" She didn't wait to voice her pain entirely and began to jog away from Keya.

Sensitivity being Keya's trademark, she instantly recognised the spite in her own demeanour. "Wait, Rads. Listen. Please wait," she shouted, hustling towards Radhika but her screams caused her best friend to speed up even more.

Minutes later, a panting Keya managed to stop Radhika, whose face was covered in sweat and tears, causing her kohl to smear way below her eyes. She looked shattered. "I'm sorry. So, so sorry," she earnestly expressed regret, holding Radhika's arms. "I honestly didn't mean it." Radhika looked away pretending to not listen. Keya wiped her tears away with both her hands and pleaded, "Say something."

"I got nothing. And you're right. If I had taken it seriously, I would have found someone myself," she replied amidst sobs, her eyelids blinking.

"That's not true. I know you've put in a great deal of effort. It's just a matter of time before an amazing person who is worthy of you comes along," Keya said in a soft voice, desperately trying to appear convincing. Cliché or otherwise, she definitely meant it. That calmed Radhika down somewhat but then she said something else.

"I'm sorry for dragging you to all those futile events but I couldn't have gone husband hunting alone."

The simplicity and innocence in that revelation deeply touched Keya. "Radhika, trust me, I have enjoyed, no, not only enjoyed but loved being dragged to every single one of those events. I swear on . . . I swear on—" she looked around and then pointing to something on the ground, said, "this used condom. I swear on this used condom that I will be your constant companion in the hunt and not quit until we have found, nailed, and married you off to the most eligible guy in the world."

With that, the tensions on Radhika's face melted away giving way to delight and pleasure. "You're crazy. You know that?" Then she seemed to weigh the situation for a second and continued, "I'm sorry, too, for saying those terrible things. I don't think you'll be lonely forever. I don't even think you're lonely now."

"I know." Both girls gave each other bear hugs.

"But I'm sticking to what I said earlier." Radhika said withdrawing herself from Keya. "I also swear on this used condom that I'm going to make you and Vivek fall in love. Don't you dare argue that."

"Okay, okay, spit out the plan."

Amidst hectic work schedules, crazy deadlines, and extended work hours, Vivek found himself observing Keya. He'd noticed her interest in him as well. First the water cooler discussions, then the IM flirts, that one quirky line from her at the end of the last few official e-mails, running into each other at coffee shops and lunches, chatting each other up until their server would indicate it was time to close for the night; all this couldn't be just by chance. Not all the time. But he wasn't certain. He wasn't sure if she was flirting and he was reciprocating or it was the inverse, but he couldn't shush the distinct voice in his head that claimed: You're smitten. Admit it and everyone gets out alive.

One evening, just as he was leaving for the day, he got a buzz from Keya's extension.

"You got plans for this Thursday evening?" she asked, casually.

"Yes, I plan to be on the flight to Mumbai. Haven't gone back in three weeks."

"Can you not postpone it by a day?"

"That would depend on how exciting the proposition is."

"I'm signing you up for a charity show. It's about—"

"Mom, is that you?"

He could hear her chuckling on the other side. Such a captivating laughter, he noted.

"It's not just another charity show. I'm involved."

"Wait, you're being auctioned?"

That same laughter again. He was charmed.

"The proceeds will go to a children's charity."

"Now that you've brought that up, can't dodge it, can I?"

"You better not."

The following Thursday evening after work, he rushed to his hotel room at The Landmark Oriental. A quick shower, followed by a stylish suit accented by a lavender tie, and a splash of cologne later, he checked into his rental car to get to the charity dinner at The City Club. The majestic venue instantly gave him the feeling of being art deco. A lift took him to the fifth floor where a massive MF Hussain masterpiece marked the entrance of the main dining room staircase. Dramatic mahogany wood details, high ceilings, and expansive windows greeted him as he entered the main dining hall. The place seemed like a milieu for the hobnobbing Ahmedabad elite. On showing his ticket at the reception table, he was guided to a round table in the centre of the hall. A well-dressed waiter immediately served him bottled water as his eyes searched for Keya, the only person he would know. Before he could make note of the ambiance, his white napkin had been replaced by a black one, probably to match his black suit.

"You're here!" Keya appeared from behind, wearing a full-length dark winter coat.

"Hi," he replied, finding it tough to contain the adrenalin that was pumping so hard through his veins.

"You're on time. The show is about to begin. Do you have the schedule on you?"

"Keya, sit. I don't care about the schedule. I'm here for you." Then quickly realising what he had unmindfully confessed, he weakly attempted correction. "I mean, because you invited me. And aren't you dressed a little funny for this event?"

"Just wait and watch," she winked and in a jiffy disappeared backstage.

Thirty minutes later, Vivek was dreadfully bored. Welcome speech, jokes so lame they made his head spin, one amateur stand-up act, a loud orchestra that made him feel like he was at a shabby wedding reception, and a short devotional song sequence that had the lady in his adjacent chair in tears; he had swallowed all this without any company whatsoever. He was baffled at why Keya would invite and ditch him.

Deciding to walk out of the venue out of sheer frustration and a desperate need to get some fresh air, he had just gotten up when the words 'and now a very special performance by Keya Singhal' fell on his exhausted ears. He let the name sink in for a moment. Then he turned around and was so taken aback by what he saw that if he hadn't had a pillar next to him for support, he'd have fallen!

Keya, the girl who always came to office dressed conservatively, had just now emerged in a red *corset* with an absurdly *plunging neckline* (he blinked his eyes), black shimmery *shorts* (his eyes narrowed), *fishnet stockings* all the way to her thighs (he gulped), a matching hat, heavy eye make-up, and bright red lips! *Am I dreaming this or am I dreaming this?*

Keya's hair was set in deliberate waves. She lay on her

back on a chaise, covering her face with one gloved hand, her legs crossed, instantly engaging the audience. When the music turned on with a bang, she slowly began to gyrate to the beats while singing some obscure lyrics that Vivek took a while to decipher. He followed her movement with his eyes.

*Ek baat maan lo tum.* She tossed her hair across her face suggestively. *Jo kahu main woh karo tum.* Each strand sequentially slid down her face onto her bare shoulders as she lowered her face to make eye contact with the crowd. *Jo karo to mera vaadaa, main karoongi jo kaho tum tum.* He was somewhat appalled, scandalised, and stunned. Realising he'd need a drink to digest what he was being subjected to—not that he was complaining—he demanded a gin and tonic from the bartender at the bar next to him.

"No alcohol, sir."

*Argh! Gujarat!* "Give me a Coke in that case."

"Wow," the bartender with ridiculously tacky blonde highlights commented while gawking at Keya. "*Ekdum mast.*"

What the hell is she doing? he wondered. She was definitely a respite after those dull acts but: *What. The. Hell. Is. She. Doing?*

He waved his hand in front of the bartender's face. "*Drink?*"

"Sorry, sir. Here."

He squinted to look at Keya in what appeared to be an appalling sequence in her act and covered his eyes as a knee-jerk reaction. She shook her body vigorously and thrust her hips out the first time with her hands stretched out in the opposite direction. With the crowd cheering, in between the fingers covering his eyes, he saw what he had never seen before. Let alone see, not even imagined. It was a raw, sexy, seductive Keya. Confident, empowered, and audacious. He absorbed that with a few swigs of Coke.

From hesitantly catching a glimpse of her, it had quickly transitioned to not being able to take his eyes off of her. Back on the chaise, she jolted her head, her hair flying, as her body did a quick turnaround while parting her crossed legs, raising them, moving them from one side of the chaise to another, and crossing them again suggestively. She pushed out her chin, gave the audience one tantalising look, and then moved away, tiptoeing like a swan to a pole that seemed to have appeared out of nowhere, just in time to be enticed by her. She used it craftily, unlike a novice, and wrapped herself around like a snake. His pulse rose dramatically as if his heart was not in his control. He was nervous, excited, and aroused, all at once. It was the classiest burlesque he'd ever seen. But that was not it. The fact that it was Keya who was doing it almost made him drool. The girl at the office was somewhat standoffish, self-reflective, and even an idealist. But this? This girl was wild, uninhibited, and very desirable. His mind overlapped the qualities of the two different Keyas and envisioned the end product. It was a pleasant surprise. A consuming feeling.

He wanted her. Now.

***

Keya settled into a plush leather sofa in the green room backstage. She would have preferred to be soaking in a bathtub, brimming with bubbles, if you please, for the act had drained her, but for now the sofa would have to do.

A few dozen tiny bulbs on the periphery of the giant mirror in the room bathed her in soft light, highlighting her features. She had changed into her normal clothes post her audacious act. Exhilaration glinted off her face.

"You rocked it, pumpkin. Put the rest of the acts to shame, you did! And . . . you look stunning," Radhika shared as she stepped into the room, instantly lighting up Keya's face.

"You think? Thanks for letting me be a part of this."

"Of course. Three years of organising charity dinners and I finally see an act I'm glued to. But we'll discuss that later. Here, take this last shot of tequila and go find Vivek."

That made her spring off the sofa. She was already feeling slightly buzzed from first few shots Radhika had forced down her throat prior to the show. It was the only way she could have gotten herself to pull off such a bold act, that too in front of such a judgmental crowd.

She took a slug of that last shot and stormed out, flapping like a butterfly, the makeup from the burlesque act still intact, creating quite a contrast to the casual outfit she was now wearing. Not finding him at the table he was assigned, she ducked to rush across the room to arrive at a good vantage point.

Minutes later, still no Vivek in the room . . .

A million thoughts collided in her head about how he could have reacted to her act. The nervous energy, which was thankfully amiss on stage, was now eerily creeping in. *What if she had overdone it?* The overly reflective, fretful, old Keya was back.

She walked out of the dining area to peek into the lobby. With her phone in her handbag in the green room, she had no option but to rely on her search capabilities and her instinct.

The lobby was a maze of people. For its size, it was hosting double the capacity. She spotted quite a few men in suits who had probably stepped out of the hall to catch some respite from the soirée inside, but none of them fit Vivek's description.

Hurriedly, she pressed the button for the lift. Perhaps he was downstairs.

While impatiently waiting for the lift, her foot tapping non-stop on the lushly-carpeted floor, a hundred thoughts raced through her mind. Was her act so appalling that he had just plain taken off? A distinct sense of hurt pride was now weaving itself with the nervous energy. *It was a huge risk*, she told herself, as she rode down to the lobby floor, *and it didn't pay off.* Just as the lift doors opened, she ran out, inadvertently bumping into a few patrons waiting to get in.

"Oh God. Watch your step, young lady." She heard a peeved woman reprove and realised she had stepped on her flowing, virgin-white chiffon skirt which was now sporting the imprint of her shoes. "Sorry. I'm so sorry," she said hoping to sound sincere and without worrying about being convincing.

She reached the centre of the reception area and did a quick spin but there was no familiar face in sight. Her heart began to sink. The all-too-familiar state of stupor hit her immediately. *I should have followed my gut feeling and not taken this plunge. I shouldn't have allowed Rads to coax me into this. It was a massive blun—* Before she could complete that thought, she saw a silhouette of a man outside the building, on the deck by the palms, smoking. Hope and excitement rushed through her veins and her heart began to pound. She walked in his direction with an accelerated pace trying to catch a glimpse. A moment later she was convinced. No two men could look so stellar. Not to her, anyway. She closed her eyes as a reflex and breathed in some fresh air.

"Ahh . . . there you are. Sneaked out? Too boring for you?" She partly accused and partly teased, surprising even herself.

"Keya! Hi. What? No, I-I was just . . ."

He was stuttering, something she had never witnessed

before. It was quite unlike him. Which, she concluded, could only mean one of the two extremes: either he had despised it or she had won him over. Now, which one was it? She shot him an inquiring look: *Don't be such a bumbling fool, Vivek. Tell me I was phenomenal . . .*

"I was—you were great up there. Stunning, actually. I had no idea you were such a . . . phenomenal dancer." He granted her wish, making her heart flutter wildly.

She noticed he drew a deep, unsteady breath and let it out slowly, appearing not in control. There weren't many people around at the moment. He took a step forward, boldly reducing the distance between them. His eyes were fixated on hers and his arm took possession of her waist, bringing her closer still. "I thought you were sensational up there, Keya." He wet his lips. Keya gasped. "You took me and everyone else in the room by surprise and created quite a stir. I . . . I couldn't—"

The lights from an oncoming car blinded his eyes, making him close them in response. She stepped back. The moment was lost . . . but his eyes, his body language, and his words had all confirmed something. She was stoked.

***

Vivek graciously invited Keya for coffee at the ritzy café next door to The City Club. A couple of frothy drinks marked the prelude to an evening of unrestrained conversation, a ceaseless stream of compliments by him, stealing glances from each other that quickly transitioned to ogling, and sparks flying high. Their chemistry was so palpable, Vivek thought even the puppy one of the patrons had brought along could probably feel it. It was undeniably an evening to fall in love.

In the darkness of the night, he insisted on dropping her to her apartment in his rental car. He discovered that she was more than a little tipsy, which exposed her low threshold for alcohol. The driver discovered this secret about her as well when she guided him like she was on a ride in an amusement park. More than a few abrupt turns and misguidings later, and after much of asking around, he and the driver were ultimately able to hunt down the answer to the big challenge Keya had thrown their way in her inebriated state.

"Good night," she said while stepping out of his car outside her apartment complex. He was slightly startled, an invitation to her place being a basic assumption.

"Let me drop you, Keya. You need—"

"No, I got it." She appeared dewy-eyed from the other side of the window. When he rolled down the window glass, she blinked, her eyelids barely able to lift themselves up, and with an impish smile added, "And thank you for an evening I won't forget until . . . until . . . I . . . umm . . . go up and crash. Right, right?"

She was high, and he didn't want to leave her alone. He felt a jab as if she was being wrenched from him. An inexplicable uneasiness followed that he didn't want to settle for. In a flash, he paid the driver, and scurried out of the car towards a floundering Keya who was still on the fourth step of what appeared to be a tedious staircase. When she realised his presence, he noticed that she stopped her upward journey to turn towards him.

"Did your driver not like your suit, too? Aww, you poor thing. What a bummer," she joked in a sing-song manner with a mock sympathetic face. It wasn't the first time she had poked fun at his dressing sense. It hadn't appeared so flirtatious before.

"You're on a roll tonight. Let's get you home safe."

He held her as she fumbled with the correct key from the bulky set of keys she was holding, trying to match them with the entrance door. Moments later, while she was attempting to try the last of the keys from the bunch, the door opened from within, disorienting her and Vivek. There stood a young man wearing a hooded jacket, busy with an electronic device.

"Keya! I'm sorry. Are you all right?" he asked with utmost concern. Keya just smiled a dreamy smile and replied, "Rosh, my buddy boy. Hiiii."

"Let's take you in," Vivek said, slightly taken aback, feeling the young man's prying eyes on him.

"I'll see you later," he heard him tell Keya.

When the lift door shut, Vivek turned around and noticed that the fellow hadn't taken the lift but was watching them from a distance. "Odd," he muttered.

"That was—that was my neighbour Kouro—" she said, struggling with her apartment door. Vivek offered to help.

"No, I'm fine. I'm fine. So, this is me," she said, opening the latch with a little difficulty. She entered, threw her handbag on the coffee table, then turned around, and looking Vivek in the eyes, asked, "Won't you come in?" He looked away, a timid smile playing on his lips as he ran a hand through the back of his head. It made him feel strangely hesitant and slightly awkward.

"I-I better take off," he finally said, ignoring the demanding voice in his head, which was pushing him to take that next impending step. "Just wanted to get—"

"Get me home safe. I know. But I'm home now. And safe. Very safe. See." She flirted with goo-goo eyes, biting her lower lip, leaning against a yellow wall next to the door, blinking softly, appearing unmindful of the world around her. He continued to look at her sparkling eyes, wishing life were simpler. If only she weren't that tipsy, he would have ventured. He swallowed to aid his dry throat, holding back on the inescapable desire to step in.

"Another time," he gasped, unsure of whether there would ever be an 'another time'. She had been a surprise all evening. What if he woke up the next morning and discovered that it was all an illusion? What if it was just a fleeting phase, he fretfully wondered. What if this was his only chance and he was blowing it off like a fool?

"Take care," he gently mouthed, and then walked away. *I'm such a wuss*, he mumbled, kicking a used paper cup that was in his way, and walked back all the way to his hotel.

When Vivek ran into Keya by the water cooler the next morning, she looked flustered at first—faltering, unable to form simple sentences, shying away—but that didn't stop her from stealing glances at him. He found it so endearing that for an instant he considered pulling her into his arms. *Already this far on the perilous path of romance, that too at a client site, so what is one more blunder,* the voice in his head asked. The cleaning crew walked in, just in time, to spare him the distress of making that decision.

All day long, images of their evening together flashed through his mind. The harder he applied himself to work, the stronger he was captivated by Keya's charm. *Damn you, woman! Is there even a way out of not thinking about you?* When he could steal a moment from the daily firefighting his work involved, he rushed to take care of the one thing that had been on his mind all throughout.

`Have dinner with me,` he typed, resisting the urge to add: *on my lap, in my hotel room, tonight, all night long.*

*Don't do that. Don't steal my thunder. That is on my to-do list. To invite you.*

*Really? I'm honoured to be on that coveted list, then.*

*LOL, stop it. Come over one of these evenings. I'm the best chef in my neighbourhood.*

*Does the offer include a dessert of my choice?* He typed with somewhat wobbly fingers.

*You're fearless, aren't you?* She followed that with a wink. *Phew, I'm safe*, he reckoned.

*I'll come if there's no alcohol.* He put down his bottom line.

*You're such a party pooper. And I never have alcohol at home in any case. Law abiding citizen and all.*

*With your threshold, it's probably a good idea.*

There hadn't been an hour in the three days that followed, when he had been awake and hadn't imagined being with her. Alone. His trip to Mumbai had never been this painful an experience. He could hardly wait to get back to Ahmedabad this time. They both had agreed on seeing each other the evening he arrived. One extra dab of cologne and a bunch of the freshest fuchsia orchids later, Vivek was ready to head out to the excitement that awaited.

It was déjà vu. He was at the same spot. Outside her door, again, and just as anxious.

"Don't overthink," she said authoritatively, opening the door for him, "just come in." He gave her a hug, both of them taking their time in letting go of each other, and handed over the flowers. She looked pleased with his choice.

As he was about to enter, he heard Keya shout out something. He turned and saw the same joker who was here the other day, standing at the same spot he had last seen him at. Before Keya could say something else, he stepped into the lift. *Odd.*

Keya turned and ushered him inside.

"Wow. It's hot in here," he remarked, as he entered her apartment, instantly feeling like a baked potato.

"Sorry. My air conditioner is broken. The air filter is dirty, I was told."

"Didn't realise it was that kind of a party. But I could undress now, to fit in," he joked, eyeing Keya's dress. She wore a sexy, ruffled black dress that barely reached her knees. His eyes hovered below her neck area, where her skin glowed. Ignoring her explanation, he began to take his sports jacket off. She let out a nervous laugh.

"That won't be necessary."

She disappeared for a flash and returned with two coloured drinks, a slice of pineapple sitting pretty on the rim of each glass. "In lieu of alcohol," she clarified, handing him the drink. This steered the conversation in the direction of all things tropical. Vivek didn't mind; this was an evening to know each other . . .

In time, she walked him to the dinner spread that blew him away. She had turned it into somewhat of a feast, each Italian dish appearing more salivating than the next. When he stopped to evaluate two servings of the same pasta dish in different bowls, she explained. "This is a *him* dish and the one next to it is a *her* dish."

"I'm intrigued. They look exactly alike."

"Well, the *her* dish is sans olives. I can't stand those."

"You're wrong in presuming I wouldn't have liked her . . . I mean the *her* dish," he intentionally confessed, looking her in the eye.

"You don't even know what the *her* dish is all about," Keya responded, catching on to his frequency.

"I think I know enough." From where he saw it, she got shy all of a sudden, and confirmed it by talking nervously without once looking at him—something he had come to realise she did only when she was feeling really bashful.

Scarlett, Kourosh, and Radhika's stories dominated the conversation all through dinner. Vivek deliberately didn't bring up work. Nothing that would remind him that the girl he was so insanely attracted to was a client. That it could have been circumstantial love at best. He knew deep down inside that it wasn't that, though. He had gone through significant inner conflict on the subject. The part that won, each time, was his heart. But . . .

Long after dinner, once they were done discussing everybody and their brother, Keya asked, "Coffee?"

"No." It was that sparkling moment begging to be seized. "You," he softly declared. His eyes took the liberty of running all over her. Then he walked towards her, expunging the hindering vastness that had stayed between them right from the start of the evening. Not being able to resist her any further, he leaned in to kiss her. The sensation of her slightly cold lips on his warm ones was electrifying. His body softly nudged her until she rested against a wall.

He kissed her, gently so, on her inviting lips like a novice. Her lower lip deceivingly offered more surface area and softness than was obvious. A low throaty sound escaped Keya's lips. She clung more tightly to him than he would have thought possible. Passion consumed Vivek and filled his veins with excitement. His kisses increased in ardour, gush written all over him and Keya, who almost threw him into oblivion with her uninhibited passion. His hands made their way through the contours of her body while hers stuck firmly to his chest.

Vivek was hot and sweaty, just as much as her, and the thermostat settings had little to do with it. The background noises—slamming of breaks by a car on the street, a screaming man, heart thumping beats coming from what seemed to be a next-door neighbour's house—were no longer distractions. Her moaning was all that registered.

His parched lips melted into hers, his tongue mated carnally with hers, and his chest meshed against her soft breasts . . . Keya's body was glued to his, mixing anxiety, eagerness, and desire smoothly. Anything else, given the situation, would be unforgivable, he concluded, as he carried her in one swift motion towards the black leather couch he'd been eyeing through the corner of his eyes. He dismissed that gentlemanly voice in his head to ask for consent. Her moans had given him more than that. They'd indicated urgency. He tenderly unwrapped her from himself and placed her on the couch. What followed was inescapable. It had the effect of a thousand waterfalls commingling into a river. Galvanising.

"Coffee?" she asked again, after she had regained something akin to consciousness.

"Still you," he replied, kissing her.

While Keya was in the kitchen making coffee after getting dressed, she felt Vivek's hands on her abs. He was holding her close from behind, his face peeking through the nook between her face and her shoulders. "I want to hear all about your life as a burlesque dancer," he teased, "now that we've got sex out of the way."

"You rogue!" She jabbed him with her elbow letting out a mischievous titter, then retorted, "I think you should come clean first."

"Ha! Aren't you little Miss Sly."

"It's the influence of your wicked company."

"Where did you learn burlesque?"

"I used to watch Helen's songs over and over again as a teen. Also, I had this neighbour in Chandigarh. Quite a talent. She taught multiple dance forms at a dance school. Moved like a gazelle and made men faint with those moves. We always did Sunday lunches together at my house. She would teach me in the privacy of my room once we recovered from food coma. Mom always thought she was teaching me something decent. Good times." Then she sported a thinking face for a moment. "Wait, I thought you were going first!"

"By the way, I love that you always put a hand or two on your boobs while you speak. It is very attractive. Not to mention suggestive."

She flung a spoon at him that he dodged in time.

Her jaw dropped open. She laughed and said, "It's my heart, you pervert, not my boobs. I always speak from my heart. Didn't realise my hands hovered around it so often."

"Sweetheart, that may be true, but from where a man sees it—" He hit himself in the heart with a sideways fist, tilting his head.

"Shut up," she interrupted, holding up another spoon in mock threat, blushing, "and stop making up topics. It's your turn to go first."

"You also shrug a lot while you do that. Just saying."

"Vivek!"

"All right, all right." He gave in and found a spot on the kitchen counter next to the coffee pot. "I'll go first. Let's see. Scarlett is getting all plump and sluggish. She doesn't like mingling with other dogs anymore. When potential romantic interests approach her at the park, she ignores them completely. All she wants is food and to be left alone. I think she probably needs some sex to kick the dreariness out of her system."

That evoked a hearty laugh from Keya. "I think I know enough about Scarlett. What about your life? There must be other interesting elements to your life besides Scarlett, no?"

He pulled her closer and told her all about his growing years in Pune and his current life in Mumbai, albeit succinctly, deliberately rushing through most parts, for his own life was not exciting to him at that point in time. She was.

"That's all good stuff. What about the bad stuff? Addictions, vices, bad relationships, jail time?"

"Okay, here's an embarrassing one. I am—rather I was—addicted to rhyming. Me and my bro. It's something we grew up doing. And it's stuck with me now."

"Rhyming?"

"Yes."

"Demonstrate, please."

"Let me think," he said with a reflective face. "Keya, you're a doll who lives in this pretty urban sprawl. It's so cool that you work with men who chase a ball. I can't believe you made dinner for an oddball. What am I hearing outside, rainfall?"

She laughed hysterically, holding her stomach, staring at him open-mouthed, and when she could finally catch her breath, she lightly clapped. He couldn't tell if he was being ridiculed or appreciated.

"I know. It's too dorky."

"No no. It's incredible." She was still laughing. "You have to teach me."

"It's really easy. Try it. You'll soon get a hang of it."

"I'll suck at it."

"I'll help you."

"Okay. Umm—where do I start?"

"Start with me. Replicate what I just said."

"Hmm . . . okay. Vivek, you're funny. But—" She went into silent mode.

"You can't take that long. Let's go to your balcony. I hear it rain."

"Okay, okay. Hang on. All right. Here we go. Vivek, you're funny and cute like an Easter Bunny."

It made him roll with laughter. In response to that, she cupped her mouth in embarrassment.

"God. That was so lame. I'm beyond embarrassed. It's all your fault."

"Seriously, it was a good attempt. But let's do this. Forget it for now. You still owe me your stories."

"What stories?"

"About you, your life," he said, making himself comfortable on the solo suede bean bag in her balcony.

"Well, I grew up in Chandigarh," she began, and told him about her family, her friends, her interests, her career.

"What's the craziest thing you've done?"

"Let's see. I once deliberately walked into the men's locker room after a Rangers' game, acting like I was lost. Saw a player stark naked. He's a very famous player," she said with mischief in her eyes, her tongue hanging out.

"You are a little troublemaker, aren't you! And just who is this naked stud?"

"I obviously can't reveal all the gory details. Not sure you can take it."

"Try me."

"Oh come on now, don't embarrass me further."

He continued looking at her, making it clear that he wouldn't leave her until she fessed up.

"Jang—"

"I knew it," he exclaimed. "Janak Goyal enjoys too much of a fan following if you ask me."

"Well, he *is* good."

"Only on the field, ma'am," Vivek decreed, making Keya bite back her smile.

"Fine, that's out. Tell me about other stuff."

She narrated her life stories in detail, her school and college years, every tiny quirk of her family members, her job, and the high and low points in her life.

"And then, there was Raj, too," she began, almost collapsing on his lap.

That name, Raj, symbolised unrequited love for Keya. It symbolised betrayal and, more than anything, it symbolised her transition from a blithe young bee to a worrying woman. It had not only altered her personality but also her outlook to a large extent. Those memories hadn't faded or turned fuzzy, hard as she tried.

It was just a couple of years ago when Raj had proposed to her in a dramatic fashion on a cruise to Singapore. He'd taken her to watch an acrobatic show at an aqua theatre inside a casino on the cruise. The show was a collection of stunning dream sequences with nifty stunts against the backdrop of rain, fire, and dancing lights. He'd bought them front row seats where they were sure to get soaked. At the end of the seventy-five minute show, as they were splashed on for the final time, three ballerinas in red swimsuits had come flying down from a suspended centrepiece, right in front of their seats, holding a board that read, 'Keya, will you marry me?' Keya hadn't experienced anything more magical and romantic than that moment. It had made her cry as she replied in affirmative and gave him an intense hug. The kiss that followed had lasted long after the audience had vacated the theatre. He had slipped a pretty ring on her finger and whispered sweet nothings to her all night, making her heart flutter.

"Raj had taken the lead on planning a destination wedding for us. It was all happening too soon," she continued in one breath to Vivek who seemed sufficiently absorbed by her narration. "My family had made several objections to Raj's lack of a definite, conventional career. He was a DJ and a master turntablist, and anyone in the crowd could vouch for his talent when he was on the job. Being born in an affluent family, he never seemed worried about who would pay his bills during slack periods. Several clashes later, I had convinced my folks about how talented he was and how I loved what he did for a living. But just days before the wedding, he decided to postpone it, all courtesy of a new assignment that required him to go on a national tour with a new band from Pune that played alternative rock."

Her hands were working through her hair, tying them into a messy side braid. "I had to face tremendous amount of embarrassment in front of my family and friends, who had all booked their travel for the wedding. To be honest, I was beside myself with anxiety; spent weeks speculating and questioning myself. I waited until the day he was back from the tour and immediately set another date for the wedding—this time it was local and with a much smaller guest list. It wasn't like the wedding was the only thing in my life but the situation had turned me desperate." She took a deep breath, composing herself, and then continued. "Gradually, I realised it was like walking on a slippery slope. He'd made one excuse after another and taken off on another tour, yet again. The frequency of calls and e-mails from him dropped. And then one summer night, it all came crashing down. There were no pieces to pick up. It was over. No explanations, no justification, just a generic 'I want different things in life now. I think this might be best for us' from him."

When she was done sharing her pain, she unwrapped herself from Vivek's arms and made way to a corner in the balcony. An incessant stream of tears was rolling down her cheeks onto her hands that were holding on to the railing firmly. She couldn't fathom why she had poured her heart out to him in one go. It was one of the most emotional nights in the recent past. From speculating about his reaction at the charity show and getting intimate with him only days later to baring her soul to him, it had wildly oscillated between ecstasy, excitement, and distress. Her eyes were shut close but the tears found their way out. When she opened her eyes, Vivek wasn't by her side, much as a part of her had hoped. He was still seated comfortably on the bean bag.

"Sorry," she said, her voice trembling, trying to inhale. "I said too much."

He was as silent as a snowflake in the night.

"Aren't you going to say anything?"

"Whatever, Keya. It's in the past." He shrugged.

"Is that your reaction?" Stunned, she turned to look at him. Could he be more insensitive?

"Wh-what do you mean?" He seemed slightly taken aback by her defiance. "What do you want me to say?"

"Something that doesn't include *whatever*." She threw a severe look at him.

"I was just—"

"No. It's not just this one time, Vivek. You've done this before." *Stop, now isn't the time,* an inner voice cautioned her but she ignored it.

"Done what?"

"Okay, I'll spell it out for you." *Shut up. Shut the fuck up. Don't do this.* "That speech in the conference room. What was that all about? Such arrogance! Then you took me for a bartender at the suite. Took off with my drink. Then you insulted me on my name. And now you think—" *Oh dear God. You are a colossal fool.*

"Keya, wait. Hold on. God, you have so much bottled up. I didn't know I had such a bad rep."

"Stop defending yourself."

A weak smile formed on his lips, then he said, "Okay, let me try this. I guess I can see why you're so aggravated. But that was work. And I have a different side to me at work."

"And what side is this?"

After what seemed to be deliberation, to her relief, he said, "I like you, Keya. I hadn't a clue I had hurt you. This is why I never mix work and personal stuff." He looked away, slapping a delicate creeper hanging from the side of the wall she shared with her neighbour.

"Well, it's too late for that," she said amidst sobs.

A few moments of awkward silence followed. She wished

she hadn't been so harsh on him. But then, her rational side argued that if this had to continue Vivek needed to justify himself.

Two young boys from the pizza shop diagonally across her building switched off the lights and rolled down the shop shutters indicating that it was two a.m. The street now appeared to be pitch dark. When she was done noticing everything else in the vicinity, she mustered some courage to look at Vivek through the corner of her eye. Waiting moves work great in chess, she'd learnt as a kid. But this seemed like stalemate . . .

Vivek rubbed his fingers on his forehead, his thumb firmly placed on his right temple, eyes shut. Keya felt lost. From where she saw it now, it seemed like a series of blunders in a short span of days. The dance act, the one too many shots of tequila, letting him come over, getting intimate, sharing her dark secrets, and now lashing out at him.

Almost an infinite amount of time later, when he hadn't said anything, she considered making truce. She'd have to find another day and place to bring up her issues with him. Just as she opened her mouth, his phone buzzed.

With a perplexed look on his face, he answered it. "Is everything all right?" And shortly after, he said, "I'll be right over." Before she could ask if everything was okay, he managed a feeble 'I have to go' and abruptly took off. He didn't look her in the eye even once.

She foundered on the floor as she saw him leave. She hadn't felt this low in a long time. It was as if someone had stabbed her in the heart. She realised what it was almost instantly. They weren't ready to come so close so quickly. She barely knew him. And she'd thrown Raj in the mix. Relived those memories.

A nauseating presage swept over her.

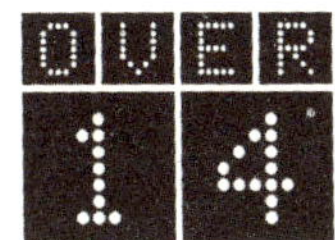

Vivek squeezed his eyes shut and then opened them. 6:58 a.m. He hadn't slept a wink in the past twenty-four hours. His eye sockets hurt, his head thumped, but his mind continued to work on overdrive. Countless cups of coffee lay strewn on his table. He had come to the stadium straight from the hotel after meeting Harsh, somewhere around five in the morning. Apart from his office, there was no activity anywhere else in the stadium. All was deathly quiet. *Not everybody's life is hanging from the edge of a precipice*, he reasoned with a wry grin.

Last night, or was it today morning, after answering that call, he had jumped into his car and scurried off in the direction of his hotel. Weekend and late night calls were hardly surprising in the field of M&A. Or medicine. It was one of the few work traits he shared with his cardiologist father. No hour was off-limits for official phone calls. It had aged his father a lot faster than he would have imagined: receding hairline, under-eye bags, worry lines, et al, and Vivek knew it was inescapable for him as well. But what had taken place was going to give him a heart attack! For the umpteenth time he replayed in his mind all that had happened.

When he'd answered Harsh's call from Keya's balcony, all he had got was an unsatisfactory 'Hey buddy, I need to speak with you right away. Come up to my suite. Twelfth floor. 1220'. That had left him feeling uneasy. Harsh had been scheduled to be on the flight back to Bengaluru the previous night. They'd even said their goodbyes right before he had left for Keya's. So, what was on fire at two a.m. then?

On the drive back, he had thought about all that could have gone wrong and realised a lot could have. This was M&A, after all. On top of that, he had begun having his share of issues with Harsh of late. Harsh's impulsive decisions had driven him to outrage and discontentment in the past few weeks. Despite him being his most-favoured client, Vivek felt he didn't really know him entirely. And that bothered him. Harsh's holding company was invested in a large number of subsidiary companies that he could never fully figure out. No marriage is stress-free, he had told himself repeatedly and moved on. Or at least tried to.

As soon as he had reached the hotel, he had rushed to take the elevator to Harsh's suite. Dressed in a robe and pyjamas, a lit cigar in his right hand, Harsh had opened the door with a blank expression.

"Is everything okay?"

"Come in, come in," he had invited him into the designer hotel room painted in orange and grey. It was a far cry from what his own room looked like. Life-sized windows offered unobstructed view of the bridges that connected the old parts of the city to the new. Had they been meeting in different circumstances, Vivek would have soaked in the view with the

And with that Harsh had concluded the dastardly meeting.

*I will. I will also figure out a way to kick you in the balls and knock you off your high horse,* Vivek had cursed in his head.

After a quick stop at his room, Vivek had headed straight to work. He had been too anxious to sleep, but now the lack of it, coupled with the stress, was beginning to get to him.

He had worked non-stop for the past three hours. Waking up people across states to get a better feel of how things were. Harsh had been correct in saying that the deal was not signed yet. So far, they just had the letter of intent and the PCCI approval. He recollected having gone through these steps multiple times in the past. The typical merger and acquisition life cycle started with the buyer looking for a suitable target, then going through a stage of due diligence to get a better understanding of the financial and operational issues associated with the target. Subsequent to which a letter of intent was signed between the two parties indicating their intent to merge or be acquired. A series of regulatory and shareholder approvals followed next that led to the legal close event known as 'Day One' in M&A parlance. Post Day One the companies were legally one.

In the past few months since they had started the acquisition process, Vivek and his team had covered a lot of ground. In a lot of ways they were far ahead in this process but in a lot of other ways they were not. Everything depended on the stakes involved. And this was huge.

Now the question was whether everything needed to be started all over again or not?

While still focussed on that thought, Vivek looked at his cell and then at his laptop for the umpteenth time, waiting for a reply from Keya.

***

There was a soft knock on her door followed by two loud ones. She stirred a bit. A volley of knocks, each sounding more urgent than the one earlier, quickly followed, stirring her to instant wakefulness. Keya considered ignoring it but the knocking only got harder, more insistent. *Do you want the house to come down?* Disoriented, running on autopilot, with a pounding head and heavy eyelids, she yelled at the door, "Coming!"

With a big yawn, she yanked the door open only to find Kourosh lingering outside.

"You sleeping?"

"Hey," she acknowledged his presence, rubbing her eyes.

"It's eight already. You no going to work today?"

"Oh god!" *Oh god. Oh god.* She had a nine a.m. meeting to run and to run to that morning. What am I doing sleeping this late? she chastised herself. Then the previous night's happenings came back to her. The wind got knocked out from her lungs, her legs buckled, and a cold, dull, depressing feeling took grip of her heart. It pained, like it hadn't in years. *No Keya, you have to be strong.* Tears blurred her eyes.

She had barely slept last night after Vivek had left. Her eyes shut as the flashes of the previous night with him went past her mind's eye.

"Keya?"

With a deep breath, she opened her eyes and noticed Kourosh look past her in her house as if searching for something—or someone.

"Looking for something?" Then it hit her. A vague memory of seeing Kourosh by the lift as she had opened the door for

Vivek. Embarrassment swept over her like an icy wave, turning her face red. She could only hope no one else had seen Vivek leave her apartment at an odd hour. Her reputation—she had a good one—in her apartment building mattered to her.

"No one. Nothing. I wait for you here."

"You know what? You should get going. It's going to take me a while to get ready."

"Keya."

"Yes?"

"Are you all right?"

How could she be after what had transpired the previous night? She'd even considered texting Rads at an impious three a.m. but had thought better of it. After cursing herself a thousand times over how she had handled the night's events, she had passed out on the balcony floor, only to pick herself up in the wee hours of the morning. Sleep might have helped alleviate some of the pain but it wasn't forgotten.

"Keya?"

"Hmmm. I-I am fine. See you later."

She reached her office at five minutes to nine, just in time for her meeting. Flinging her handbag on the desk, she got herself coffee and sat down in her cubicle to compose herself, trying to make sense of what had happened. The scalding hot coffee burned her tongue, but she didn't realise it then. Her mind and thoughts were on Vivek. He hadn't even called or left a message. *Wait, I haven't checked my cell since last night . . .*

She speedily opened her handbag to check for a voicemail. Zilch. Then she looked at the office phone. Nothing blinking there either. She logged into her computer to check for her personal e-mail account. No luck. Then she opened her

Outlook and there it was, an e-mail waiting for her. She had received it at 4:55 a.m.

`Subject: Hey, it's me.`

It was from 'Vicky' Grewal's personal e-mail account. *Vicky, of course, that's what they call you*, she mouthed. Then she read the body of the e-mail, expectantly. All she got was an unsatisfactory: `Let's talk when you come in.`

She slouched into her snug chair and swivelled around in it. The e-mail was such a let-down; it got her more aggravated than she was before she had read it. Fury consumed her, making her want to smash her laptop on Vivek's head. Walking out on her last night was unforgivable enough.

Irately, for lack of an effectual plan, she printed out the e-mail and stormed in the direction of the conference room. She didn't know what she wanted to talk about or what she wanted to hear from him. Right now the only thing that her numb mind processed was that she had to see him. She knocked loudly at the locked conference room door, venting part of her rage at that piece of wood. Seconds later, Omar opened the door just enough for his narrow head to peek out.

"Is Vivek here?" Disgruntled, she demanded.

"Yes, he is actually on a call. Can I—"

Before Omar could conclude his thought, Vivek emerged from behind him, nervousness splattered on his face, a look she had never been privy to before. His face looked lifeless and his eyes bloodshot.

"I got this." He signalled to Omar to leave them alone.

"You wanted to talk?" she asked in a cold, impersonal tone.

His eyes narrowed at her tone. "Can't talk here, Keya," he whispered with clenched teeth, looking stoic. Banging the door shut behind him, he began to walk in a random direction, pulling her by her hand.

"Where are you dragging me? I have a meeting to run at nine," she resisted.

When they passed known faces, Vivek ensured a nod whereas she just kept her head down and walked alongside, hiding the hand that was so authoritatively holding hers. Once out in the lobby, Vivek turned around to look at her, his face still steely.

"*What are you doing?* I have to go. I'm really late for my—"

"Is there no safe spot here?"

"I don't care. I just—" Her voice rose a notch higher each time he initiated dialogue. He shushed her and dragged her to a small vacant conference room by the corner. Then he tugged her in and kicked the door shut.

"Why were you creating a scene? Couldn't you just come along with me minus the drama?" Vivek angrily questioned, his voice deliberately low.

"Why are you dragging me when I'm telling you I'm late for a meeting?"

"Let's talk for a minute."

"Fine. Talk. Tell me what this crap is all about." She flashed the printout at him.

He took a deep breath. "Let me explain. Last night . . . look, I—"

The conference room door knocked open with men in ties on the other side. One man acknowledged Vivek's presence with a smile. The other one said, "Oh, pardon me. I guess we had this room at nine. We'll wait outside."

Before Keya could put a spin on it, Vivek handled it effortlessly. "There's no safe spot to interrogate Rangers' employees, is there, gentlemen? Please come in. We are just wrapping up."

"No safe spot on our turf," one of them responded to Vivek's joke as they made their way in.

After walking halfway through the office, Vivek abruptly pulled her into a corner and hit a button. It was the freight lift. Once inside, he pushed another button to make the lift doors close.

Vivek held her by both her arms. His face softened but the worry lines didn't completely go. Keya was unable to speculate as to what was coming her way.

"Keya, look at me."

She didn't. She focused her gaze on a notice stuck on one of the walls that cautioned about the maximum capacity of the lift.

"Keya," he said, turning her face towards him, gently. She resisted.

"Listen, I am so sorry for last night. I can completely understand your anger towards me. I didn't mean to bail out on you. But the truth is I had no option. I *had* to leave. I am sorry it all happened that way." He took in a short breath and carried on. "Also, I didn't know what to do when you broke down. I didn't mean to sound like a jerk but I guess I did."

He held her eyes for a long time and finally asked, "Can you forgive me? I like what is there between us; let's give this a chance. Please?"

For her part, Keya just stared at him in utter disbelief. This man befuddled her, making her wonder if he was the same person who had been such a jerk the first few times they had met . . . the same person who had left her hanging all by herself in her balcony the previous night.

She focussed on the present and realised his words had made her feel better. Last night, before the flare up, wasn't a mistake. *Thank God!* She needed to know that she hadn't gone ahead and jumped into the sack with the first man she had been attracted to since Raj. It wasn't about getting physical but about having the right feelings pushing her towards it. It was a balm on her conscience that Vivek had felt something, too. He still had a heart that functioned without a defibrillator. In no mood to confront, she blinked softly. He would have to do all the talking today.

"I have to admit that I was taken aback when you confronted me about all the past incidents. No one has ever told me that I am being a jerk, not to my face at least, and not since high school. And I never realised I was being insensitive or hurtful. I didn't mean to come across like that."

Hearing this Keya wondered if he was giving her excuses for his inexplicable behaviour. As he confessed more, she discerned that he was owning up to it. All of it.

She stood there, calm and composed, but with wet eyes, absorbing his confessions. She had never heard him disclose so much about his faults or his feelings. Or about his feelings for her. He embellished that with "and last night, before the drama, was beautiful."

She smiled, the first she had managed since morning.

"Say something, Keya."

"It's my turn to listen."

"Haven't I said enough?" He held her face in both his hands.

"Maybe . . . but I'm just being greedy."

It made him chuckle. He seemed to have realised it as well. The worst had passed. He lifted a strand of hair covering her face and tucked it behind her ear. "It just hit me how special you are to me."

"I want to believe you."

A beat passed between them.

"What made you leave so hurriedly last night? You never told me."

Vivek's features hardened on hearing that. The worry lines were back on his face . . . more deeply etched, if that were even possible. "Just a little emergency at work. Nothing serious," was all he let out.

Keya knew right then that he was lying. But what all was he lying about?

Looking outside the window of the conference room, with both hands in his pockets, Vivek sported a very agitated expression. The ultimatum Harsh had given him was rather disconcerting. He had moved heaven and earth to get to the bottom of things, without letting anyone in his office know what was actually happening. But this clandestine behaviour had set his teeth on edge. He couldn't rely on any member of his team, not because he didn't trust them but because he couldn't chance a slip-up from their side and have this deal fall through. He had finally managed to get a meeting with Sashikant Dubey, the Rangers' General Manager after pushing him hard to shift around his existing meeting and pencil him in.

Hours later, Vivek was outside a corner office with a golden nameplate that read Dubey's name. He gently knocked on the door which was left ajar.

"*Aa jao bhai. Andar aa jao*," Dubey invited him graciously. "*Hum mil chuke hain na pehle bhi?*"

"Yes, right after the deal was announced," Vivek said, shaking hands and taking the seat right across from him. Harsh had given him an accurate portrayal of Dubey. A short, pudgy man. Hideously dressed. Talked with his mouth full. A *paan* nuzzled in his right cheek was hard to miss. Life-sized posters of several popular Rangers players graced the wall behind Dubey, as did the team posters.

"Harshji must have told you about Janak Goel." People seldom referred to Jango by his real name. Janak Goel didn't go with his personality one bit.

"He did. I'm here to get to the root of the problem," Vivek responded in Hindi, sensing Dubey's inclination for the language.

"*Haanji poochhiye poochhiye. Chai piyenge?*"

Before he could politely refuse, Dubey was already on the phone. "*Bete do cutting chai bhijwa de. Shakkar alag se.*"

Vivek opened his tablet in case he needed to make notes, which he rarely did. Typically, he would make mental notes during meetings and upon returning to his team, share the details and leave documentation to them.

Over the next half an hour, Vivek was bombarded with a generous share of information from Dubey. Jango was keen on winning a championship. The Delhi team hadn't made it to the finals in all these years and were looking for good talent to win that championship that had been eluding them. They'd offered him a slightly better deal, too.

"Isn't it a bit early to be luring players for next year . . . not to mention illegal?"

"What's early and what's late in unofficial business? *Yeh lijiye chai aa gayi.*"

Overlooking Dubey's slavish attitude, Vivek began to verify Jango's deal details. Jango was on a ten point one crore contract with the Rangers. When Vivek brought up the question of any under-the-table amount given to him in addition to the salary, Dubey resorted to shrugging, and then added, "*Chhodo unn baaton ko.*"

"We're all a team now, Dubeyji."

"*Ab kya bataoon mein.* You'll make me lose my job."

"No worries, we'll leave that for later. But, tell me this, did you expect it at some level?"

He told him that it had always been a hanging sword and that he'd be lying if he said he hadn't seen it coming when the Rangers hadn't made it to the playoffs last year.

"I still don't get it. Why Delhi? They have an equally bad track record, if not worse. They won—what was it?—four games last season. Not to mention a constant exodus of their top players."

"*Tabhi toh acchhi team ka jugaad ho raha hain auctions se pehle hi.*"

Vivek clenched his fists and began to tap his feet, raising his eyebrows. He remembered the day Harsh had asked him the same question when he had pitched the proposal of acquiring Rangers to him. 'Rangers have a single star player, Jango, to carry their entire weight forward. What if he leaves?' he recalled Harsh asking him categorically. He also recalled telling Harsh that there was only a slight chance Jango would ever leave. There was too much at stake. Everyone knew he was destined for greatness. Money wasn't all that he was after, he was emotionally invested in the Rangers. He had been with the team for four years after all. Vivek had studied his interviews intently. Jango had always maintained that he would retire with the Rangers; good or bad times could never shake his loyalty to the team.

So, what had changed now? Maybe four years of not

making it past the quarter-finals were beginning to deter him. Vivek recalled the entire conversation with Harsh distinctly. He felt like a fool for not taking this angle seriously. What business did he have to take Jango at face value? A piercing fire truck siren on the street brought him back to reality. He had let his thoughts drift away arbitrarily. Bygones, he told himself. He had made a bad judgment call but Harsh was right. There was always a way out.

"What about his endorsement deals?"

"He has contracts with Reebok, Coke, Gillette, Sony, McDonald's, Palmolive, and Tata Motors. Every brand will be evaluated, as is the routine. Some will stay, some will not, and some will get transferred; it all depends. But one thing is certain; Janak is not one to get bothered by all this," Dubey said, flicking his wrist in the air. "Do you know that he made it to Forbes' world's hundred richest sportspersons list last year? Was at the forty-fifth number. He earned over a hundred and seventy crores from endorsements only."

"I read that. What about his private life? Any personal motivation to go to Delhi?"

"I believe personal motivation is the biggest reason. *Unki wife jo hai*, she is the niece of the new CEO of AMR Group—the company that owns the Delhi team."

"Oh, really? That might be a compelling reason. Isn't he worried about his public image? Quitting when the team needs him is weak," Vivek asked, baffled.

Dubey laughed. "At the age of sixteen, he was arrested in Germany for smoking ganja in a public place. Last year, an MMS got leaked about his extramarital affair with a model in London. You think he cares about public image?"

Vivek loosened his tie and began tapping his feet rapidly.

All of this was discouraging. Half an hour into the meeting and he'd not hit a single ray of hope.

"Have there been talks about extending his contract?"

"Of course. We can't afford to lose him."

"What are the proposed contract terms, Dubeyji?"

"Eleven point one crore next year. A crore more over his existing contract. But that was prior to the acquisition."

"That's all the information I needed. Appreciate your time. If there's any new development, please keep me in the loop."

Vivek left Dubey's office and headed straight to a coffee shop across from the arena. He gulped down a double espresso shot at one go, the top layer of the rich golden cream promising stress alleviation from where he saw it.

The bitterness of the drink lingered in his mouth long after. He felt like the drink itself: pressure-brewed with a bitter after-taste. His mind was all over the place thinking of options regarding Jango. It was a unique situation, his first, where he did not possess the requisite skills to solve the problem. Not one to give up, he began to think out-of-the-box.

His cell beeped. *Keya.* He let the call go unanswered.

***

Vivek was just in time for his seven a.m. breakfast meeting with Harsh at their hotel. As he walked past the steel walls and décor, the pink and purple night-lights caught his attention. The design of this newly-opened restaurant could have been the big talking point over breakfast today, if he had no agenda. But he did. And it was one *helluva* agenda. He had been doing a mental dry run of what he wanted to convey to Harsh all through the shaving and showering process, back in his room.

An elaborate spread of breakfast options—a large variety

of cereal, fruits carved in interesting shapes, idli, breads, and assorted condiments—greeted him as he entered the dining area; but food was the last thing on his mind. Having known Harsh for this long, he was far too familiar with how he operated. He hadn't a doubt that Harsh would want to dive in straight to the meat of the matter. Vivek would need to play hardball and paint the big picture first.

He picked up an egg sandwich, at the insistence of the headwaiter, and headed over to the table where Harsh was seated. He looked as fresh as the breakfast spread. Vivek's attention was drawn to all the four plates he had been working on, plates that now looked ready to be skated upon. They exchanged pleasantries and indulged in small talk about everything from the downward slide of the Sensex to the Eurozone crisis. Harsh seemed in no hurry to get to Jango's story.

"I've thought of some options." Vivek finally got to the point.

"Does it meet my bottom line?"

"Hear me out." He shared what he'd learnt from Dubey and other sources, relaying the potential reasons behind Jango's willingness to move and what he was being offered. Then subtly, he pitched his plan to Harsh. "This is the moment for the Rangers to figure out how they want to hitch their wagon to Jango—"

"Well, breaking news, my friend. We are the Rangers now. Unless I want to let this deal turn sour, what are our options?"

"Jango is clearly the best player in town. He is twenty-eight, still has at least four-five years of peak performance left in him. We should talk about re-signing him and lure him in with the best possible deal."

"Look, buddy. Unlike some of us in this breakfast area, I don't have any rich uncles who have left me a palace in inheritance, just in case you're thinking I'll pay for that new contract."

"If that was for me, I have no rich uncles who've left me a palace either, Harsh." Vivek enunciated each word calmly. Just a little too calmly. And then laughed to inject some levity into their conversation. "Hear me out. Let's address the immediate cause for uncertainty first. Make a new offer to Jango; take it a notch higher. Re-sign him verbally and give him the maximum allowable for the next year. Second order of business is to give him the confidence that the new management will have his back. That they will be willing to put in the investment needed to build a better team around him. We'll need to assure him that he won't have to carry the team's weight for the next four years like he's been doing for the past four."

"Even if we ignore the money aspect for a second, why would he *re-sign*?" Harsh questioned with a serious face.

"It's clear what he's after." Vivek was confident of his proposed solution.

"I'm not so sure it's that clear. He wouldn't be leaving otherwise."

"Here's the thing. Th—" Vivek noticed Harsh getting distracted by the waitress picking up his dishes. "Thank you, sweetheart," he said, all the while ogling at her rack. "Coffee?" she enquired, to which he smiled, all his teeth on display, and said, "Sure, if you feel like it." Then he winked at her and let out a monstrous laugh. For a moment, Vivek contemplated pouring the burning hot coffee she had just placed on their table over his eyes.

"*Harsh*, here's the thing."

"Yes, yes, I'm listening."

"The Rangers' performance is at an all time low. Jango averages forty-two runs per game. No one's more reliable and consistent than he is. And yet, look at the team's graph over the past few years. He'd be God if he didn't get frustrated."

"Wait, hold on. What was this 'build a better team around him' bit?"

Before Vivek could attempt revealing his plan, Harsh's phone ring interrupted. "What's the news?" he asked someone on the phone, anticipation sketched on his face. "Sweet. I like the sound of that. Make it another twenty grand on my behalf. All right, buddy. Speak soon." Then he turned to Vivek. "That's my pal from Macau. He's been handicapping thoroughbreds for both of us since last week. Making me good money. Have you tried horse racing yet?"

Getting Harsh focused was tantamount to getting a toddler focused. Or maybe worse. Vivek pretended to not be annoyed. "No, I haven't, Harsh. One day, when I have enough time and money."

"Sounds good. Let me know if you need tips on figuring out which horse is worth a wager."

"Sure. Appreciate that." Vivek had never been more riled with Harsh. "Coming back to our discussion, one idea is to get two good players next season."

"And who exactly are these miracle workers, these two players?"

"I don't know, Harsh. We'll have to scout."

"Nah. I'm not convinced. And don't you listen? Two new players means more money. I haven't factored in paying for two better guys."

Vivek smiled into his cup of coffee. *He had him.* With

Harsh pushing back, this was playing out exactly as he had suspected. Knowing the right buttons to push and having learnt to manipulate at an early age, Vivek felt in control of the situation. He savoured the feeling for a moment, before proceeding with the rest of his plan

He knew Harsh was convinced that even at ten percent above the market price, they'd got a great deal on acquiring the team. It was the cheapest way to own an IGL team. They'd gotten in at sixty percent of thirteen hundred crores, with Harsh's private equity partners paying for the rest forty. He knew the Rangers had tremendous potential. All that was needed was to tighten up a few loose ends.

"If we lose Jango, we lose the benefit of owning a team with potential. The second Jango leaves, this team will be worth nothing," Vivek began.

"Buying the cheapest IGL team and then paying more for two expensive players. That's just bad business sense." Harsh's hands emulated a balance scale.

"Our revenue projections have factored in no elimination rounds for at least two years given the feeble state of the team. I believe if we get two more star players, there's a good chance the collective performance will lead the team to playoffs. Playoffs could mean significantly higher revenues than what we've projected for the next season," Vivek said, finally laying all his cards on the table.

"That's a huge gamble."

"Life's a gamble, Harsh. It's the odds you play that count. The way I am looking at it, the odds are pretty good. You've always taken calculated risks and they've paid off."

"Let me think about it. Put all major activities on hold until then."

After that spiel to Harsh, Vivek knew he had to get down to ensuring that the numbers tallied. He had brazened it out in the discussion, creating one castle after another in the air, all in the hopes of just selling the idea to him. Not that all of it was hogwash, but a large percent of it was. And it was his responsibility to add credence to all the tripe he had spurted out. Harsh was about to demand detailed analysis. He needed to be one step ahead.

Vivek sat at his desk revising revenue projections if the Rangers were to make it to the playoffs in the next two seasons. It would make for a fair comparison chart.

His phone beeped. It was Keya calling from her extension.

"What's stud boy up to?"

"Hey," he whispered, given that his team was surrounding him like aggressive bees hovering around a beehive. He noticed Omar looking up, something he did each time Vivek was on a personal call. It was as if he had a sixth sense about entirely insignificant matters. He considered walking out in the hopes of getting some privacy but the clock was ticking. He wished the conversation wouldn't last that long; he had a lot to pack in a short frame of time.

"I miss you."

"Umm, yeah." Omar was now audaciously staring at him and smirking. It got Satyen's attention, too.

"Why are you whispering? Ahh . . . let me guess. The boys are around."

"Yes."

"Aww, you poor little coy thing," Her tone took on a naughty edge. She was clearly enjoying his fix. *Sadist.*

"Let me call you later." Before he could disconnect, Omar

got up from his chair, which was adjacent to Vivek's and leaned in to get better access to his cell phone. Then, in an entirely unprecedented move, he screamed into the phone, "Your boyfriend is touching other men inappropriately. Help!"

Vivek, astounded, stared at Omar for the tacky act he'd just pulled off. The others were laughing hysterically. *Bloody madmen!*

"Let me call you back." He hung up the phone, then looked at Omar with the sternest expression anyone in the room had ever seen on him, fury unfolding on his face. Omar, having retreated to his chair, was now pretending to be busy with some printouts like nothing had happened. His lips were tightened, holding back laughter. "WHAT. WAS. *THAT*?" Vivek questioned in the meanest tone anyone had ever heard him use.

There was no response from Omar. He continued to be in a make-believe bubble which by no means was a safe haven.

"Omar, we're a respectable consulting firm, not a *freaking fraternity*."

Omar looked up at him, slowly, appearing not the least bit affected by his admonishment. "I was just—"

"You were what? And who do you think it was?"

"Umm . . . your girlfriend?"

"My *girlfriend*? Do you even know if—do you—God! Satyen, you deal with this joker. Knock some sense into his head if you can. I'm done here." With that, he stormed out of the room.

It was Omar being Omar but Vivek had had it with his immaturity. When he'd hired him, he'd thought of him as his golden boy. Which is why he excused him for things no one else would be able to pull off with Vivek. Clearly, Omar knew it too on some level and took unfair advantage of it. Annoyed, Vivek walked into the corridor towards the building exit to get some fresh air. *The nerve of him to—*

Just then his cell phone rang, again, cutting the diatribe in his head effectively. It was Harsh.

"Let's do this. Use the Jango-quitting risk as an angle. Lower our initial offer from thirteen hundred to twelve fifty and we've got ourselves a deal."

"Harsh, that's not a good idea at all. We were—"

"I am not one bit convinced this was a good deal as it is, Vivek. Jango might leave. Auctions may be made mandatory for all players next year. For all I know, there might be some sort of a shitty sting operation video about to be released about the Rangers losing on purpose or something," Harsh casually remarked.

*Sting operation video? How do people pull things out of their asses and use it as an argument?* "Look, Harsh, there's just no way Rangers will agree to that kind of a price drop. It's completely absurd—"

"Find something. What are you for? Find a huge flaw in the team. Or make up a media story and use it against them. That'll get them to accept it. Look, the bottom line is that I no longer feel comfortable paying that kind of money for this team. I'll have to swap my Bentley with a Ford if I make wrong decisions."

The verbal thwack in Vivek's mind that had stopped with Harsh's call got renewed with new-found ardour. This time it was directed at Harsh. "Let me think about how we might present this," he replied after a moment.

"That's not good enough, Vivek. Make it happen. You know you need this deal more than I do. I could walk away anytime I like."

That last statement hit Vivek hard. This was his third

time he was working with Harsh. Never before had this man come across as so arrogant, so bastardly. Why was he being so overly aggressive in this case? He had been tough on previous negotiations but this was almost as if he was viewing Vivek to be the enemy now. He would need to get to the bottom of this later on.

"Yeah. I'll keep you posted."

"It's Tuesday. I want something concrete by Thursday."

Vivek almost smashed his phone on the pavement.

Vivek was on the first flight to Mumbai the next morning to meet with the 'deal team': the suits, aka lawyers and the bean counters, aka financers, among various others. If an alternate deal was to be worked on and the outcome presented to Harsh in forty-eight hours, long distance wasn't going to cut it.

Landing at Santacruz domestic airport at 7:30 in the morning, Vivek picked up a couple of newspapers and a cup of excessively sweet syrup they sold in the name of coffee, as takeaway. He was already late for his meeting and had a flight to catch in the next few hours back to Ahmedabad. He had flown in and out of Santacruz airport so many times, at all possible hours of the day, to the extent that some of the airport cleaning crew had started looking familiar.

Just as he reached his office, Alisha, his secretary, relieved him of the stuff he was carrying. She walked with him towards the conference room, trying to keep up with his pace.

"Everyone is here—the corporate counsel for the Rangers, the CPAs, and a support cast of lawyers. Harsh's private equity partners are here as well. We have Neal from our internal team to support you. Oh and all the files on Rangers are already in the conference room on your side of the table. I'll order lunch from your favourite restaurant, Piccadilly. And will bring your mocha right away. Do you need breakfast?"

"No. And you're the best." He winked at her, trying to lighten himself up in the process. This was going to be a big meeting and he wanted himself to be in control and in good spirits. Any sign of hesitancy and the sharks in the room would smell blood and it would all be over before he knew it.

Everyone who was scheduled to meet was already seated in the conference room with files, calculators, power points, and an array of popular conference room gadgets surrounding them. He glanced around from left to right. The lawyers looked ready to bombard the attendees with legal ramifications in coma-inducing terms. The corporate council had perpetual seriousness on their faces. Then he glanced at Harsh's private equity partners. They looked like they were at a court, attending a murder trial. Vivek's boy, Neal, was the only stress-free guy in the room looking like he was at a movie; relaxed with slight anticipation on his face.

"Good morning. It's never over until it's over, isn't it?" Vivek said, occupying the centre chair.

"It's what we live for," the senior lawyer joked. Everyone in the room chuckled.

"Thank you everyone for making this happen at such a short notice."

"Hey, as long as there are no early morning flights involved, we're in," a young banker said in jest.

"I'm happy to pull my weight. Those flights are strictly my prerogative," Vivek gibed. "So, anyway, here's the scoop. There have been some developments in the Rangers at the team level which are—I'm not going to lie—concerning."

"And to offset the risk from that Harsh wants to revise the offer?" The first private equity fellow completed Vivek's thought for him.

"How much lower are we talking about?" The second private equity chap interrupted.

Vivek inwardly smiled. It never failed to surprise him how tuned the deal guys were. Anytime a last-minute meeting was called in an ongoing deal, everyone knew something was not right and a new price needed to be agreed upon. He had not hinted at the offer at all and yet everyone had sensed the meat of the matter.

"You guys are good detectives," he joked. "Significantly lower. Twelve fifty." Vivek intently watched the reaction of the Rangers' corporate counsel and Head of Corporate Development. They didn't look like they were expecting a major change.

"This is better than a windfall at a casino, *if* there are no caveats. What are the caveats?" one of the banker's questioned.

"Increase Jango's salary and factor in two new high-rated players next year."

Silence befell the boardroom as if someone had just jumped out the ninth floor window. A few people looked at each other in what could only be described as unadulterated shock.

"We certainly weren't expecting that," the senior banker began, pushing up his glasses with his index finger. "The terms were very lucid on the onset. It was a one-time, concrete initial offer. There was certainly no room for potential future investments. This is rather perplexing."

"I understand. But the very basis for chasing this deal is in question now. Needless to say we've considered all available options. This seemed to make the most sense," Vivek tried to convince them.

"Let's see all the cards on the table."

"Very well." He walked the team through Harsh's new proposal—the logic behind it, the modified projected revenues, the assumptions, and every minute detail involving it; not once fumbling, not once under confident, not once failing. One banker pushed back into his chair, his arms crossing as he listened to him. The other banker sported a frown as he heard him talk so intently.

"You can't be serious about having a revised offer done in the next few hours," the senior banker lashed out after Vivek had completed his pitch.

"I wish I had a different answer."

"There are multiple issues with what you have suggested, Vivek. First off, we're not prepared, psychologically or otherwise, to commit to any additional investment, whatsoever. Secondly, Harsh should have been here personally to discuss all this. And thirdly, even if a new deal has to be agreed upon, and I stress on if, then within the stipulated time it's just too ambitious."

It felt as if it was just Vivek and the bankers in the room. The others had ceased to exist. Vivek had to make this happen, he had to keep pushing. He didn't have much time or much choice. "I have some rather promising revenue projections here," he continued, undiscouraged.

"Vivek, lets save your time and ours. We've got some semblance of where your head is. But this is where the rubber meets the road. I'm afraid our stance remains unchanged."

"I understand where you're coming from." A face-off with the bankers never led to any good. He'd learnt that the hard way. "But here's why it's important to all parties involved. We're going fifty crores lower than the first offer. That in itself is worth chasing."

"I appreciate your breaking it down. Fact of the matter is, on a pervasive level, this didn't look like a lucrative deal to us." He let that sink in. "Why don't we do this? Let's reconvene another time when Harsh is in town."

"Gentlemen, let's not take any hasty measures."

"This deal that you want reworked and signed in the next two hours isn't hasty?"

With that, both bankers walked out of the conference room. The others, who had acted like audiences at a tennis match, looking at Vivek and the bankers alternately as they spoke, appeared astonished.

With no time to waste, Vivek followed the bankers out. Resolution marked clear on his face.

***

"I survived the bull fight," Vivek told Harsh over the phone, referring to the nasty meeting with the bankers. Despite his best endeavours he had missed his flight back to Ahmedabad and was now waiting for the airlines staff to announce the names of those lucky stand-by passengers who'd be put on the last flight of the night. The only saving grace was that he had the coveted third spot on the list, his elite status with the airline coming to his rescue yet again.

"Did you grab and hold the bull by the horns?" Harsh hurriedly enquired.

"I had to do some dangerous manoeuvring at the risk of

being gored or, worse, trampled."

"Don't they slaughter the bull at the end of the fight?"

"Ha! Not in this case. The bull is our cash cow," Vivek said, alluding to Harsh's bankers.

"Ahh, yes. That minor detail. Tell me what happened."

"Nothing good. The bankers walked out on me. I chased them out and—" His racy narration was interrupted as he saw his name move from the stand-by list to the approved list on the screen. He rushed to the counter to get a boarding pass and then to the woman scanning those passes at the gate, and flashed it at her. She gently took possession of it, scanned it, and wished him a good night.

"All that noise! Are you at Essel World?" Harsh scoffed.

"Give me just one second to find my seat amidst these Essel World characters." He followed the long queue of people waiting to shove their luggage in overhead compartments, some doing it slower than a herd of snails travelling through butter. His cell beeped. Keya was calling him. *Not now.*

His heart sank as he made his way through the Business Class seats all the way back to the Economy Class, the other side of the world. Luck was clearly not on his side tonight, he realised. What else would explain missing a flight with a perfectly-contoured Business Class seat screaming out his name and instead being put on stand-by for an Economy seat where his long legs never fit?

"By all means, take your time. I have nothing going for me this evening," Vivek heard Harsh take a cigar puff over the phone, his voice dripping with sarcasm.

"I'm sorry, Harsh. So, yes, the financers were outraged. They weren't willing to budge at all. Literally walked out on me," he began, giving the account of the exhausting episode as he ducked to get to his extremely tight window seat.

"I'm listening."

"Their financial commitment for this deal remains unchanged. If we can get the Rangers to agree to the new offer, the bankers have left it to our discretion to use the balance amount towards acquisition of new players or increased salaries."

"That's not good enough. Who's paying for the rest?"

Just then, a woman with an infant occupied the seat adjacent to Vivek's. A man carrying an enormous diaper bag, a pink blanket on his shoulder, pink baby boots in one hand, and a milk bottle in another, sat next to her. The squealing baby along with the chatty parents invaded Vivek's space like flood water gushing in. He tried to focus.

"Well . . . uhh . . . their financial year is about to end and they're unable to commit any more funds. I sat them down and showed them the upside to increasing Jango's pay and getting two good players. They are somewhat interested. In fact, they are open and quite willing to—"

Before he could complete that sentence, his phone was no longer in his grasp. The baby in the next seat was now standing on her mother's lap, her tiny hands just long enough to reach the phone Vivek had been holding a second ago. In one quick motion, she had grabbed the attractive piece of technology from his hand and begun cooing into it. The mother seemed completely oblivious to this appalling situation, screaming at the husband, who just didn't have enough hands to carry all the belongings he was burdened with, as he fumbled through the diaper bag.

Vivek, aghast, not knowing baby-conversation etiquette, tried to do a one-up on the little girl by trying to snatch his phone back but the baby didn't oblige. He could hear a loud 'hello' from the other end on the phone line. Harsh was probably yelling into the phone. The baby had turned her back on him, amusing herself by pressing a variety of buttons in quick succession. Vivek rose from his seat, bending over her to reach out for his phone, trying to set the record straight with the baby about who the rightful owner was. No luck. Both parents still seemed astoundingly oblivious to the entire event so he finally launched a complaint with them.

"I'm sorry to bother you but I'm just trying to get my phone back."

"Oh, I'm so very sorry." It took a moment for the mother to realise what had just transpired. "Extremely sorry." Embarrassed, she tried to gently seize the phone back from her kid. The baby was now holding it firmly with both hands, refusing to let go. In an unprecedented scene, Vivek watched two adults wrestle with an infant to get her to give up the phone but she didn't give in. Had that not been his phone and had that not been his life on the line, he would have thoroughly enjoyed the situation. But, well . . .

The mother now forcefully held both hands of her child while the father gently peeled away the little fingers that engulfed the phone. When Vivek finally got his phone back, he realised the baby had not only managed to disconnect the call with Harsh but also launch half a dozen apps as well. *Great!* Just when he returned to the home screen and began dialling away, ignoring the loud screams, the baby sputtered in a precise trajectory, spraying a stream of saliva droplets on his face and jacket.

He felt an uncontrollable urge to punch someone, the father of the child being his obvious choice, but restrained himself. They apologised to him again, several times so, offering him scented tissues that he wiped himself and his phone with. A quick sniff later, there was little uncertainty that he now smelled like cucumber. Ignoring all the downsides, he dialled and got through to Harsh.

"What was *that*?"

"Nothing really. Let me quickly wrap up before they make me switch off my cell."

Before he could articulate the rest half of his story, he was whiplashed by a piercing announcement by an air hostess in a raspy voice.

"Please turn all your electronic fruits off," she announced, eliciting laughs from fellow passengers. Another one positioned herself in Vivek's aisle, her body language that of a boot camp instructor, signalling him to cut off all communications with the outer world immediately, if not sooner.

"Your boys just didn't budge. Their financial year ends—"

"Sir, please. Your phone needs to be turned off."

"Just one more second," he implored. "They aren't open to any additional funding in the current financial year. They didn't warm up to the news of Jango quitting, so unless something—"

*His cell beeped. Call waiting. Keya again. Dammit!*

"Sir, please. We're ready for take-off. You need to turn it off," the air hostess said sternly, staying put and politely giving him dirty looks. The little girl next to him saw inexplicable humour in the situation and began to giggle, reaching out for his phone again. Great, he was being harassed by two women now. And then there was this third one he was sure he had managed to miff.

"Got to go, Harsh. Unless Jango stays, they aren't open. For this year at least. But I have an idea. Let's talk over breakfast tomorrow. Bye now." He pressed the off button with all his might, trying to drive the point home to the vexing air hostess who would just not move.

"Please power it down." She gave him attitude one last time before walking off.

"You realise we could have met someplace else? Where there were not hundreds of people screaming in our ears. Right?" Keya asked, snuggling next to Vivek, her head tilted to rest on his left arm. They were at the Fourth Test match of the England tour of India, being played in Ahmedabad.

"Brilliant," Vivek gleefully cheered. She looked up to check the scene. The English team had just dropped a simple catch making the crowd cheer wildly. She yawned and went back to resting her head on his arm. It was, in a way, their first date post the events of that night. She just wished it was more intimate than this. Why he had picked a game for their first date and why she had allowed that to happen was beyond her.

"Vivek," she screamed, for there was no other way to be audible. "I just said something."

"What, sweetie?" he mechanically questioned without looking at her.

"I just said something."

"Oh. Yeah. That's because this is the best way to mix business with pleasure. I had a meeting with

Harsh and a few others. They chose to continue the discussions alongside the match. My work was done and I didn't see a reason in suffering through a match with them. And you are fast becoming my favourite partner these days," he rambled on, his gaze still fixated on the game.

"Where have you been so occupied all this while? I mean, I didn't catch even a glimpse of you."

"Missed me, did you?" he enquired with a heart-melting grin.

"Ha! Don't delude yourself. I was just saying," she responded, biting back her smile.

Before she could probe him further about his absence and the busy state of affairs he seemed to be swamped by, the game broke for drinks giving way to the crowd-pleasing activities inside the stadium. The camera moved swiftly from the front row all the way to the nosebleed section in the end, capturing the crowd; the clips of animated people being projected on the centre screens. After that came the distorted images of the faces of the audience via the distortion lens, breaking the crowd into laughter. Keya had been far too familiar with the routine, having been to the game several times.

"I can smell a cheesy proposal next," she sneered.

"What?"

"Watch."

Just then, flashing on all four screens across the stadium were the words: Shalini, will you marry me? The camera then zoomed to a young man's face in the audience who was apparently proposing. The girl seated next to him looked visibly shocked, both hands covering her mouth, the typical beauty-queen-winning-the-crown expression. The camera switched back and forth between their faces as the crowd rooted for them, chanting 'say yes, say yes'. Then the girl got all emotional as she nodded her head in agreement, tears strolling down her plump cheeks. The man squeezed in to sit down on one knee and slipped a sparkling ring on her finger. That shot was covered with a pink heart on the television screens across the entire stadium and everyone applauded as if they had just witnessed the royal kiss.

"That was cute. But when did we get all American?"

"No clue. And, please, that was annoying," Keya scoffed. "Hold on. Did you just say cute? You *never* say words like cute. What is wrong with you?"

He laughed. "What is wrong with *you*? What are you so provoked about?"

"Because that, my friend, was a load of bull. Why would anyone want to make a public spectacle of something that was supposed to be so pure, beautiful, and personal? It's just a dirty little trick played by guys to coax girls into agreeing to their unreasonable demands. What poor girl will be able to say no in front of so many people? That was just lame," she vented out in one breath.

He signalled her to lean in. When she moved her head closer, he whispered into her ear, "What if I said all that in front of all these people right now? Would that be lame?"

"Huh?" Utterly speechless and bemused, she squirmed and gave him a quizzical look. *God, he was joking, right? She couldn't be imagining this.*

"Tell me."

"Huh?"

His propensity to perpetually catch her off-guard was not something she appreciated. Before she could articulate her questions, he pulled her close to him and squeezed her, then looking into her eyes, his breath on her, he said softly, "Tell me you don't believe it's lame. Because I could give this idea a thought, you know."

Was he playing her with words? It was so evident. Or was it? She felt her skin tingle. Her heart began to flutter. Ecstasy mixed with incredulity could be oddly discomforting. Add to that a strong dose of déjà vu and she didn't know what to say. "Really?" was all she managed to ask, her eyes wide.

He stared at her for a moment, then said, "Oops, sorry, just kidding." Then he got up, shrugged, and began to take off.

From the corner of her eye, Keya continued to look at him with a stricken expression. Was this supposed to be funny? Had he not learnt anything from her confession about Raj?

Vivek turned back to say something to her and she believed that that was when he saw her reaction. Maybe understanding dawned, for his next words were, "Keya, I am sorry. I didn't mean it that way."

"Yeah, I am sure. I'd like to leave now."

***

"You're asking me to go to Brazil with you in Feb? It's too soon. I can't go," Keya said, declining Radhika's offer, after contemplating on it in between the rapid mouthfuls of soup she took.

The girls were back at Maharani, indulging in their Friday night ritual. The dark red on the brick walls came to life through the ornate lanterns hanging all over the place. Tiny dashes of flowers and leaves etched on the metal allowed light to sparkle through the lantern and onto the walls, forming fascinating shadows.

Radhika had turned herself into a flesh and blood

equivalent of the new breed of food websites that offered ratings on food, décor, service, cost, and surveys for restaurants. Her free-spiritedness often manifested in the worldly cuisines she chose to indulge herself in on a weekly basis; reading up about the country and culture beforehand and dressing up with accessories that blended with the cultural elements. Not that there were many restaurants serving world cuisines in the city; all it took was a new dish on an existing menu for her to go try it out.

Today she wore a bright kaftan with smoky eyes and a heap of gold jewellery, the direct outcome of that being her becoming the recipient of several admiring glances from the servers and the restaurant patrons.

"You are quite a dish tonight," Keya said, impressed, as usual, by the level of effort her friend had put in to her appearance.

"I'm just a tease."

"Not the ultimate fantasy?"

"Actually, I'm the lure."

"Until they discover what you're all about?"

"Precisely."

Both girls laughed at the inanity of their conversation. Keya's mind drifted to Radhika's proposal from a few minutes ago. A three-week trip to Brazil and Argentina in the beginning of the year was what Radhika was after. Set up base in São Paulo, road trip to Rio de Janeiro and back, fly to Iguazu Falls followed by a few days in Buenos Aires and the neighbouring cities. Absurd ideas being Radhika's trademark, she'd even proposed Kourosh in the mix. The trip idea had sounded fabulous, in theory only, to Keya until Radhika had mentioned him. It was beyond her to understand how anyone could suggest something as ludicrous as that, given her already twisted life. She had shared with Radhika all that had taken place with Vivek, down to the meeting at the match and all that he had said. If after that also Radhika wanted to complicate her love-life by factoring in a very-besotted Rosh, then God help her, for she was ready to strangle somebody. And Radhika was great to start with.

"Thinking of strangling me?" Radhika asked, so bizarrely tuned-in to her thoughts.

"Get out of my head, will you?" she replied, giggling with amazement.

"Babe, you need a break. Your work is getting to you. Don't over think. Just say yes."

She was right about that. Keya's work continued to be a concern to her. She equated it to the anxiety and trauma of waiting to be hit by floods instead of being in the midst of it. Once hit, you could look forward to survival and plan how to cope with the anguish and damage, if any. But this, what she was going through, was the anxiety of waiting for the kill to take place. And the anticipation of the kill was killing her.

She was sure something was wrong somewhere. With barely enough work force to sustain her vertical, she had enough reason to think that she wouldn't be shown the door. It wasn't exactly how she felt though. LHF's absence pinched her just as much as Harsh's presence did. She had a bad feeling about Harsh and just his proximity bothered her. That man was getting heavily involved in the day-to-day operations and she frequently had to face him in meetings.

She'd often tried to bring it up with Vivek, subtly sliding it in during conversations, to get a sense of whether things were stable. But, nothing. He seemed unaware, too. Or perhaps unconcerned. When speculations had turned futile, she'd found a way to pacify herself. *Unless there's an elephant in the room, I'd rather be in denial,* she'd convinced herself. It had worked until she had an epiphany once. There indeed was an elephant in the room. The man she was dating. Until Harsh and Vivek were around, the dust could never settle down. She had deliberately zoned out of that web of thoughts, but not forgotten it. And over the last couple of weeks, her sixth sense was telling her something was happening . . .

"Hey, look, Jhumka is out," Radhika exclaimed, pointing at the dancer who had just made an entry to a pulsating score, an exquisite clay pot placed on her head.

"You know the belly dancer by her *first name*?" Shock didn't begin to cover it for Keya.

"I've been here before. And that's not belly dancing. It's Rajasthani folk dance. How uncultured *are* you!"

"I don't even know my neighbour's name and you know the belly dancer's! Unreal."

"Yes, you do. Your neighbour is Kourosh and he is in love with you."

Jhumka rotated to the beats, revolving around a few centre tables at first, showcasing her lissom belly, and swung by the rest of the tables soon after. The way she moved, actuating every muscle in her body with elegance, she had the entire crowd in raptures, including a few men who couldn't resist yanking out crisp notes from their wallets and flashing them at her. She smiled and moved on in a fluid motion, her little helper boy running around behind her to pick up the tips.

"Family restaurant—that's what you called it, right?" Keya laughed.

"So what do you think? Are you sold on the trip yet? If

you want to finish that sad, little book of yours, you're going to have to move your butt."

"Wow, you're in assault mode today. I can't say I'm not tempted."

"But?"

"But it's too short a time to cover two countries. I'm not big on touristy stuff, you know that already. I certainly want to see the Rio beaches and Corcovado and the museums in São Paulo and indulge in Argentinean feasts that include intestines and other glands. But I also want to do the quaint spots. The stuff that locals do. I need time to research before I visit. And write while I'm there."

"This is exactly why we should take Kourosh. You do what you want and take all the time you need. We both will leave you alone. Brilliant plan, right?"

"Wait. How did Rosh get into the picture?"

Radhika for all her glibness shut up at that question. She began studying her nails and let on a facade of studied indifference. Keya was flabbergasted. "Rads!" she shrieked. "Are you telling me you like him?"

"That's bull. And you don't get any information unless you go up there and dance with Jhumka. I want to see a folk-burlesque combo."

"You are demented. And do not side-step my question."

"I am not. You are seeing what you want to see. I mean, it would be very convenient for you if that goofy character and I got together. That's all," Radhika spelled it out clearly for her. A little too clearly.

"Oh, okay. So, what about my work?"

"Screw work."

"What about Vivek?"

"I'd say screw Vivek too—oh wait, you already have—but you'd call me a cliché. Speaking of the devil, where is he?"

"In Mumbai. He keeps on shuttling between Mumbai and Ahmedabad a lot these days. I just don't know why . . ." her voice trailed off.

"Love, don't fret over it so much. It took me a while to understand this, but *Que sera sera* baby. Words to live by."

As crazy as Radhika was, she got Keya thinking. Vivek aside, that promise to self made earlier in the year of wrapping up the first draft of the travelogue by the end of the year was a constant discomfort. A trip was needed to materialise before the goal could be met and Radhika was offering her just that. It had sounded so achievable back then. It was almost the end of the year and no remarkable event had occurred. Yes, she'd found love—or something close to it—but with Vivek acting so distant and self-involved at times, she wondered if her life was on the right track. Maybe she needed to invest her energy in her heart's deepest desire and not waste it on random pursuits.

"I'm game. Let's go," she told Radhika, blinking hard a few times to dissipate the wetness.

***

Vivek could never get used to the wetness.

He watched the unseasonal rain descend bountifully from inside the chauffeur-driven car that was whisking him to his next mission. For a moment it made him feel like he was part of a spy movie, his life turning into a series of challenges, each challenge a new territory. If only consulting had the sex appeal of being a spy. Just for the sake of it, he drew a question mark with his index finger on the foggy window glass, his way of asking the universe the outcome of his current mission. Not that he was remotely superstitious. The universe apparently mulled over it for a few moments, for soon after the question mark got erased. It made him grin a bit. *Thanks for having my back, big guy*, he mentally uttered, looking up at the sky through the window.

He was on his way to meet Jango's agent at his residence in the Oshiwara area of Andheri. Presenting the new deal to the Rangers would be a huge uphill battle and a potentially counter-productive one, unless he played a few cards right first. There were too many issues. Issues he had oversimplified that morning for his team who weren't entirely in the loop. "Here's the puzzle, guys. Harsh wants Jango to stay. Jango potentially wants a better team. A better team would mean more money which Harsh's investors aren't willing to pump in. Harsh also wants to use Jango's quitting angle to lower his bid. And, in this game of unrealistic expectations, no one has thought of a way to get the Rangers on board with the revised offer. So unless you guys have any earth-shattering suggestions, I'll be inaccessible till late afternoon."

Earlier that morning, he'd stood under the waterfall-esque shower for a rather long time, thinking of options. *You've got to take some risks and not lose hope*, he'd told himself. What he was about to do might be labelled as bluffing but he had limited choices. It was a classic Catch-22 situation, with each party involved requiring a confirmation from the other before proceeding. He didn't know all the answers yet, *but* he'd figured out one question for Jango's agent.

Being apprehensive before a big meeting was a given, but this time had Vivek feeling strangely anxious. For one, he had only read about Indian sports agents in newspapers and never seen them in action, unlike their foreign counterparts who were always seen escorting their star clients, especially when the stars were in messy court trials.

Attempting to meet Jango for any sort of business proposal would have been naïve. He knew that. So, he had dug up the details on the sports management firm that represented him. A Trimurti Sports Management that had an Avinash Khanna assigned as Jango's agent. Vivek had been part of business meetings that took place from conference rooms to restaurants and from bars to airport lounges, but never at someone's residence. Certainly not at someone's he had never met before. Earlier that morning when he had called up Avinash to fix a time, the man had mentioned that his office was getting a facelift and had invited him to his home instead.

The cab pulled up in front of an establishment that could easily be labelled as a state-of-the-art masterpiece by a commoner. The house appeared enhanced by extensive use of concrete, steel, and glass; a work of art in itself. Vivek, for the first time in his life, felt apprehensive about entering someone's home.

"Can I get you some coffee or *lassi*? I'm from Punjab. *Lassis* are our big selling point." Avinash broke the ice, walking fast and talking faster, guiding Vivek to the formal living area as they passed through the entrance hallway that seemed more like an art gallery. Several pieces of abstract paintings adorned the mauve walls, with coloured lights reflecting from the ceiling bringing them alive. A solo piece of steel bench, shaped like a wave, rested in the middle. *Ostentatiously modern*, Vivek thought to himself.

He took a seat on the bright red couch in the living room that had a thick layer of steel covering each wall, the place giving him a feel of being inside the locker area of a bank.

Avinash, with his dark brown henna-coated hair, shirt open to the third button, and silver trousers appeared camouflaged with the modern space they were in.

"Appreciate your time, Avinash."

"My pleasure. How can I help?"

"On behalf of the new owners of the Rangers, I wanted to discuss an offer for Jango, one that we're all very excited about. He's clearly the most valuable asset and the new management has nothing but praise for him."

"Yes, I hear good things about . . . Harsh, is it? Haven't had a chance to meet yet."

"Yes, Harsh. We hear that Jango is in talks with another team. Harsh and the team are keen on not only offering Jango the most money but also building a championship team around him, as early as next season."

He searched Avinash's face for signs of a negative or neutral reaction to his proposal. But that man was by no means new to the industry. At thirty-eight, he still was one of the younger sports attorneys in the business who had started out with negotiating media contracts. He'd long since established himself as one of the leading sports attorneys in the country. His clients included three Indian cricketers and one Australian. He had negotiated cricket and media contracts as well as created many different kinds of sports marketing relationships. Jango was one of his biggest clients.

"I'm sure Jango will be pleased to hear that," Avinash responded, stroking his chin with his right hand, not making eye contact. His disinterest in the proposal was obvious, the perfunctory words notwithstanding.

"We've all been privy to the rather disappointing state of affairs in the past few years with the Rangers, despite Jango's exceptional efforts. We realise why he must have felt compelled to take this route. But the new owners are about to turn things around. They're willing to bring new coaching talent if required, bring a couple more established players, and change the structure of the team."

"That's great to know. It might be a little late though."

Vivek took a sip of the chilled *lassi* to counter the acid reflux in his system. This meeting was giving him all sorts of unsettling sensations. "I appreciate your honesty, Avinash. But from where I see it, things haven't gotten to the point of no return. I'm sure you—"

"I'll speak to Jango and see where his head is at," he interrupted, crossing his legs, leaning further back in his chair. Impatience in his tone was unmistakable.

"Hear me out on the offer," Vivek persuaded.

Nothing. He didn't even fake interest anymore. Vivek took a deep breath. He had got to break the limbo and Avinash's dodge-mode. Stalemates frustrated him to no end, especially during a career-challenging time like this.

Where until now his voice had bordered on the expectant, Vivek now dispensed with it. This was man to man. And he'd be damned if he didn't make this man see his side. And agree to it too! "Look Avinash, here is the deal. The first part of the deal is that Harsh is offering him eleven point one with a ten percent increase each year for the next three years. The second part is to get Prasad and Akshay into the team next year. Talks are under way and we've persuaded them and got their verbal 'in'. I hope this strictly remains between you and me. It's obviously confidential information."

"Really?" Avinash's face had turned serious but he was still silent, perhaps analysing the offer in his head.

Vivek's butt prickled with the bluffs he was so effortlessly producing. He knew deep down inside that if Jango stayed, getting two solid players, if not Prasad and Akshay, wouldn't be a big deal during the auctions. He presumed it wouldn't take much to turn his bluffs into a reality. Harsh's propensity to shell out cash to get the best had been legendary.

"Harsh is willing to make that investment, time and money wise. He and his investors are very passionate about this team—its glorious past and the promising future it holds," Vivek added, leaning in a little closer to Avinash.

He had one shot with this person and he was not going to leave until he promised consideration. From behind Avinash, a blown-up photo of David Beckham in front of the goalpost—head stretched out to kick the ball mid-air, an intense expression on his face, both feet up in the air with a tilted body—stared at him. Vivek, with an erect back and a serious face, narrowed his eyes slightly to get one good look at it. It gave him strength, inspiration. He shifted his attention back to Avinash. He had to nail this one. He wasn't about to tell this guy all the facts. Like how badly the Rangers needed Jango. That there was no Rangers without Jango. That Harsh was willing to do whatever it took. Nothing that would indicate desperation. No.

"Avinash, talk to me, man. What am I missing here?"

"You want to know the truth?" the agent questioned after a few seconds of silence.

"Yes. Absolutely."

"The truth is, Jango is done with this team. He's given them four long years. That's a lifetime in this business. It just doesn't do it for him anymore. It's not where his heart is. I'm afraid I can't convince him to stay."

There it was. The entire truth. For a moment, Vivek wanted

to nod in agreement, exchange business cards and take off. It sounded like the only sane option. That's not what winners would do though.

"I hear you, loud and clear. But let's not overlook the fact that it's essentially new management. The owners are dead serious about turning this dysfunctional team into a cohesive one. They're going for the big dream. Jango could, too. It could be very rewarding."

"I-I'm not sure," Avinash responded with pronounced head shaking.

*Come on, give me something to work with here,* Vivek said in his head.

"Would you consider discussing it with him?"

"Look, Vivek, I don't mean to be rude—"

*I'm not taking no for an answer.* "Think about it, Avinash," Vivek coaxed fervently. "Here's an opportunity for Jango to make it big, just like his good old ODI days. No empty stadiums. No booing from the crowds. No one-man army."

Vivek finally saw his eyes sparkle. He jumped onto that frequency. "You know what drives Jango, right?" He had his undivided attention at last. Vivek went in with his trump card, "It's not money."

Avinash nodded. That was Vivek's clue to push it hard. "Harsh and the team are focused on making it to the finals next year. They're committed to making this a revenue-generating team. And they need *you* to make this happen." Vivek could feel the force from within. His hands were in loose fists under the table, his shoulder muscles felt contracted, and his eyebrows were raised in anticipation.

There was silence in the museum of steel. Avinash collapsed in his chair, his hands pressed together, pointing upwards like rafters of a tall church roof. His fingertips and thumbs joined and disjoined alternately. He looked away for a bit, his gaze fixated on something outside the window. Then he turned to Vivek and said, "Can't promise anything but let me talk to Jango and see what I can do."

"Here is a rough draft of the offer." Vivek's fist turned strong as he breathed a sigh of relief.

"I don't understand. How did you convince the Rangers to accept the low offer half way through the deal?" Keya enquired, curling next to Vivek on her bed on their movie night in, munching on popcorn. It was a dull, windy night that she decided she would much rather spend in, watching a movie he had picked. The idea had sounded so romantic when it had occurred to her, until the point where he'd picked *300*. With the central theme being the big war between Persians and Greeks, lined with blood and gore, the movie was nowhere close to her idea of a compelling romance. She grudgingly diverted her thoughts to other serious matters. Earlier that evening, Vivek had hinted about some issues between Harsh, the Rangers, and Jango. She only knew bits and pieces from the grapevine and the speculations doing the rounds in her office and in the media. "Tell me, how did you convince my CEO?"

"I . . . that was a slip of the tongue. Forget I said that, baby. Let me make you some coffee." He tried to roll out of the bed but she pulled him back by his nightshirt collar. His proximity brought along the whiff of a delightfully tart note that felt like a heady current of lime, lotus, and freshly-cut wood. She could get used to this.

"Not fair. You shouldn't have said anything in the first place. It's killing me now."

"It's completely unethical and against all contracts I've ever signed," Vivek said, rubbing his temples. "You'll get me in trouble, hon. It's no fun. Will just lead to a shotgun—to my head."

"No pulling a fast one. You exaggerate a ton. Come on, don't shun."

"Home run!"

"Oh my God, I did it. I rhymed!" Keya was suddenly as excited as a little girl dressed in her favourite princess costume, momentarily forgetting everything else.

"You're learning. Impressive."

"Okay so it might get you into trouble," she resumed her line of questioning, "but I'm worth the trouble, right?" Saying that she winked and pulled him closer. She now lay comfortably by his side, her face supported by her palm. She studied his smiling face and suspected that he was probably thinking of a way to summarise it without giving away details. He didn't look like a man who would let the cat out of the bag.

"Not falling for that one." He shook his head.

"I know what it is. You have trust issues," she exclaimed, forwarding the bloodbath scene in the movie. She knew she was being unreasonable. It was against the explicitly written M&A rules to share details of such deals with anyone unless it became public knowledge, after all. She also knew how uncomfortable it was making him. But on some level, she was deriving great pleasure out of this. Watching him in a fix was turning out to be immensely entertaining.

"Ha! You watch too much *Oprah*. I just prefer to follow protocol." He snatched the remote from her hands and rewound to the bloodbath. "This is the best scene," he argued impatiently.

"Fine." A mock frown accented her face and she stuffed a handful of popcorn in his mouth to get even. He got up coughing.

"God! This is the spiciest popcorn I've ever had."

"That's what you get for being so secretive." She watched him jump out of bed and run to her kitchen. If spice tolerance level was a factor, they would have been deemed incompatible. He was a dreary two and she almost a nine on a scale of one to ten. She had overlooked that when she had glazed her popcorn with butter and generously sprinkled red chilli seasoning all over it.

When Vivek returned to the bed, she sat kneeling with her legs bent backwards, her toes touching each other, and her fingers playing with her loose curls that fell carelessly on her face.

"I honestly can't share much. There's probably someone from the PCCI hiding out in your balcony waiting for me to commit that crime," he argued.

Keya watched him collapse in the bed as he made himself comfortable, not taking his eyes off the television one bit. She wondered if this was a good time to bring up the topic of downsizing that she had been longing to discuss with him. For weeks now, alongside Vivek's absence, what had also rankled her was how she had come to lose and gain back her position with the Rangers. She couldn't silence the demons anymore, not since they had become involved. She had been curious to know initially how it had all panned out. But now it was a necessity. She couldn't help but wonder if he ever felt she was in this relationship for a reason: to have a secure future. That would kill her. She would just have to muster the courage to bring it up.

She wanted to verify if it was indeed his decision to lay her off back in the day, to learn the basis on which he had made that decision. What was going through his mind when he had offered to hire her back? Or when she'd fought it out? What he thought of it all, quite frankly. She couldn't silence the inquisitiveness inside her to learn what Vivek thought of her calibre, her job function, her competence. Had she passed the test when he had evaluated all employees with his magnifying glass? Or had she failed it and he had still decided to bring her back on board? A huge wave of insecurity swept over her.

"I have a question," she finally muttered, looking away, shifting her weight from one hip to another. That did the trick. It distracted him momentarily from the movie she was slowly beginning to detest.

"I love the pillow hair on you," he said, gently brushing a few strands away from her forehead.

"Are you listening?"

"Yeah."

"I . . . umm . . . I don't want you to feel like—like you should ever—I hope you haven't already—because that would be—that would be wrong."

"If this was an audibility and coherence test, I failed both."

"Never mind," she sighed and began to roll to her side of the bed. Vivek pulled her by the edge of her nightshirt.

"Try me again."

She did, this time with a tad more articulateness. When

she was done, he held her face with his warm hands, his eyes piercing hers, and then gave her an impassioned hug.

"You make me want to be a good guy, you know that?" She rested her face in the nook of his neck, her eyes closed, feeling relieved. She was so lost in the moment that it took a while for her to realise that he hadn't answered any of her questions.

"What if I was responsible for it? Would you be able to forgive me?"

She pulled apart and stared slack-jawed at him for a second. "That's a good one." She laughed hesitantly, gullibly.

"No, seriously. Hypothetically, what would you do? Fling your shoes at me, right?"

She continued staring at him, puzzled. A nervous twitch fluttered on her cheekbones. She wasn't sure if he was just teasing her anymore.

Vivek's eyes closed voluntarily. Unwittingly he began to trace his journey. There was a big expanse of black initially. Gradually, the faces emerged. He saw Jango, Harsh, Dubey, Krishnan, Harsh's investors, Jango's agent. He saw them all, standing upright, their arms crossed, frown pasted on their seasoned faces. Things had been happening too fast. Pushing Avinash—Jango's agent—had worked in his favour. Vivek's gut had been accurate. Jango wasn't leaving for more money. Frustration had begun to manifest via rash decisions. Avinash had succinctly conveyed to Vivek a week later that Jango wished to remain married to the Rangers. Of course, there were conditions. Seemingly minor conditions. Like a three year under-the-table contract equivalent to Delhi's offer. Like building a team before the beginning of the next season with his say in it (That was a tough one for Vivek to crack.

Players had no role to play in selection of new team members. In theory at least. Not unless the fate of the team depended on you. Then all bets were off. 'Of course' had been Vivek's response to Avinash on that.) And like a new head coach and an assistant coach who Jango had worked with in the past and shared good rapport with. That was a startling demand as well. Vivek knew he had to pick his battles. Nitpicking would lead to being stuck in a rut. Not that he had the luxury of making a call on which conditions would get accepted. But he sure had the luxury of influencing Harsh.

When Vivek and Harsh had a strong indication from Jango about accepting the new offer, they had set up several rounds of meetings with Krishnan. Vivek had skilfully dropped the bomb on the board of the Rangers. It was all exceedingly simple. All the regulatory approvals had been obtained and they were close to official close of the deal. Jango was considering quitting. Harsh could withdraw anytime unless the Rangers would accept Harsh's new offer of twelve fifty. There was shock, raised voices, debates, high emotions in the meetings that followed but no one needed convincing that if Jango left, the team would be instantly worth nothing. Harsh was holding the wild card, their only saviour. Only he had the money to bring Jango back. Of course, there was still the question of getting additional financing for Jango, the two new guys, and the coaching team. Harsh's bankers hadn't budged. But that was the least of Vivek's current concern. Harsh had enough money to buy three such teams if he wanted to. He was also backed by several private equity firms in a variety of his businesses. He could arrange for additional cash in a heartbeat when he so desired and that too from multiple sources. After weeks of going back and forth with Krishnan, Vivek and Harsh were very close to getting him to sign the new reduced offer. It wasn't a done deal yet but he could smell the finish line. And—

"I'm waiting," Keya whispered, her interruption a welcome relief from the chain of thoughts that had engulfed him. He turned to face her. His heart skipped a beat. She painted a fetching picture and for one crazy moment he considered sharing everything with her. Looking into those expectant eyes, he ran a finger across her forehead, down her nose, and onto her lower lip, pushing it down slightly.

"I wouldn't do a professional favour to you unless you asked. I know how much it would hurt your self-esteem, your idealism. And I didn't even know you when I turned in my recommendations for downsizing."

"Wait, what does that mean?"

There was no easy way to dispel her confusion and misconceptions. Vivek didn't have the heart to tell her he'd put her name on that list then. That it was by sheer luck that Keya's boss wanted out and their names were swapped. He'd have to bring it up to her one day.

"I'm kidding," he smiled. Apparently he could bluff his way out with Jango's agent, but not with this beautiful woman who was increasingly making his heart swell with affection. Or was it love? "My job was to cut the fat. And as far as I can tell, you're the meat. I'm glad I realised that, although a little late." He pulled her closer by the waist as she giggled and planted a kiss on her alluring lips.

"Wait. Me and team aren't out of the woods yet, right?"

"You know too much."

***

Vivek was meticulously typing an update e-mail to the group. Day One, the official 'seal the deal' day was exactly a week from now. Given the amount of twists and turns this deal had incurred, it had been more like car racing than any regular M&A deal. But it would all culminate soon enough and that made him smile. He continued typing relentlessly, and popped in a piece of chewing gum to fight the three p.m. slump. Funny, in the past few months he hadn't even had one moment that he could lay to waste, and here he was, fighting an afternoon slump. He grinned again at that and started humming a tune.

The conference room door, which was ajar, swung open. It was Harsh, appearing . . . disgruntled. *What now?*

"Vivek, I need to speak with you right now. Guys," he said looking at Omar and Satyen who were working on desks next to Vivek's, "give us a few minutes." They obeyed him and walked out immediately.

"This may come as a shock to you. Just a little warning there. The thing is, I want to . . . I actually need to back out."

Vivek, who had been sporting a smile until now, turned impassive. His features took on a glacial expression and his eyes turned cold. A nerve ticked in his jaw.

"Now?" *You got every fucking thing you asked for. Why do you continue to drop these bombs on me, you fucking moron?* If they were inside a boxing ring, Vivek would have rendered Harsh unconscious.

Harsh pulled a chair across from him and tossed him a few papers.

"Have you seen this?"

It was the front page of *Deccan Herald*. SPLIT DECISIONS, the title of an anchor story read. Alongside was a picture of Harsh and a woman. A quick scan through the article explained it all. That woman was his wife and she had filed for divorce. He quickly glanced at the other couple of online newspaper printouts Harsh had hurled at him. BENGALURU BILLIONAIRE'S EXPENSIVE DIVORCE, HARSH DESAI—IT'S A WRAP. Several other similar headlines confirmed the story.

Vivek looked up at Harsh, aghast. "What is all this? When did it happen? I'm-I'm sorry to hear that."

"Yeah, well, she has landed me smack in the middle of a financial mess. Two hundred fucking crores! That's what her jerk of a lawyer has slammed me with for settlement. Ladies and gentlemen, I am officially *fucked*," Harsh fumed, uncrossing his legs, shifting his weight on both, and finally crossing them again. All this while his hands massaged his forehead.

"Wow. I've never heard of such huge settlements, in India at least."

"It's complicated. She has an eye on my foreign investments, too."

"No pre-nup I presume?"

"No. I'm *that* stupid."

Vivek picked up a bottle of water from the side table, handed it over to Harsh, and leaned against the table next to the chair Harsh was sitting on.

"Two hundred crores? Is she out of her mind? I don't sleep on a heap of notes. It's all invested in businesses and properties and mansions around the world that *she* visits and decorates. I don't have it neatly stacked up for that gold digger."

Vivek had never before seen Harsh so vulnerable.

"I understand."

"Anyway, look, this will only get more ugly and nasty. She is vengeful and will publicly castrate me. It's going to be a losing battle. Now isn't the time for me to commit to new businesses. Do what you need to do. Get me out of this."

There it was. Extraordinarily simple. Vivek's destiny clearly sketched on the front pages of those newspapers. He could pretend to not read those words but the reality was that it was over. Harsh had already made up his mind.

There had been several times when deals had fallen through half way, but each of those times there had been a logical reason. Vivek's client, whether it was the buyer or the seller, always had a range of concerns and reasons for backing out which would be deliberated upon as a team. This pulling the plug in a heartbeat was a first. A disturbing first in his entire career.

Harsh's abrupt withdrawal made absolutely no sense. Okay, it did a bit. He got that Harsh was in a financial soup, but there were ways of salvaging the deal. If he really, really wanted, he would not let this slide. That's what it was, wasn't it? Harsh wasn't keen on the acquisition. He never really had been. It was Vivek who had been bulldozing him all along. It shattered him immensely.

In the days that followed, Vivek kept to himself, attending only to crucial e-mails and phone calls. Every waking hour, every waking minute, he replayed everything in his mind, right from the very beginning, and every time he came to the same conclusion. Luck. That's all it boiled down to. He used to joke that he had had everyone's share of bad deals in Mumbai, including the beggars and the pimps; well he had just added Ahmedabad into this *blasted* privileged league. *Good fucking Lord!* His association of years, months of effort on the project, his aspirations; all reduced to ashes in an instant! This felt a lot beyond project failure. It almost felt like a *personal* failure. This had been the project of his dreams, an opportunity he'd been eyeing for so long . . .

***

Omar had been assigned the task of following every story that involved Harsh in the public eye. If there was more to this than what met the eye, he was going to figure it out.

Vivek, in his hyperactive state, was thinking wildly of options when his phone rang. It was Krishnan.

"Can you come by?"

He knew it. Krishnan was going to ask him and his team to vanish faster than he could say vanish. He'd already taken the initiative. It had all been too catastrophic.

"Ahh, Vivek, yes, come in. I wanted a quick word with you."

"Sure," he said, occupying the black leather chair across from Krishnan.

"It's been almost a week since Harsh backed out. I'd like for you to—"

"I understand. I'm almost done wrapping—"

"Not so fast. I'd like for you to extend this project. Wrap up the previous one. Create a new SOW. Essentially, treat it as a separate project."

Vivek, taken aback, blinked in confusion.

"What . . . what exactly did you have in mind?"

"It's still very early and strictly confidential. We've had interest from another private equity," Krishnan let him know, leaning in a little bit, his voice dropping.

"Great! That's just great. I had no doubt about this eventuality." *What? Already?* It had barely been a week since

Harsh had given them the boot.

"Yes, it's encouraging news. Harsh's withdrawal news is all over the media. It was the cover story of several newspapers last week, domestic and international, including the *Wall Street Journal* sports section. I'm sure you saw that."

"Absolutely." *How the hell did he miss that?* Omar was going to hear from him about not filling him in with the media news.

"Unfortunately, Harsh's prior lowball offer is out in the open, too. We'll see how the negotiations go. Where you fit in is with the due diligence aspect. We've already gone through this once and the management feels you've been a great asset. I'd like for you to continue in a new capacity, on behalf of the Rangers this time around. Thoughts?"

If there was one thing Vivek had learnt in his long-established career in the industry, it was that rare were these golden days when projects fell from the sky like tiny pieces of liquor chocolate straight into your open mouth. If they ever come to you, you say yes!

"I'd be happy to."

Over the next few days, Vivek learnt a great deal about the new developments in the pipeline. The new investor was the distinguished private equity firm, Westside Capital, based out of Mumbai. Westside had engaged a firm, B&W Consulting, to lead the efforts. It was a company he had never heard of and that unsettled him. With the very suspicious exit of Harsh, the entry of Westside and B&W added more layers to the mix. Too much was happening too soon. And he couldn't make sense of it.

***

By the end of the first few weeks in his newly-appointed position, Vivek was drained. Both mentally and physically. He had no idea when one day ended and when the other began. Life was a blur. A hurt Keya, miffed parents, demanding new bosses; could life get more berserk than this? The only silver lining was that finally, after numerous entries and exits, the deal was on.

Drinking away at a bar in Bandra one night with Omar, life began to feel like a freshly-filled beer mug to him. Steady and predictable at the bottom, fizzy and rapidly changing on the top.

The initial weeks with Westside Capital and B&W had been very demanding, his role defined as the hard negotiator. From working on Harsh's behalf to acquiring Rangers for thirteen hundred initially and going down to twelve fifty later, he had witnessed the tables turn as he was made to push Westside Capital to raise their offer from a meagre eleven hundred to a somewhat respectable twelve.

Life had come full circle for him in a short span of few months and not in a good way. Everything was an uphill battle at the moment. Day after day he found himself at the same table, saying the same things in different words to the same people, pushing his way through but not making much progress. Receiving more than its share of media coverage for all the wrong reasons hadn't helped the Rangers one bit.

Harsh's backing out had created a false sense of desperation in the market for the Rangers, which predators like Westside Capital were making the most out of. In one way, it was almost as if Westside and B&W, by some unknown power, had dug up every modest detail that made the case weak for the Rangers. They'd come prepared with statistics on everything—

from cash flow to ticket sales and from player contracts to disproportionate bonuses. But that wasn't what intrigued Vivek. It was that their quotes were always *just* a shade different from the previous deal's. They hadn't displayed knowledge on the actual numbers—that would only be insider information—but they had exhibited their insights into it by asking the hard questions. It'd left him more baffled than anything else.

"I know what it is," Omar spoke, alluding to an apparent epiphany he had just had. "They've planted a spy in the Rangers. This is totally rigged. There's no way they would know all the details they seem to otherwise. Have you talked about this with anyone?"

"Omar, you watch too many spy flicks, and I am this close to losing it," Vivek said, pinching his thumb and index finger very close together.

That shut Omar for a brief moment. But soon after he resumed voicing out his thoughts and questions with, "And what's with that Xiang Bhutia dude? I'm afraid to say anything to him. I feel like he's going to cry if I ask him a hard question."

Xiang was the senior director from B&W. A petite man with spiky hair, he dressed straight out of *GQ* except for the thick diamond-studded gold bracelet that jingled each time he wrote something, Xiang Bhutia had the kindest smile. In a room full of sharks, Xiang's presence was a welcome respite. His seemingly unwary eyes invariably sparkled behind his eyeglasses and his short frame, the shortest in the group, often reduced the threatening vibes that everyone else from Westside and B&W effortlessly exuded.

"Omar, shut it man. I'm dead."

***

Vivek didn't believe in miracles but when he witnessed the shaking of two sets of familiar hands with the words 'It's a deal' falling on his jaded ears, it was the closest he'd felt to seeing one. After much push and pull, the Rangers had been sold, again, this time to Westside Capital for a figure of twelve hundred crores.

Even selling a dozen toothpicks could seem like victory if one had to slog at it for too long, and this was an IGL team, the thought had crossed Vivek's mind. The prelude-to-a-kiss phase had lasted rather long, stripping the kiss completely of excitement. Vivek showed his amicable side to both parties, smiling, congratulating them verbally while lashing out at them with the choicest expletives mentally.

"Let the good times roll," Xiang said with a firm handshake. "Look forward to working with you on the real stuff."

"Likewise," Vivek reciprocated, relief showing on his face.

"We'll have the contract sent over to you by tomorrow. Once the formalities are done, you and I should sit down sometime this week. I want to start with the work you'd done for the previous buyer on staff reduction."

"I could brief you on it. The Rangers have already gone through the first round of—"

Xiang cut him off firmly. "Westside typically kicks off with restructuring. It'd be helpful if I could have that list from you."

And just like that, Xiang Bhutia ceased to be the gentle dude with unwary eyes.

"I can't get over the fact that it's your last day in town," Keya said. They were meeting at a coffee shop near her place. Vivek had proposed the idea of catching up at her house or maybe even his hotel, but she had refused. Although things were going fine, on the face of it at least, but something somewhere was still off, and she didn't want the privacy these places offered unless he came clean with everything.

Vivek was gazing intently at the screen opposite him where a cricket match was being telecasted. The straw from his cold coffee rested on his lips, apparently forgotten. For a good twenty odd seconds he hadn't even blinked his eyes. Keya doubted the sanity of her decision to meet here.

"Vivek," she spoke a little more loudly, "I just said something."

"What?" he mechanically questioned without looking at her.

"I just said something."

"Oh, yeah? Repeat, please?" he requested with an embarrassed grin.

"I said I can't believe you are leaving tomorrow."

"Good. Because I am not. This isn't my last day in town. I might have to be back next week," he countered her fears, but his gaze was still fixed on the game. He had mentioned earlier that day that he wasn't needed here any longer and that he was being pulled into another high priority project in the Mumbai office, but clearly that was not the case. Either, he hadn't thought this through or he just loved giving her mini strokes.

"Oh. Okay. So what happens to us when you leave tomorrow?"

"You will miss me and I'll be back soon."

***

"I miss him too much. It sucks," Keya said to no one in particular, shutting down her laptop after typing a mail to Vivek, the umpteenth one she had composed and not sent yet. That man had broken her in. Or maybe she'd let her guard down . . .

It was the first night away from Vivek and she was alone at her home waiting for her friends to turn up. Kourosh had volunteered to pick up Tiramisu from The Crust and Radhika was bringing Chinese take-out. For her part, she had arranged for a warm ambiance by lighting a few citrusy candles and a Moroccan henna lamp that dispersed soft, romantic light, and then laid out maps of Brazil and Argentina. They had a trip to plan, after all.

Kourosh and Radhika came a few minutes apart from each other. Between good food and good friends, Keya began to have a great time. She let her anxieties about Vivek and her job stay out of her mind. Tonight was not the time to focus on that.

Half way through dinner though, she started to catch unmistakable signals from Kourosh. She had caught him staring at her while circling his fork around the noodles, laughing too hard at her non-jokes, and pouring her Coke to the rim of the glass. It was these little things he always did that made her uncomfortable. She had postponed it for too long. She'd have to have a word with him tonight. No, scratch that. Right now.

"Rosh. Patio. Please?"

"Wait, let me grab my drink," Radhika butted in, trying to pull down her tight dress that had rolled half way up her thighs.

"Just me and all the Parsis in the room, Rads. Two minutes." She smiled at Radhika, who in turn deciphering what this might be all about, gave her a thumbs-up and mouthed "good luck."

Kourosh followed her out quietly. Keya didn't get the feeling that he was thinking through this at all. She didn't have the heart to tell him that there was no point for him to be hopeful. That she was taken, in a way.

"I . . . umm . . . Rosh, I don't know how to say this."

"What's up, Keya?"

She was looking away, not being able to make eye contact. She didn't know why she was feeling so guilty. She had never led him on, never promised anything. Never hinted at anything. Have I, inadvertently? she wondered.

"Have you met Vivek?" Hell, she wasn't even sure where that was headed and here she was using him as a ruse. *Good girl, Keya!*

Kourosh seemed to rake his mind for a moment, moving his shiny blonde hair away from his face, and then said, "Oh, yes. I think so. At your Christmas party last year. Chubby guy.

Kinda old. Wore a moose sweater. Bad sweater. What happened to him?"

"*What?* Who are you talking about?"

"I don't know. Someone from your party last year. Who are *you* talking about?"

"Rosh," she said with an indication of anxiety in her tone, "Vivek is my boyfriend."

It was an unexpectedly calm moment. No knee-jerk reaction. No drama. No broken heart. Kourosh appeared stoic. He was staring at her, his arms tightly folded across his chest. Then he turned his face away from her, slightly . . . slowly, but his eyes never left hers. After a brief period of silence, he laughed.

"I get it! You're joking, yes?"

Keya felt the pain he was about to feel. That's how well she understood him. It had hit her several times how genuinely she cared for him, but it was always in an amiable way. She blinked repeatedly, not being able to articulate anything. He must have noticed the seriousness in her eyes because something wiped out the smile from his face.

"When?" he asked softly.

She drowned in an ocean of guilt, the waves snatching away her ability to speak. She sniffed, looking down, pursing her lips.

"Keya, say something." He grabbed both her arms and gently shook her.

"It just happened . . . a few weeks back. I'm so sorry. I wanted to tell you earlier. But I-I wasn't sure myself."

In the sparse light provided by the street lamps and a half moon his eyes sparkled. Soon she noticed the sparkle intensifying from the wetness. She took his hands in hers in a feeble attempt to pacify him but in reality, it was she who needed to be comforted. Big, dense tears were forming in her eyes.

"I'm sorry," she said one more time as a lone tear rolled down her cheek.

"You don't have to. It's okay. I'm okay," he said, barely audible.

She gave him a warm hug hoping it would do the trick and give them both the closure they needed. Just then, Radhika pushed open the glass door and peeked out, like a squirrel from behind a bush.

"Group hug?" she asked, carefree, and joined them.

Later when it was just the girls, Radhika nudged her and enquired, "You've released him, right? Because I'm going in, baby." The wink that followed confirmed her intentions.

***

"Be aware of your breathing. Slowly take it in. Focus on connecting it with your thoughts. Try to relax. And let go of all the burdens," said the silver-haired yoga instructor in Gujarati, then repeated it in Hindi. In a dimly-lit room, that passed for a gym in Keya's neighbourhood, accompanied by what sounded like subdued Tibetan music, sat Keya inhaling just the way she had been instructed to. But to no avail. She *couldn't* relax or keep her mind focused.

Restless, she opened her eyes, her pose nowhere close to the butterfly pose everyone in the room was conveniently sporting. In her clumsy state, she looked around for some other failure besides herself but no one else seemed so disengaged. She tried finding her centre of gravity as instructed and bending her back one more time but the stiffness in her spine was invincible. "Flutter away, all you butterflies. I don't have time for this crap," she murmured to the room full of people. Yanking the purple yoga mat from beneath her, she walked out of the class. Yoga wasn't going to be bringing her stress relief anytime soon. That much she had figured out.

The acquisition process had left her exhausted, what with no boss and her team squeezed to a mere three. In a parallel universe, the workload would have decreased along with the team size, not in the mad world she inhabited, though. New management had brought in 'visionaries', people who came solo with a truck load of ideas and no team to implement them with. On some days, it felt like she reported to half a dozen bosses, all asking her for the world, concurrently. It not only kept her up at night but hijacked her life to a large extent.

She reached home, hung her key, and tossed the mail on a side table that served as catch-all. Just as she was about to turn around and proceed towards her bedroom to crash, her eyes fell on a glossy black card. She leaned forward to pick it up and noticed another one, just the same, under the first one. RANGERS, PRIVATE EVENT, it read. Instantly, it hit her. Vivek had scored two passes for Keya for a pre-season Rangers' party, one for her and the other for Radhika, given that he wasn't in town. Four years of working for the Rangers had not translated in a single opportunity to attend such a glorious event. It had taken a Vivek to score. It made her feel small, insignificant. Dismissing the self-pity, she immediately dialled away Radhika's number to tip her off about the excitement that awaited them later that night.

"It would be evil to crack such jokes. My heart just skipped a bit," Radhika accused in disbelief, playing up the drama quotient.

"No, I'm serious. It's at a five-star hotel. I'll pick you up at 10:30."

After waiting for what seemed like an eternity in the rickshaw, she noticed Radhika finally walking towards her, looking smug and cheerful in a yellow strapless body-hugging dress and cheetah print heels. It instantly made Keya worry about the adverse effect of that teeny-tiny dress on the driver.

They got dropped a few yards away from the hotel and noticed a few media folks outside who seemed to be adjusting their equipment and focusing on an invisible red carpet by the entrance. Keya gasped at the beauty of everything around. The men appeared dapper in their designer wear and most women had some serious skin on display. She checked her reflection in a car window and beamed; she wasn't looking so bad herself. A shimmery bandage dress, uncomfortable heels, and shimmer on her eyes and lips made her feel self-assured.

Stylishly done in horizontal stripes in shades of peach and grey, the ballroom at the hotel was lit in a soft purple hue. Luminous chandeliers hung gracefully from the ceiling at measured intervals. Jazz in the background set the mood. Keya took a few more steps in search of familiar faces, pulling Rads along with her, who oohed and ahhed at everything they passed: the tables laid out with drinks and hors d'oeuvres, the guests in their splendid dresses, and especially the cricketers in all their glory. Rads held Keya's arm tight as if to prevent herself from tripping when Jango appeared in sight. Keya glanced at Jango, scanning him from head to toe. He definitely looked like the star of the evening.

"Sweet Lord! I'm about to faint. That man is my new

religion," Radhika declared. "Can you introduce me to him?"

"Umm . . . Jango doesn't actually know me."

"Uhh? Who could you introduce me to then?"

"No one knows me here, Rads. Just a couple of big bosses. And I don't think we should be going near them. They'll suspect I'm gate-crashing or something."

"Gosh, you're so useless."

Keya made a note of everything around, comparing it with all the stories she'd heard first-hand of such parties. The crowd, the conversations, the ambiance, the music; it was all a first for her. She was suitably impressed.

"Hey listen, where are all the cheerleaders?" Radhika greedily enquired.

"Good point. I actually have no clue."

"And why are there just a few cricketers? I only see the married ones. Where are the young hotties?"

"I honestly have no clue. Stop attacking me with all these questions, Rads. I already feel like I don't belong here."

"Oh you know what? Someone told me that ever since that Gabriella girl busted the cricketers, boom! no more cheerleaders. Perhaps that's why the hotties stopped coming."

"Must be. Let's get something to drink."

As the girls waited in line for the bar, Radhika continued yapping away in amazement. Keya felt quite the opposite. Being quite a party girl during her college years, she'd seen it all; bars, nightclubs, farmhouse parties, alcohol, drugs, foreplay. It wasn't her scene anymore. Now, she'd much rather be in a place with friends where screaming wasn't a prerequisite for a fun evening. She didn't even want to say it to herself but she was bored. Dreadfully bored at her first glam party.

Radhika dragged her all the way around the room, slyly

checking out her target, lending her ears to private conversations within cliques. Barely a few sips down, her eyes sparkled.

"I just heard VIP. Did you hear VIP?"

"VIP what?"

"You think there's a VIP party going on simultaneously?"

"This is the VIP party. Look," she replied, pulling out the two invitation cards from her handbag. "Check this out. One VIP admission. Radhika Mehra."

"You're right, but no harm in checking, right. What if it's somewhere around here and we're missing out on all the fun? This party looks so dead anyway."

Keya knew better than to argue with Her Highness. Giving in usually worked out best for them both. She shrugged, duly displaying her willingness to play Watson to Sherlock.

With mischief dancing in her eyes, Radhika dragged Keya outside the ballroom and straight into the reception area. Keya noticed how Radhika decisively picked the young male receptionist out of the three available ones. She signalled him to lean in and promptly went for gold, "Where's the VIP party?"

"Ma'am, I don't—"

"We're Neil's friends. He's asked me to check at the reception," she said, namedropping a young batsman from the Rangers' team.

"Oh, this way ma'am."

In a surprising series of events that followed, the young receptionist walked out from behind the desk and escorted them to the lift. *It is on the topmost floor*, he whispered so as to guard the big secret. Then he pressed the button for the eighth floor and gave them a warm smile. The lift door closed and Radhika said animatedly, "Didn't I tell you?"

They scrambled out of the lift on the eighth floor and stepped into, what could only be called, an alternate universe. It was a smaller and edgier group of people, mingling under neon lights and swaying to pulsating music. Keya walked in, slightly hesitant, her face heating up. It was exactly how she'd imagined a real IGL after-party to be like. Except this wasn't an after-party. It was a much younger demographic as compared to the crowd in the ballroom and a lot more alluring. The young, single cricketers looked elated and sloshed, holding wine glasses or doing shots, laughing throatily as sexy, exotic girls hung onto them.

"Oh my God," Radhika jubilantly exclaimed, stretching out each word. "This is like a dream. Unreal."

"Shh. Can we please not act like gate-crashers?"

Radhika ignored that plea entirely and walked in with a swaggering, slinky style.

"Look over there. Cheerleaders! I think they got them through the back door to escape all the media attention. This is un-believ-able," she loudly proclaimed.

Keya walked alongside Radhika, squirming, uneasy, gazing at the newness around her. When she felt her heart rate steadying, she indulged herself in the unfolding urban entertainment.

"Can I get you ladies a drink?" A handsome stud appeared from nowhere breaking up their little clique. When he began flirting with Radhika and she merrily reciprocating, Keya started to feel like the third wheel. Excusing herself, not that they even heard, she headed out to the rooftop open area to drink in the scenic views of the city's skyline and to escape the discomfort.

In an attempt to appear busy, she yanked out her phone

and pretended to play with it. She moved along from one railing to another, ignoring the few admiring glances that came her way, trying not to come across as a lost puppy. She noticed people from Westside Capital but didn't know them enough to strike a conversation. She also spotted a few consultants from B&W. The only person she had occasionally worked with from B&W was Xiang Bhutia but there was no trace of him. She missed Vivek. Terribly so.

Sporadic fireworks lighting up the eastern sky caught her eye. She moved further in their direction to catch the entire show. There was nothing more enchanting than a sky lit up with sparkling, glittering lights, albeit for a brief period. Spotting a chance to get still farther away from the madding crowd and closer to the reprieve of a quiet space to enjoy her private show, she took a few more steps deeper into the softly-lit corner. Some bustle and murmur fell on her ears. It was probably someone, just like her, desperate to get away. Or maybe someone was making out, she mischievously concluded. She diverted her attention back to the fireworks.

"Yes sir. I'll definitely fax it to Mr Desai tomorrow morning. Yes sir. No, Vivek is not in town." Keya heard distinct words from a voice that seemed to be approaching towards her.

Vivek . . . such an exceptionally common name. The being-out-of-town bit sounded familiar as well. Too much of a co-incidence, the thought suddenly hit her. Curiosity got the better of Keya, and she decided to peep and catch a glimpse of who was there. She leaned forward and saw a man in a black suit walking towards her. Her stomach twisted at the prospect of being deemed a prying loner. Having lost Radhika to carnal pleasures with random strangers, the last thing she wanted was to be caught at a party she was grate-crashing. She ducked instantly, cocking her head in the opposite direction and stood still. She pressed herself harder against the wall so as not to be seen. The voice came closer and eventually passed her by. Then the man stopped walking and leaned against the railing, just a few feet from Keya. She thought about turning away from the spot when she grasped who the male figure resembled from behind. It was Xiang Bhutia! She laughed inwardly. How silly of her to hide from the one person she knew in the whole party. The eeriness of the situation vanished right away. She waited for him to wrap up the call so she could walk up to him and say hello.

"Mr Desai did call me a while back in regard to that. He's back in Bengaluru. Right, sir. I'll see to it that he has what he needs. Good night," Xiang spoke in one breath into the phone.

Something was wrong. Terribly so. *Mr Desai? Bengaluru? Vivek? Not in town?* It was an odd mix of names; names she hadn't heard being uttered in the same sentence ever since Harsh Desai had backed out of the deal. It sounded sketchy and gave her an uneasy feeling. She ran her hand through her hair and pulled them on her face, turning away from the balcony and towards the wall. She brushed past him inconspicuously and walked away, a scowl glued on her face. When she reached what she thought was a safer zone, she inhaled sharply and replayed the past few minutes in her head. *Mr Desai? Harsh Desai? Xiang was going to fax documents to Harsh Desai? What on earth did he have to do with Harsh?* Harsh had backed out weeks ago and the new owner, Westside, had brought in B&W. Vivek was in the mix, too. She couldn't erase the bad feeling the night was conferring her with. Something was fishy.

The next day dawned bright and clear but Keya couldn't

clear the confusion in her mind. She mulled over what her head referred to as a non-issue, but her heart just wouldn't budge. Why did Xiang take Vivek's and Harsh's name in the same breath? Xiang had no business knowing Harsh, as far as she knew. What were they up to? When Harsh was in the process of acquiring the Rangers, it had been too hard on her. Things had seemed to be going smooth with the Westside acquisition process up until that night. What ordeal awaited her and her team this time around? It seemed like a vicious conspiracy. What was it about Vivek that she didn't know? It wasn't a mere fling anymore. She was undeniably in love. And with the kind of person she always wanted. It had all been so rosy and magical, despite his staying so occupied with work lately, that the slightest of snag felt like a catastrophe.

Keya suddenly felt suffocated. Fresh air! That's what she needed to clear her head. She took the lift down and began to walk towards the nearby coffee shop. A few swigs of coffee later, she made the call she had been dreading ever since she had reached office today morning.

Vivek wasn't able to speak for beyond a few seconds. "I am driving Keya. Let's talk later. Okay?" Before she could respond to that or even hint at what was troubling her, he had hung up.

The nerve of that . . . that . . . *cheat*, her mind filled that last word in.

Keya shivered in the scorching sun.

It had been a long wait. The kind where time froze and so did the brain, not permitting rational thoughts to break the limbo. Keya knew herself well enough to comprehend that until she had educed the truth from Vivek about what Xiang had said that night, she was not going to be able to go about life normally. It was as if she had become her own worst enemy. What could have been a perfectly good weekend had now reduced to stories about a burnt toast, a mixed-up laundry load that ruined all her delicates, and being behind on paying bills.

Vivek hadn't returned her phone call over the weekend. She'd reluctantly left it at that. Monday wasn't far, after all. Although the project was over, some post-merger issues had surfaced. Vivek was to make a trip back to Ahmedabad for that the following Monday. She had never looked forward to a Monday as much.

Trying to appear casual, she walked by the conference room that served as Vivek and his team's office but didn't hear Vivek. She repeated that at five-minute intervals for the next hour and was greeted with nothing but dejection. Much after noon she overheard his unmistakable voice originating from the lobby somewhere and ran back to her office to call him.

"How was the weekend?" she asked, unruffled, the goal of ferreting out valuable information high on her agenda.

"A little jacked up but all good."

"Good. Umm . . . I had a question."

"What's up, sweetie?"

"Are Xiang and Harsh connected somehow?"

There was a pause. It didn't feel like the kind of pause that one normally required to rack their brain. Rather the kind in which one needed to create a carefully constructed lie.

"No, I don't think so."

"Are you sure? Maybe there is something you have forgotten about? Or maybe a tiny detail you do not want to get into in front of me but know nonetheless? Why do I get that feeling that you know exactly what I am talking about?"

"I take off for one weekend and you turn into CBI?" He seemed dismissive.

"That's not the answer to my question."

"Why the sudden interrogation?"

"Interrogation? It's a simple question!"

"It's Monday morning, Keya. If you don't have anything important to discuss, I'll call you later." He bluntly disconnected.

That was all the validation she needed. Where on one level she had scored, she felt hopelessly defeated on the other. How could her newly-formed relationship fall apart already, she deliberated. It wasn't like she expected him to stand in the rain sans an umbrella holding a bunch of red roses waiting for her to return home. An honest relationship would have more than sufficed.

She was just glad she had work to pour herself into.

A monster of a Monday behind her, much after sunset, Keya gulped down what was left of her espresso that she'd picked up mid-afternoon. The appetising part from the liquid had gone missing and she could taste something cold, bitter, and disgusting.

She knew Vivek was just a few offices away from her but he'd not made one effort to drop by, call, e-mail, IM, or use any social media to reach her, if not apologise for his rude behaviour. He could have sent good vibes at the very least. She would have caught those.

Radhika had called earlier that day and said something only she would say."There must be so much sexual tension between you two at work. Clandestine affair and all."

Unfortunately, it was just tension.

When exhaustion triumphed emotions, she shoved some reports into her laptop bag and headed out, ignoring an unbearable desire to drop by the conference room he was in, just to catch a glimpse of her boyfriend. But each time she thought of that term, boyfriend, a question mark immediately followed in her head. He had never openly declared anything till now, but she had felt they were going somewhere. And then today happened. He had suddenly turned so sketchy, so unpredictable.

She scampered into the lift and hit the button for the lobby level. But instead of going south, the lift doors opened again. It was Vivek, in all his glory, standing right across from her. It felt a little surreal for a second to her.

His face broke into a big smile at the sight of her. "Hey sweets, I was just about to stop by and ask for dinner. Where are you headed?"

She stared at him, trying to decipher the motive. "Home," she replied and slammed the button again. It obeyed her and instantly did as directed, leaving Vivek with a rather creased forehead and an incredulous expression. He acted in the nick of time, pushing his hand between the almost-closed doors. The sensors immediately recognised the action and parted, allowing him to enter.

"What was *that*?" he asked, aghast.

"What was what?" She hit the button for the lobby level, watching the doors close again, carefully avoiding eye contact as Vivek entered her space. It was just the two of them in the lift.

"Are you trying to avoid me?"

"No, I'm trying to dodge your questions. Just like you dodged mine."

The lift stopped and the doors opened. They were at the lobby level already. Right across from them was the security desk where two security personnel were stationed. Keya, taking advantage of the set-up, hurriedly walked out. He followed suit, she gathered, from the tapping of his shoes right behind her. It was dark outside and insanely windy. She turned left towards the bus stop, her hair flying wildly across her face. The winter chill in the air made her shiver slightly as she wrapped both arms around her chest. Her hand got pulled making her turn around. It was him.

"Stop walking and talk to me for a second, will you?"

"No," she said, freeing her arm from his grasp. Turning around, she began to walk again.

"Goddammit, stop this drama, Keya. I'm trying to have a conversation here. What the fuck is the matter with you?"

"Conversation? Really? Okay, let's have a conversation, Vivek." She was now facing him, the wind threatening to uproot her but she was pressing down on her heels. "What is going on between you, Xiang, and Harsh?" she asked him point-blank.

He looked at her, one eye at a time, with an expressionless face and then suddenly exploded.

"*What?* You are out of your mind!"

"I knew it. You don't have an answer, do you?"

"Huh? I told you, nothing was going on. What on earth is your problem? What is it with Harsh? That bastard ditched me. Left me in the middle of all this mess. He turned this into a fucking deal from hell. What else do you want to know and why the fuck do you even care? Gosh. It's like you're already the nagging wife. Get a life," he yelled, using his hands to drive home his point as if the expletives weren't enough.

"My problem? My problem is that you are a bloody liar." She was loud enough to get puzzled looks from bystanders. She turned away and began to run. She couldn't hear footsteps following her anymore. Having spotted an auto rickshaw across the street, she ran across the intersection even when the walk sign wasn't on. A quick glance had confirmed the idea wasn't that dangerous, so she ran. But out of nowhere, a car came zooming towards her, and almost ran her over. "*Oye marna hain kya?*" one of the boys in the car yelled. She speeded up to get into a rickshaw, finally catching a breath. She peeked out one last time to see if he was around. No such luck.

Keya threw back her head against the headrest and inhaled. It invariably started small. Just like with her ex-fiancé. And before she could know what was happening, her world would come crashing down.

How could she be so unfortunate to be on the receiving end of two dishonest relationships?

Keya avoided Vivek all week and he did the same. They would run into each other several times during the day but one of them would be quick to move away. She debated whether she should try talking to him again, but concluded that it wasn't a minor thing that she could just overlook. This was lies; one thing she could never make her peace with. Especially from someone whom she almost believed to be the love of her life.

Keya closed her eyes and put the pillow over her head. She wished she could just sleep away her Saturday but there was so much work to do that she didn't know where to begin from.

`Doll, make sure all your travel documents are ready today. We don't have many days left. Okay?` She'd received this text from Radhika earlier that morning reminding her of the impending South America trip.

Keya dismissed the thought of taking a shower and looking civilised before heading to office. Time was of the essence! Moreover it was a Saturday morning and she'd be lucky to see another soul in her building. A few quick official e-mails followed by printouts for Brazil was on her agenda for the day.

As she reached her office, she quickly printed a stack of documents and walked to the printer to retrieve them, only to find it jammed. Frustrated, she tried for some more time, shaking it vigorously, at the same time hoping no one would catch her in the act, but nothing. Then she went around it and cranked it open to troubleshoot.

With her head ducked between the dusty printer and the wall, she heard a rattle from a distance and looked up to take a look. Who was as unfortunate as her to show up on a Saturday? There wasn't a soul in sight but she was sure she had heard footsteps. Out of sheer curiosity, she tiptoed to the other side of her office that overlooked the open space, and saw a man's retreating figure. She craned her neck and instantly recognised the spiky hair. It was Xiang Bhutia . . . She rushed back to her office, grabbed her handbag, and ran back to the exit, taking the stairs down.

If she had to get to the bottom of it and clear her doubts, however insignificant, she had some digging around of her own to do. There were high personal and professional stakes involved. She couldn't just let it be! Since the night of the IGL party, she'd been keeping an eye on Xiang. His needing her help with several assignments had only made it easier. She had read and re-read all his e-mails looking for a clue, swung by his office couple of times a day under false pretexts, checked the printer, the photocopier, and the fax machines after he used them, just to see if he had unintentionally left anything behind. So far, she'd had no luck. But this could be promising . . .

She stormed out of the main entrance door and speedily walked towards the cross street, looking out for Xiang. Evidently, he seemed clueless and went about life as usual. She followed him for about a minute or so and watched him enter a tiny photocopy shop.

The shop had copiers lined up in one corner, desktops and printers in another, with rest of the space doubling up as a coffee shop. The commercial area that the centre was in brought in a large amount of customers. There had always been a queue each time she had been here. Luckily it was a weekend today and there was hardly any rush.

Xiang was standing by one of the fax machines, arranging his documents and sending them off. She saw two available desktops and using her hair to mask her face reached out to the closest one. She initiated the printing process, then walked up to the printer to pick up the copies. On the available side table, she separated them out by itinerary, hotel confirmations, flight tickets, and must-see suggestions, but her eyes were on him all the time. Then she grabbed her stack and took it to the copy machine next to Xiang's fax machine. He seemed preoccupied with what he was doing.

She thought through it for a moment, the hare-brained plan that had formulated in her head, and then using her elbow pushed his wallet off the fax machine. It startled him, he turned, and as his eyes met hers, he turned white. Keya for her part apologised profusely. He bent to pick up his wallet, his brows furrowed, giving her the perfect opportunity to glance over at the document stack. Time not by her side, she pushed the stack out, too.

"Sorry, I'm so very sorry," she said, feigning regret.

Xiang stayed put on the floor, trying to collect all the documents flying over him. Keya jumped at the opportunity, seized one of the documents on the fax machine and craftily slid it under her stack. She hadn't a clue about how any of this was going to help. She was just letting her intuition guide her. When Xiang stood up, she noticed the large frown on his face, his gaze brutally intense. She apologised again, repeatedly, asking to help him out but he shunned her. He turned his back on her and began arranging all the documents. She even heard him counting the page numbers on the stack.

Panic instantly hit her. She broke out in cold sweat. He was going to figure out that she had pulled a page out! Those numbers won't lie. To save herself the embarrassment, she picked up her own stack and rushed to the desktop next to which she had kept her handbag. She looked out at him through the corner of her eye, shuddering, feeling foolish, waiting for him to yell at her or call her out for stealing his paper.

Nothing.

He just collected his stuff and took off, not even waiting to say goodbye. Still seated, she tilted her neck as far as she could and watched him walk away. When he was out of sight, curiously, apprehensively, she pulled out his paper. 'Confidential' was the second thing that registered. The first thing which not only registered but somewhat disoriented her was 'Harsh Desai'.

She glanced around to see if she was being watched. There was no one around. Reluctantly, she began reading it. It was on B&W Consulting's letterhead. Why would B&W write to Harsh? *This couldn't be happening!* There shouldn't have been any communication whatsoever between them. She shushed herself so she could read ahead. As her eyes followed the letter, all she found was a little bit of nothing.

*Dear Harsh,*

*Requested documents are attached. A separate copy has been mailed to Westside Capital Partners.*

*Regards*
*Xiang Bhutia*
*Sr Director*
*B&W Consulting*

Her mouth dropped open as she stared at the document, her hand cupped her forehead in utter disbelief. She hadn't thought enough to comprehend it all. Perhaps it didn't need much comprehension. Or maybe it did. But it sounded all wrong. She'd never know all the acquisition details but all she knew was that B&W was hired by Westside Capital after Harsh left the deal mid-way. The three of them working together seemed like a disaster waiting to happen. She bent down again looking for other relevant documents. Under the printer, under the desk, away from the copier, all over. There was nothing there.

How did Xiang not figure out she had stolen his paper. It hit her after a while. What she had got hold of was just the cover page. The meat of the matter was numbered. *Phew*, she breathed a sigh of relief.

Did Vivek know? Was he behind all this? Was he fooling everyone—the Rangers, her, his bosses? It just dawned on her that this was a bigger conspiracy than she could have ever imagined. Till now she had just heard people allude to IGL as dirty, foul, corrupt, etc, and never really seen that side of it. *This* changed everything . . .

She tried to gulp but her mouth had gone dry. Her head spun, thoughts hitting her faster than she could process them. Her body felt immobile. No, she must move. Put some distance between her and him.

Inserting that paper in between her pile of papers, she ran out—walking in a random direction, breathing faster, trying to come up with a plan. She needed to confide in somebody. She had to otherwise she would go mad! But who? Vivek—her supposed boyfriend who was probably behind all this? If he wasn't, he was a liar at the very least. There was no way she could trust him. The only other person would have been LHF but he was history now.

Who could she talk to about this?

Keya called, what she referred to as an 'emergency meeting' with Radhika and Kourosh at a nearby café. Generally not one to spill out work stories to friends, she had found it much too difficult to hold on to what she had discovered via Xiang's document.

She narrated what she could, dumbing down the complicated story in parts when she caught Rosh scratching his head and Rads getting busy with her compact mirror. To catch her attention, she somewhat exaggerated the bits about Vivek's alleged involvement. That startled Radhika, her expression dumbfounded.

"Oh, honey, confront the bastard," she growled. Kourosh nodded in agreement. Not that it added any additional value. Lately, Kourosh nodded his approval with pretty much everything Radhika said.

"Wait, hold on for a second, have you two been . . . *hanging out*?" Keya stared suspiciously at Radhika and Kourosh. Radhika sheepishly grinned. Kourosh did, too. The cat was out of the bag. Wow!

"Anyway, we'll talk about that later. You really should confront Vivek. Right now."

In the heat of the moment, furious, Keya dialled away.

"You really thought you could slide through this, huh? Can't believe you'd do it. I'll expose you, Vivek." She spewed fire with her opening line.

"Hello? *Keya?* What are you on about?"

"Fine. Pretend. Pretend all you want. But I know about Westside Capital and Harsh now."

"What about them?"

"Vivek, really, you don't have to act anymore."

"Just stop with your foolishness for a minute and talk sense. What the hell are you talking about?"

"Oh, you poor innocent guy. Tell me you have no idea that Harsh and Westside Capital have joined forces. That B&W has been hired by them both."

"*What?* How did you find out?"

"So it is the truth!"

"Keya, just hold onto your spiteful words and tell me the whole thing. Please. This is news to me."

"You're busted, Vivek. B&W has been hired by Harsh, isn't it?"

"What?"

"Just like you are, too."

There was silence on the line for a few moments. All she got was an audible exhalation. "Listen, I know you're mad at me. But this is important. I really have no clue."

"How do I know you're not lying again?"

"When did I lie *before*?"

She hung up the phone immediately. No confessions, no clues. It was as simple as that.

Immediately, he called her back.

"Don't hang up, Keya. There was nothing to tell."

"Likewise, then."

"Keya!"

"I'm right here."

She heard another sigh preceding brief silence. "Look, you're making a big deal out of nothing."

"Then stop calling me."

"This is absurd," she heard him mumble. "At least give me a chance to explain."

"I did. Three chances. Did you forget?"

"There was nothing to tell. I just hate being bugged with work questions when it doesn't involve you . . . I mean someone. So I ignored them. Now will you please tell me what you know about Harsh?"

What kind of an unjust rule was that, she wondered. How was he so interested in getting to the crux of Harsh's story and not even spare a thought to coming clean first? It disturbed her. For a moment, she felt completely detached from him.

"Whatever, Vivek. I don't even care anymore. If you just want to know about work stuff, fine. I found a document from Xiang Bhutia by the fax machine. It said something about mailing documents to Harsh and Westside. That's all I got."

"Documents? What documents?"

Irritated, she retorted, "I don't know. I just saw one sheet." She didn't have the nerve to tell him she stole it. Unethical as it was, she had good reason. Her intuition.

"What exactly did it say? Can you fax it to me right away? I can't even believe—this is huge if it is what I think it is." Hurried, distressed questions. She could sense his restlessness. Only if he could sense her resentment.

"I'm not mailing you anything."

"This is not the time for drama. Just please tell me what exactly did it say?"

"Get lost, Vivek. And I told you already. It was from Xiang, addressed to Harsh. It said he was sending documents to Harsh and a copy to B&W."

"God, Keya! Give me something else, this—"

"Yeah? Take this. It said: Vivek is a bloody cheat and a bloody liar." With that she hung up, tears streaming down her face.

Vivek called her incessantly but she ignored all his calls. A voicemail was what she got a little later. *I didn't mean it that way. I am sorry for acting like a heel. What I said was inexcusable. Please forgive me. Just that this is huge and I need to know everything you know to act on it. I will explain it next week.*

*Good luck finding me next week.* She texted him.

*What? Where are you going?* The war had now taken shape through texts.

Some place pure where there are no lies and deceit.

You've lost it, Keya. Call me when you calm down. You're presuming too much. And could you please leave that document from Xiang on your desk? I really need to see it.

She switched off her phone and flung it on the couch.

From his mid-twenties till now, Vivek had come a long way in his professional life. Each passing year had exposed him to more than his share of mucky situations—situations where stingy businessmen played badasses and asked for the world, and if you didn't deliver then it was your ass on the line; situations where other consultants, his colleagues, pimped out their contacts, friends, and family for more money in their accounts; situations where top entrepreneurs hid behind the veil of public-service to make a quick buck; situations where one minute the deal was on a smooth track and the next in jeopardy for no discernible reason except politics at the top level—and he had dealt with each and every deal that came his way with confidence and resilience, and emerged unscathed. He was fiercely competitive but not in the ugly way Keya had just implied. Moreover, he was not a cheat, never had been. But he just couldn't wrap his head around what was happening. Life had dealt him a double-whammy. And for once in his life Vivek Grewal didn't know what to do . . .

Nursing a glass of wine, he made his way to his joke of a balcony. His mind drifted to Keya's revelation about Harsh. The fourteenth-floor winds swept through his hair, clearing his head and helping him make sense of the obscure information that had come his way.

Could Keya be mistaken? He hadn't seen a copy of the alleged letter by B&W addressed to Harsh himself. Granted, she was mad at him but would this be a prank she played on him just to mess with his head? It didn't feel like something Keya would cook up herself.

He traced it as far back as he could. Harsh backing out half way through the deal had, certainly, made him suspicious. It was quite out of Harsh's character, at least what he knew of it, given that he had found a way to meet all his demands: the lowering of the initial offer, making Jango stay, convincing his investors to pitch in the extra money for building a capable team around Jango in the following year. Harsh's divorce alone wasn't enough to make him get out of it this way. What else could have the motive been then? And what was B&W sending him? If any relevant documentation from the process that Vivek had undergone for Harsh was missing, they should have contacted Vivek. Was B&W two-timing Harsh and Westside Capital?

He went inside, powered up his laptop, and began typing in word combinations on search engines he felt might throw up something conclusive. Nothing. Zilch. Thoughts clouded his mind, sapping all energy. He needed to be alert, awake. He stepped into the shower, relying on it to help him.

Minutes into it, he was still under the potent bout of water, his hands awaiting his brain's signal to pick up the bar of soap and start lathering. Just then an image flashed in front of him.

It was that of an older gentleman posing with Harsh. There was something about the man that had registered in his brain, while he was running an image search a while back.

Hastily, he wrapped a towel around himself and rushed out to his laptop. He ran the image search again. A few drops of water from his wet hair fell on his keyboard. With no tissues in sight, he blew some air to make them disappear. Going back and forth a few times on the image search, he ultimately stumbled upon the same picture. There was no mention of the event or of the names of anyone in the picture other than Harsh. It was a photograph of two men: Harsh on the left side of the frame with that familiar face on his right, his arm around Harsh's neck as they laughed. Vivek narrowed his eyes, willing himself to remember. Then it hit him! It was the same person he'd run into at the Independence Day event, one who was throwing a party for the actress sisters and their mother. The same guy who'd invited Vivek to his pool party and graciously offered him his swimming trunk! They'd exchanged business cards, he recalled.

He scurried to his desk and pulled out the card holder. He'd been good about sticking in all the business cards he had got over the years. You never know when you need someone, was his motto. He searched fretfully, first alphabet wise, then randomly, to look for a card with a name that he didn't recognise. When he couldn't locate it, he just groaned, half convinced that he was wasting his energy on something that didn't even seem like a clue. Perhaps it was just a hunch. But perhaps it was more. He did vaguely recall the guy talking about owning a private equity firm in Mumbai. Maybe it could lead to a clue. He must get to the bottom of it. Anyhow.

Without verbalising his doubts, Vivek put his top two people on the detective job. Satyen had been assigned Westside Capital and Omar B&W Consulting. They'd been doing the relentless digging around to catch the slightest of clues. It'd been speculations galore, for sure, but neither of them had convincingly been able to put a finger on Harsh's, B&W's, or Westside's motive.

It had crossed Vivek's mind several times to involve the Rangers' senior leadership and their legal team. But there was nothing concrete so far. The only proof he had was the single piece of document Keya had been nice enough to leave on her desk—a letter from Xiang Bhutia to Harsh. Jumping the gun would lead to no good.

Vivek was caught in limbo. Despite carefully scrutinising all documents, e-mails, and web searches on Harsh, B&W, and Westside, he had still hit nothing. He kept on looking at the same picture of Harsh and the gentleman from the Independence Day celebrations, but despite raking his mind he couldn't think of a way to reach The Schmu—. His body stilled. That was it! *The Schmuck!* Yes . . . *Mr Deshmukh*! He would definitely know!

Vivek dialled his mother's number, mentally thanking Alisha for giving this man such a nickname, else the name would have easily escaped his memory. After almost a mini-investigation, clearly dissatisfied with the answers or the lack of what he had furnished, his mother finally handed over Mr Deshmukh's number to him.

"Mr Deshmukh?" He called right away, not worrying about the in appropriateness of the hour. "This is Vivek. My mother, Mrs Pammi Grewal, had put us in touch just before the Independence Day parade. You might recall."

"Ahh . . . yes. Of course, of course. Tell me."

Vivek began the interrogation, careful about not coming across as desperate. After narrating the gentleman's physical description and a few reference points he could remember, Mr Deshmukh finally located the name.

"It sounds like you're looking for Amit Gupta."

"That name sounds familiar."

It took Mr Deshmukh another few minutes to place Amit Gupta's employment details. All he gave Vivek was a vague 'some financial company'. Then Mr Deshmukh got all suspicious and spun a web of questions around Vivek's inquiry. Vivek dodged the all-too-familiar third degree that he'd come to believe was his fellow countrymen's infamous trait.

"I really can't remember any more. I'll ask around and call you if I find something."

That was enough fodder for Vivek to begin the online search again or so he reckoned. Amit Gupta. Could it have been a more common Indian name? A million Amit Guptas showed up in the Mumbai region. After scrolling through the first few pages, he threw in the towel.

His phone rang again.

"Vivek. I have some information. Gupta Financial Investments."

"You made my day! Thank you, Mr Deshmukh," he responded, pleased with the clue that had been offered to him. "Appreciate it." He hung up and searched again. There it was. *Mr Amit Gupta. Owner, Gupta Financial Group.* A tedious, uninspiring website surfaced with a shipload of details on their business, their clients, their vision, their management team, and everything else under the sun. He clicked on the 'About Us' link. It jarred him. He saw a very familiar name, conspicuous against the dull grey background. Gupta Financial Group was listed as the subsidiary company of Westside Capital. Amit Gupta and Harsh Desai were no strangers to each other as was evident from the telling picture he had stumbled upon. *What did that mean?*

Millions of neurons were firing away in his head, presenting him with all kinds of possibilities, and none of them sounded comforting. He shook his head in denial. He could feel his pulse rising, blood rushing to his face, and his mouth going dry. Hard as he tried, he couldn't swallow. He walked back and forth from one corner to the other.

An hour later, he was convinced. This had to be the most logical reason. This was the biggest fraud he'd ever witnessed firsthand. He had got to stop this deal. In a heartbeat, he picked up his cell phone.

Vivek boarded a flight to Hyderabad the next morning and a couple of hours later, checked into a cab towards Banjara Hills, passing by hotels, ritzy restaurants, and shopping malls. Hard as he had tried, he couldn't decide on the best way to confront Harsh. In the end, he had called Harsh's office in Bengaluru, only to learn that he was working out of his Hyderabad office that week.

The taxi dropped him off outside an aesthetically appealing skyscraper that was made up entirely of stained glass. He'd spent months working in this office during one of his previous projects with Harsh, so he was familiar with every inch of it. Not waiting to check in at the front desk, Vivek walked through the corridors of Harsh's swanky office, ignoring the questioning looks from employees.

"May I help you?" he heard a female voice ask him, but disregarded it and continued walking.

Standing in front of Harsh's cabin, he pushed open the

door and barged in. Harsh was in the middle of a video conference as was evident from the large flat screen.

"Vivek," he said, startled. "What are you doing here?"

"I'm here to get some answers," Vivek said defiantly, hurling his laptop bag on the chair across from Harsh.

"What answers? I didn't know you were coming."

"You're busted, Harsh."

"What? What are you talking about? I'm in the middle of something, actually. Do you mind waiting outside?"

"I'm not going anywhere."

"What is this bullshit behaviour? It will not be tolerated in my office," Harsh warned, then glancing at the television screen where the video conference was in progress, said, "Let's catch up later, guys." He disconnected it with a remote and stood up from his chair. "What are you doing here?"

"Why did you do it, Harsh? Why did you fool me? Three fucking years of loyalty gets me *this*?" Vivek slapped the table hard.

"What crap are you saying? I don't have time for this. Go wait outside. I'll call you when I have a breather, if you're in a mood to talk in a *civilised* manner." He picked up the receiver and pressed a button. "Sheila, escort this gentleman out of my office right now."

"I am not going anywhere. I need answers. Why did you puke all over the deal? You really thought you could make it fly? It's all—"

"I don't know who's planting these insane stories in your head. I don't owe you any explanation," he raged at Vivek from around the table, his teeth gnashing, his eyes drilling into Vivek's.

Just then, the door opened and a young woman walked in.

"Sorry about that, Harsh."

"Sheila, escort him out right now."

"Sir, please—" Sheila turned to Vivek.

"Until I walked in here, I refused to believe that you could stoop so low. That you could bloody resort to insider information. All for a few bucks? Was that what this deal meant to you? I put my heart and soul into it. Eighteen fucking hours a day, for months, all I worked on was this account. Gave it the best I could. And you just crushed it? Just like that? Fucking ridiculous. It's like I don't even know you anymore."

"Sir, please—" Sheila pleaded to Vivek.

Turning to Vivek, his index finger almost in Vivek's eye, Harsh retorted, "Don't you dare raise your voice with me. I told you the divorce was costing me too much. If you can't get that straight in your shitty little brain, keep your stories to yourself. And get the hell out. Get your stinking brown ass out of my office."

"It's too late, Harsh. It's all out in the open now. Your misdeeds will be all over the papers tomorrow. I won't spare Westside and B&W, either. All three of you will go down. Mark my words."

"Shut the fuck up. Talk to me when you have proof. Sheila, call security and throw him out."

"That won't be necessary. I'm out of here. But I'll see you in court." With that he walked out, slamming the door behind him. He took the lift down to the lobby level and knocked open the main entrance door, the sides of his jacket flying as he stormed out.

As Vivek stood outside, catching his breath, his mind continued spewing thoughts one after another. This wasn't how it was supposed to pan out. Harsh was supposed to deny all the accusations. He was supposed to appear clueless, shocked. He was supposed to take interest in the matter, to help clear any misunderstandings, to provide him with some answers. Not admit sabotaging it. Not shrug it off.

Not having thought through it entirely, he was left clueless about the consequences of this unprecedented situation. He would have to quickly work out a remedy. But what could he possibly do? First things first. He needed someone to confide in. Krishnan? His boss in Mumbai? Should he be going public? Talk to the press . . . or PCCI? They'd all ask for evidence.

"Taxi," he called out, waving at a driver across the road who seemed to be looking in his direction. A few enraged steps towards the cab later, he overheard someone calling out his name.

"Wait, Vivek. Hang on." He turned around to find Harsh standing right behind him. "Let's talk."

"There is nothing left to be said," he lowered his head to see the taxi driver at eye level. "Airport?" The driver nodded in agreement. In one swift motion, Vivek entered the cab.

"Don't be so dramatic. Let's talk." Harsh grabbed the rear door.

"I think I know all that I needed to know." That was far from the truth. But he was so furious he might have kicked Harsh in the nuts for stultifying him, if it were a different setting.

"Stop being hasty," Harsh persisted. "Let's go to my office and talk."

"Look, Harsh, unless there's going to be a revelation, I really don't—"

"Calm down. Come."

Vivek threw him a sceptical look, but that did nothing to disrupt Harsh's composure.

"*Arre aaja yaar. Itna mat soch.* Come," Harsh commanded with a hand gesture.

With eyes clouded with mistrust, Vivek followed him. Both carefully avoided each other's gaze in the lift. A sinister kind of silence befell, making Vivek tap his feet and blink repeatedly. From the corner of his eyes, he checked out Harsh's body language for clues, but there wasn't a hint. Appearing calm and relaxed, Harsh lit a cigarette. Then he walked to his office, occupied his plush executive chair, picked up the phone and instructed his secretary to not let any calls through.

"Sit. Tell me what's bothering you," he demanded unflappably, his face resting in the curve of his palm. That whipped Vivek into a frenzy.

"I'm not starting from scratch. Either you fill me in or I'm out of here." He meant it.

Harsh sat in his chair, blowing smoke rings into the air. He threw Vivek a curve ball by avoiding the issue.

"You're a good guy, Vivek. I like you. Always have. But you're young. The world is a strange place. And you—"

"Harsh, let's leave the philosophy for a rainy day. Talk about Westside and B&W."

"What about them?"

"All right. You know what? I'm out of here." He had run out of patience.

"You're overreacting, man. I'm just asking what you know." Harsh shrugged, raising an eyebrow, pursing his lips.

"I have a copy of a letter from Xiang Bhutia to you," he baited, his stance firm and expression dangerous.

That caught Harsh completely off guard. His face turned pale, colour draining from it completely. Vivek sneered. He was sick to his stomach with all of Harsh's despicable antics, so much so that it made him want to retch.

They stared at each other in silent acknowledgement, distaste, and disgust. Vivek was spoiling for a showdown.

"So? I-I-I had left behind something that I needed and . . . and I wasn't aware you still worked for the Rangers. Yes!"

Vivek folded his hands across his chest, waiting for a better alibi to surface. He cocked his one brow up at him. Harsh looked away for a moment. Apparently having decided on something, he glided closer to him and bent his head to lean in closer.

"Here's the deal. I'll give you the details and reward you for safeguarding them."

"Really?" A nerve ticked in Vivek's jaw.

Harsh smiled a saccharine smile. "I'll make you an offer you can't refuse. But before I proceed, I want confirmation that you'll be there for me."

"Haven't I always been?" Vivek asked in lieu of an answer.

"Yes, yes. You are right. I shouldn't have kept this from you. It's all water under the bridge, right? Happens. The best of us make mistakes. I want to give you something. A crore sounds like a good idea? I'll send over that little gift to your apartment tomorrow. You bury this whole thing, cover it up, and we'll call it—"

That shook Vivek right up. "Harsh, you're wasting time, yours and mine."

The sickeningly sweet smile erased off Harsh's face and something disturbingly menacing replaced it.

"Don't play with fire, Vivek. You don't know how well-connected I am. Take the money and stay quiet."

Vivek let out a yawn, stretched his limbs, and cracked his neck.

Harsh glowered, his eyes seeming to pop out of his sockets.

"I am waiting for you to realise Mr Harsh Desai that you do not have a bloody fucking option left. That letter was only the beginning."

"Talking in threat-speak? Who else knows about this?"

"Pretty soon everyone will."

Silence followed. Harsh was vigorously rubbing his forehead with his fingers.

"Okay, how about two crores? Five?"

"Are you serious?" Vivek growled, narrowing his eyes in disbelief. "You—I'm not here to—you don't know me at all, Harsh. After working together for years, you still don't know me. It's a shame, really."

"Think about this rationally. It doesn't matter what you know. Pretend it doesn't exist. Take the money. I know how hard you work for a good life," Harsh said with conviction.

"I'm done here." Saying this he got up. Harsh, too, jumped out of his seat.

"What are you going to do? Talk to the media? My connections are stronger that you'd ever know," he said shouting at him. Spit flew from his mouth, his face blood red.

"You still don't get it, do you? I don't care how strong your connections are. I don't care that you have enough money to silence the entire media. I'm here because I wanted to see it to believe it. You shouldn't have betrayed me, Harsh. I'll never let you forget that." With that he walked out.

"You're making a big mistake."

"Fuck you, Harsh."

Vivek checked into a taxi and left for the airport. The adrenaline that had been pumping through his veins a few minutes back was now subsiding, bringing in its wake a sweeping realisation of his foolhardiness. If he knew anything about Harsh, it was that his words weren't meant to be taken lightly. And his threats even less so. At the end of it all, he felt like a fool. Why did he have to confront him this way? What was he expecting Harsh to do? Own up to it all or shirk it entirely? It wasn't like he himself had a plan. It was just a knee-jerk reaction that had compelled him to travel to Hyderabad for the face-off. There hadn't much time for thoughts, he had to let it out.

But what now? He had to choose wisely. After reflecting on it for a while, he decided it was time to let Krishnan know. But before that, he had to make another call.

"Omar, do you remember that sports journalist who wore long kurtas? That lanky bugger who followed me around in Ahmedabad during the initial part of the deal? Shailendra something? He is with Ahmedabad Chronicle. Find his number and call me right away. It's extremely urgent."

Omar called him back within minutes, providing him with all that was asked from him. Not wasting any further time, Vivek gave a detailed account to Shailendra through the hour-long drive to the airport with the assurance of it showing up the next morning without any red tape or other political issues. He relayed the details to Krishnan immediately after.

Vivek felt slightly relieved and a bit in control when he reached the airport. He now had a plan. It may not have been the best plan but he had a plan. Ideally, he should have had this discussion with a few people in the hierarchy above Shailendra. But, it was done now.

His taxi pulled up in front of the Rajiv Gandhi International Airport in Hyderabad.

"Crazy traffic. Is it always so bad?" Vivek made small talk with the cab driver.

"*Kaadu, sir. Pradhana Mantrigaru evala vusthunaru. Anduke ee hadavidi.*"

"Huh?"

"Prime Minister coming, sir. Many police here."

After much honking and swerving, the cabbie found just enough room to squeeze in and drop him off by the curb. The long queue of people by the airport entrance frustrated him, but then his flight wasn't until much later, so he wasn't really that bothered. He went and stood at the end of the line.

He was busy texting Omar back and forth when he felt something hard thrust against the lower right part of his waist. He was about to turn around to tell the person behind him to mind himself, when he heard a harsh voice whispering in his ear, "*Peeche mat dekh.* Parking lot *ki taraf chalna shuru kar.*" Immediately, it dawned on him that he was surrounded by at least three people, possibly more, who were all tough-looking, forceful, and were pushing him without being too conspicuous about it.

"What a bummer that they don't speak English over here. At all," Radhika complained to Rosh, after unsuccessfully asking a little shopkeeper boy for a bikini top with extra padding, her hand gestures eliciting a laugh from the boy and his friends. "And where are all the Brazilian supermodels they keep boasting about? Haven't spotted one since we landed."

Keya smiled at Radhika's reaction. They had been in São Paulo for a week now and heard this on a daily basis from Rads. When the three of them had landed here, Keya was the only one who had felt a prickle of disappointment. The city seemed to be a concrete jungle, not what she had expected.

The visitor guide she'd yanked out from her suitcase immediately after being seated in the taxi told her that it was one of the largest cities in the world. She could feel the enormity as they drove through barren land at first and then through a sprawling city. There were crumbled houses in myriad colours, messed up construction sites, and clothes hung to dry in the balconies of high rises. The skyscrapers made it seem Mumbai-like, difficult to spot where downtown was. As the cab whisked away the three of them from the airport to the heart of the city, Keya's eyes had begun sparkling in wonder.

She noticed that Radhika had focused her energy on shopping and nightlife, dragging an unsuspecting Kourosh along with her. Privy to Radhika's intentions in regards to Kourosh, Keya found solace in the fact that he was only unsuspecting, not unwilling. It was the perfect little arrangement. She was a sexy kitten and he a lovelorn victim. It left her with plenty of time to explore, to detoxify her life, and absorb the vivacity around her.

She chose to take off early in the mornings, while Radhika and Rosh were still asleep, walking through the city, looking around, soaking it in. The locals seemed to be a warm lot so just a few words in their lingo did the trick. The weather was splendid; warm and humid, just the way she liked it. Work, Vivek, and other testing issues seemed like a distant memory already. A café, a lemon tree, the porch of a museum; no place was too foreign to set up base and scribble the musings of the day. Satisfying and liberating, it brought her tremendous joy.

They travelled to Rio, feasted their eyes on the Christ The Redeemer statue, sunned themselves on the world-renowned Copacabana beach, and had an enjoyable time everywhere. Swimming in the bluest waters with the hottest bodies in the warmest weather is a sin one must commit, she later wrote in her book.

"What's on the laundry list for today?" Keya asked Radhika as the girls took a break to drink some coconut water from a roadside stall after an early morning jog.

"I'm going to propose to Kourosh," Radhika anounced with élan.

"Woo. I'm so stoked." Keya's eyes widened with excitement. "Let me feed you the right words. For utmost impact, ask, *you will marry me, yes*?"

"Propose is a wrong word. I'm going to confess. That I might be falling for him."

"You're going to tell a guy that you *might be* falling for him?"

"Not just that. I also wanted to gauge his feelings for me. Actually, not gauge. I want to know for sure."

"Radhika, my love, your mind is all over the place this morning. Why don't you first figure out what it is that you really want to discuss?"

"You think he likes me?"

"I can't tell if he's smitten but he does seem to admire you."

"Do you think he still has feelings for you?" Radhika posed a hard question.

"Nah. I don't—he didn't—actually, I'm pretty certain he's moved on. It has come up a few times, inadvertently. He said he's happy for me."

"Okay, *pheeeew*. I'll have to think about this."

"But wait, is he really the guy for you? He's younger and he'd disqualify on most of your prerequisites. Where's that list you bump all the suitors against?"

"I know," Radhika agreed, oblivious to the mischief in Keya's eyes. "I've finally come to terms with the fact that if I go around with that list stapled to my forehead, I'll be waiting for eons. My new strategy is to go with what feels right in my heart. I like Kourosh. I really do, Keya. He's so honest. So genuine. So caring. And ridiculously cute. We'll see how it goes in the end. But I must give love a chance."

Those words infused delight in Keya's heart. Those were the exact same things she'd said in Kourosh's praise when she'd become acquainted with him. Two women, one opinion. Rare as fitted hats.

"Okay but don't ask him before the Carnival tonight," she instructed. The exuberant festivities centred around the eminent Brazilian carnival were to commence that evening and they'd bought expensive tickets for the opening night. "Just being a little self-centred here but God forbid any of you end up being hurt after that talk, our Samba plans will be ruined. Please?"

"You're a nut."

The Carnival marked the highlight of Keya's trip so far. Hundreds of majestic floats, samba dancers of all ages in creative costumes, topless beauty queens with glamorous feather wings, and sparkling heels preceded every float. It was all about celebrating the spirit of the people, she learned. A spirit that lingered on in the air even after the carnival was long over. A spirit that was so contagious that one couldn't help but get painted in. A spirit she wanted to put in a bottle and take back home with her.

With a heavy heart, they wrapped up Brazil and reached Iguazu Falls in Argentina. There weren't many things that could have made this vacation any more phenomenal for her than what it already was. Perhaps her family's presence, if they could have made it. And Vivek. She had been consciously ignoring his memories that popped in her head time and again, the twitch in her heart that made her shudder, and the fear of a lonely future. No negative feelings, she'd promised herself on the onset of the journey. So she pretended as if none of that pain existed.

Days later, on the Beagle Channel, surrounded by water, sky, and mountains, in the beach town of Ushuaia which was the closest city to Antarctica and called itself the 'End of the World', Keya, beaming with pride and delight, reached the end of her travelogue. It transported her to a bubble of bliss. Nothing else seemed to matter for the time being. A long-cherished dream had rewardingly culminated . . . Seated on the therapeutic sands of the beach, dressed in a bikini top and shorts, she threw both her arms up in the air, faced the sky, and took a deep breath of the balmy ocean air. And then let out a liberating scream and spent the day indulging in little treats like massages and cappuccinos.

This trip had done more than putting the ugliness with Vivek behind her. It had provided her with the much needed food for the soul. It wasn't just about the beaches and palm trees and coconuts and the lingering fragrance of orchids in the air. More than anything, she had been able to re-establish a connection with herself. The peace, the calm, the fulfilment of a life not defined by professional failures or personal relationships but brought about by indulging in the little joys of life. It had made her grasp that what she was after during the onset of the journey was merely a consequence now. What she had gained in addition to that was incomparable. Truly satisfying. And with any luck, long-lasting.

***

Her body ached, her head throbbed, but she had never felt this good in a long, long time; maybe years. "Heck. Maybe never," Keya said out aloud and giggled.

It was a Monday night and she had just returned from a remarkably indulgent three-week trip to a depressingly rainy day in the city. But there was sunshine in her heart. Clichéd but true. It seemed like an era had passed her by. She cranked up the air conditioner in her apartment and settled into her couch. The tags on her wet bags that read EZE -> AMD were gawking at her. Mocking her, or so she felt. Sleep was all that was on her mind, but she couldn't sleep. Maybe if she picked herself up and carried herself to her bedroom . . . Right then her bell rang, jarringly so.

As she peeked through the keyhole, an all-too-familiar face looked back at her, astounding her into inaction. It wasn't something she had expected, which was saying a lot considering she prided herself on having a fertile imagination. It was a very wet Vivek with anticipation sketched on his forehead. She narrowed her eyes to get a closer look. It drove away all speculations that this might be an illusion. *What on earth*, she muttered, *I don't want him here.* She shuddered, motionless, feeling infuriated. The door bell rang again. She opened the door passively.

"Hi," he said, exploiting the pièce de résistance that his smile was. Holding an exquisite bouquet of red roses, he stood, dressed in a dark suit, dripping from head to toe, his wet hair accentuating his face and making him look savagely gorgeous in the bargain. But . . . *scars* ran deep on his forehead, right cheek, and below his lower lip. There was also a beige sling over his left hand. It was hard to gauge how long the sling ran. His suit seemed oversized so as to cover it up.

"These are for you," he said, extending the roses to her with one hand, breaking Keya out of her trance-like state.

"Sorry, I'm a mess. Didn't know the rain would come down so hard."

She blinked a few times, feeling mentally paralysed, her hand mechanically reaching out to accept the flowers. It seemed too surreal to be true. The image which had flashed in her head countless times—her ultimate fantasy—of him standing on the side of a street with a bouquet of roses sans an umbrella waiting for her in the dark, while it rained pitchforks and hammer handles, had come to life! Serendipity, she was certain; but it made her heart flip.

"What are those bruises on your face? What—how did—is everything okay?"

"Yeah, I just tripped over the stairs at the gym. Nothing serious."

She contemplated over his answer for a brief moment, then asked, "What are you doing here?"

"Why didn't you tell me you were going to South America? I learnt from the office couple of weeks back. Tried calling you several times before they told me. Guess you hadn't turned on the international service."

"Vivek, what are you doing *here*?" She rebuked this time. The aversion in her voice evident.

"Can I come in? Please?"

"Look, I just returned from my trip. I'm dead tired. Can we talk tomorrow?" She only had enough energy left to silence the loud thumping sensation in her heart, not enough to sit through his reasoning.

"I'll be quick, I promise."

"Not right now, Vivek." She banged the door hard on him. She heard a few knocks but resisted.

***

Soaked, somewhat defeated, Vivek leaned against the stained wall outside Keya's door. He was more resilient than she credited him to be. He wouldn't leave just because she threw him out. But he didn't necessarily feel the need to push her on it. If she wanted some breathing time, he was going to have to give it to her. He turned his face to look out at the darkness through the circular opening in the wall and felt uneasy. It was as if water was stagnant in his right ear. He moved his head back and forth as he tilted it, tugging on the earlobe so as to open the canal wider, and then tapped the opposite temple with his wrist. A few tiny drops trickling out through the right ear brought some relief. Then he leaned against the wall and banged the back of his head softly but repeatedly against it. The way his life had changed in the past few weeks had been too unsettling. He hadn't been able to wipe away those memories.

His eyes closed at the recollection of that wretched afternoon.

***

When she felt slight remorse for slamming the door on Vivek, Keya pushed herself to rise from the couch and walk towards it. She glared through the peephole, standing on her toes to get a better vantage point, looking over the stairs, then on the other side, but there wasn't anyone in sight. Her forehead creased at the possibility of him taking off. *Couldn't he have attempted truce again?* Abruptly, Vivek appeared in the peephole view, disorienting her. He knocked gently, his fingers running through his wet hair causing a few droplets to roll down his face. She opened the door reluctantly.

"Keya, two minutes? Please?"

She raised her eyebrows and threw her hands up in the

air as a sign of mild protest. Physical proximity with him had tremendous power over her, much like a tiny sail boat struggling to hold its own against a mid-ocean storm. Unconvinced about her own possible reactions, she turned around and began walking towards the kitchen.

He eased himself in, from what she saw through the corner of her eye. He didn't follow her or pull her towards him or anything else for that matter. He just stood there, making a small pool around him.

"Would you just hear me out?"

She found the farthest wall from him and leaned against it just to symbolise what she was feeling. He seemed respectful of that.

"You probably haven't read any Indian newspapers on your trip. A lot has happened in the past three weeks," he began. "Cannot thank you enough for tipping me off about Harsh." He'd taken her silence for an affirmative response.

A clueless expression was all she could manage.

"Actually, Keya, I am still stumped. You are the only one I am owning this to. Harsh! I've known the guy forever—and for him to do this—just didn't seem real, you know? Never saw it coming."

"Can you not look so tortured and just tell me plainly what he did?"

Vivek looked mildly taken aback. "He partnered with Westside Capital. Such a fuckball. Bloody skunk."

"I don't get it."

"That conniving bastard left the Rangers deal mid-way, deliberately, hooked up with Westside, and got them to put in an offer on the Rangers independently. Westside was paying less for Rangers than Harsh had offered. It was actually way lower than Harsh's initial offer. He got a huge cut out of this."

"Wow! That's . . . that's serious fraud. Why did he need to stoop so low, but? Wasn't he a gazillionaire or something?"

"He was certainly pretending to be one and doing a good job of it. He'd backed out on the grounds of his wife thwacking him with a massive divorce settlement. He used the legal mess excuse that would ensure a harmless exit from the deal. Turned out he'd planted that story in the media himself."

"He *forged* it? Really?"

"Believe it! What has come to light now is that he'd done some reckless deals and owed big money to investors. It was one nasty game he played. Gave insider information on the Rangers in return for a fat cut from Westside Capital and also got a stake in the Rangers via the same deal but through one of their subsidiaries—Gupta Financial Investments. Anyway, the Rangers have filed a lawsuit against him. He'll have to testify. The lawsuit is against B&W Consulting as well. They are neck deep in this shit."

"Is there evidence against him?"

"Yes. All because of you! Thanks for leaving the proof on your desk by the way." He grinned.

"What proof?"

"That sheet from Xiang Bhutia. When the Rangers fired B&W and took legal action, B&W changed their story and claimed not having known that Harsh was a prior buyer. They maintain that they assumed Harsh was a partner in Westside Capital. Completely preposterous."

"Wait, was that enough proof?"

"No, but it was a start. The lawsuit details are out in the open now and Harsh has been all over the newspapers. There's intense scrutiny going on with all three firms. If convicted, it's going to be a few memorable years in jail. It'll take some time. For now, Westside Capital is out."

"That's unreal. What happens to the deal now?" She was doing her best to absorb all the details.

"The upside is, since there has been so much media coverage, there has been some interest from other investors. It's a deal from hell, if you ask me. But there are a few things in the pipeline."

"What about you? Did you get dragged in because of Harsh?"

"Ha, he'd love that, wouldn't he? I'm safe," he assured, nodding his head.

There was an awkward silence. She wasn't sure if she entirely believed the story. Harsh's story was probably the least relevant to her. Big deal that Vivek was innocent in that matter. Good that he wasn't a cheat, but what about other things? Things that mattered for both of them, *if* there was to be a 'both of them', her devilish mind corrected. She wasn't even sure she wanted to hear him out. On one hand, she was dying to know his justification. But on the other, she knew if she heard it, he'd make her believe it. She was sure he would have a perfectly valid-sounding reason for everything. He was a consultant and a pretty good one at that. *Why couldn't she hold her own with him around?*

"One down; I owe you one more," he said with frayed enthusiasm.

Keya freaked momentarily. He was getting better at reading her mind.

"You want some coffee and a towel perhaps?"

She sat on the couch holding a couple of cushions, her

hand running through the brand new bangs she had got herself in São Paulo. He sat on the tiled floor, few feet away from her, next to the lit candles that lent him an orange glow. It was not just the candle wicks burning in the room that night.

He looked washed-out as if he'd been splashed with disappointment. She wanted to sympathise with him but all she could think about was her skull-splitting headache. The sleepless flight and one too many explanations from Vivek were unsettling. Was he an honest guy? Or a flaky guy with shades of honesty? Could her future with him be anything better than bleak? Will they ever be able to re-ignite their love or will a solitary life engulf her? It all seemed too complicated to be figured out right then and there. All she wanted was a shower and a nap.

"So, what do you think?" Vivek seemed eager to make up.

"Is that all?"

He looked away for a bit, then nodded.

"I probably have bluffed my way through harmless little experiences and deals on the professional front. It's nothing out of the ordinary though. Everyone in the business does it. Ultimately, it's not those things that get you your way. They merely act as a starting point, sometimes as a catalyst. It's what you build on it that cou—."

"I am not talking about business. I am talking about things at a very personal level. And even if we have to talk about work, then Vivek, I don't understand all this. I'm a very black and white kind of a person. From where I see it, either you're honest or you're not."

"Keya, please."

"I need time to think."

"Don't say that."

"We're two conflicting personalities. And if there is going to be something, it'll be long distance now. I don't know if we can—"

"You're too precious for me to lose. And I'm willing to do what it takes."

"For instance?" She was not taking anything at face value, anymore.

"Like cleaning up my act."

"Vivek, we could talk in circles all night and have nothing come out of it."

"What if I gave you a specific plan?"

"I guess I'll have to hear it."

"Okay. Here's the deal. You'll probably be tempted to think that I'm making this up. But it's genuine, one hundred percent. There have been several talks within my firm about having presence in Gujarat. It's the kind of idea that got tossed around in every bi-annual all-hands meeting. Nothing ever came out of it mainly because there was no one from the senior leadership team who wanted to shift base and set it up. But there's someone from the senior leadership who's just had a change of heart."

"Nothing promising so far." She shrugged.

He placed his hand over hers, leaned in, and said, "I'm not done talking yet. So someone's had a change of heart. And he is going to push this through—get his ass over to this city and set up a new office. That way, he could be closer to . . . this girl." He let a beat pass before he put his arms around her neck and asked, "Sounds like a good idea?"

It took a while to sink in. He'd said a lot, but still not the one thing she wanted to hear. She knew for sure now that he felt it. But couldn't he just say it already! "All that sounds too easy and convenient, much like an empty promise."

"He'll make it happen. You will just have trust him on this one."

"And just who is this elusive guy you keep referring to?"

"Someone who loves you, immensely." His forehead lightly brushed against hers. His breath was on her now. He'd been dry for hours but she could smell the rain on him.

"I don't know what to say."

"Say yes."

"Being cheesy, are we?" She scoffed out of semi-frustration.

"Only the truth."

She looked away.

"I'm not trying to be a smart aleck, just trying to lighten up your mood. I'm well aware of the distress I've caused you. And I'm deeply sorry about that, Keya. But that was my past. Do you remember I told you once that you make me want to be a better person? You really do. I'm willing to do what it takes. Give me a few months. I'll make it happen. I just need one chance. Just one. And I need you to be by my side."

"I'm not sur—"

"Don't say that. Give me a chance to redeem myself. I won't fuck this up."

He squeezed her hand gently. She looked at his face. For once, she saw sincerity gleaming on it. And love. She didn't have the heart to turn him down. Not after what he had promised.

"Forgive me, please."

Tears escaped her eyes and rolled down her cheeks. Words failed her. She nodded, her eyes blinking, her lips quivering.

"Actually, before you forgive me I have one more confession."

"Vivek!" she shrieked, "Haven't you hurt me enough?"

"During the first round of evaluations, I-I don't know how else to say this—I had included you in the 'pink slip' group. But it had nothing to do with your expertise or experience. It was just based on my interpretation of everyone's job functions."

She cupped her mouth, utterly shocked. It took her a while to respond.

"Based on your interpretation of my job function? Did you even—" Could he have been any more insulting? She always knew this at some level but she wasn't prepared to have this discussion with him.

"But here's the truth. I wasn't the one who got you laid off. In my defence, I didn't even know you then. Then Aman offered to be laid-off and I thought you were saved."

"Then why didn't he? I don't understand."

"It's a long story. I thought you were safe. But Krishnan had other plans. Aman and he had been working together for years."

A deep cleansing breath. It did nothing for her.

"Honest to God, it had nothing to do with you. It's just the nature of my business. But ultimately I wasn't responsible for firing you. I know that's what you thought all this time."

She involuntarily bit the inside of her lower right lip so hard, she could almost taste blood.

"Say something, Keya."

She attempted to swallow her hurt pride. It wasn't his fault, she knew that. But the embarrassment of being picked to be laid-off by the man she considered her life, impounded her. The only saving grace was that she had got her job back on her own terms.

"Vivek, if you did me a favour and saved my job, please tell me now."

"I swear I didn't do anyone any favours. Feel free to check with Aman."

She had lost all energy to process information. She'd just have to take it at face value for now and later find a way to get it out of her system.

"I'm going to make some Maggi," she said an indefinite amount of time later to divert her mind off it. With any luck, Maggi would alleviate much more than hunger.

***

Vivek mulled over the fact that Keya had brought up 'honesty' way too many times. It was a loaded term as far as he was concerned. He'd initially planned on telling her about what had happened between him and Harsh. That Harsh had sent goons who had captured him while he was waiting at the Hyderabad airport and beat him up brutally in the parking lot. That they'd taken away all his belongings . . . his laptop, his phone, his wallet. That without uttering a word, it was made clear to him that Harsh was not to be messed with. That it was by sheer luck that there had been increased security due to the Prime Minister's visit to Hyderabad that afternoon and some cops had come to his rescue. That he had spent a night in a hospital near the airport and his wounds had bled profusely for days. That he couldn't move for a week and was left to suffer a hairline fracture in his left elbow. That he had to ask for police protection thereafter when he returned to Mumbai. If he told her all that, she might feel sorry for him and forgive him for the wrong reasons. He wanted her to be fair. For once, he wanted to have her ideals.

The only saving grace had been that Ahmedabad Chronicle

had carried an extensive coverage on Harsh's misdeeds and the other papers had been quick to follow suit.

***

It'd been hours into the truce process. Vivek had been talking and she had been listening.

"Won't leave me, will you?"

After much contemplation, she didn't resist shaking her head in affirmation. She had got to give this beautiful liar a chance.

"Thank you." He squeezed her with one arm so tight she could barely breathe. "I love you, Keya. I love you so much." Magic words, she thought.

"Oh my, this cast runs all along your hand! What—"

"Yeah, it's nothing."

She stroked it gently. The warmth of his hug stripped her of her anxieties and uneasiness and surprisingly, for a split second, she experienced inexistence. It was as if she wasn't a separate entity any longer. His actions leading up to their issues now seemed organic, his efforts to pacify her seemed earnest, his apologies seemed sincere and heartfelt and his love—his love for her seemed unfeigned. Unadulterated. Unembellished. Just the way she liked it. She had moved over to the other side. There was nothing else left to be said. They'd said it all. There were only assorted emotions to be felt. At some point in this space-time continuum, he pulled her away and said, "Will you go shopping with me?"

"Shopping?" she asked in a voice not her own, the lump in her throat still hard.

"I need to buy a ring. Need a woman's perspective."

It better not be what she thought it was. They weren't there yet. Not after what had just transpired.

"Scarlett's getting engaged," he added to clear the air.

Her heart smiled, a first in days as she hugged him again. Moments quickly dissolved, an eternity passing before either of them felt the need to tear apart from each other. Her eyes opened, the euphoric embrace pre-empted by the chirping of a bird on her window. The view outside the window caught her attention. The soft light of dawn had eventuated in the pink-blue sky. They'd made it through the stormy night. The rain had ceased to exist. Everything, tangible and otherwise, suddenly seemed clear. Unmistakable. Bright. It was a new life, bursting with promises.

"You're on probation starting now and you have six months to fix yourself," she declared playfully.

# EPILOGUE

After an extensive probe by the governing council of the PCCI, a judge in a special court convicted Harsh Desai of four criminal counts including making false statements, conspiracy, obstruction of justice, and misappropriation. Harsh was sentenced to five months in prison and two years probation for his unlawful acts.

Westside Capital was convicted on similar counts and was criminally prosecuted. A senior partner involved in the Rangers acquisition was sentenced to three months in prison and had to pay punitive damages to the Rangers.

The jury was still out on Amit Gupta.

B&W Consulting was convicted of facilitating misappropriation, and Xiang Bhutia served a two-month jail sentence. A separate civil lawsuit found B&W guilty of several employment malpractices.

With all the press about the Rangers, several sources of funding surfaced. Eventually, it was acquired by a Mumbai-based investor who had just sold his stake in another IGL team. Jango was acquired by the Delhi team in the 2013 auction. The new owner of the Rangers sourced good talent and built a promising team, paving way for the Rangers to finally make it to the playoffs a few seasons later.

Keya is still with the firm and now works as a Marketing Director. She also got a coffee-table version of her travelogue printed, just for herself, complete with all the pictures taken by her and her photographer friend from her previous visits to South America. The book serves as a great conversation starter for guests in her cosy apartment, lighting up her eyes each time she sees it. A sense of pride and delight was all she ever wanted out of it.

After a year of dating, Radhika and Kourosh called it quits. Radhika is happily married to a businessman from Delhi who splits his time between India and the US, giving her plenty of time to be married-but-single and utterly eccentric. Kourosh still lives next-door to Keya, and in addition to working for a local designer, he volunteers at the Parsi Community Centre of Ahmedabad, organising social events geared towards preserving their culture. He's dating a young Parsi dancer who trains at the centre.

It took Vivek about a year but he set up an office in Ahmedabad to establish his firm's presence in the lucrative Gujarat market. Omar and Scarlett moved along with him. It was going all too smooth between Vivek and Keya until he broke the news about his decision to marry Keya to his mother. The wedding drama in the Grewal household has just commenced, driving Vivek insane every step of the way.

# FiNGERPRINT! DIARIES

| Author | Parinda Joshi |
|---|---|
| Date of Birth | 26th March |
| Sun sign | I'm the overfriendly Arian they warn you about |
| Hometown | The heart of Gujjuland, Ahmedabad |

# The Author

Parinda Joshi is the author of *Live from London* (Rupa & Co, 2011). She blogs for *GQ* (India) magazine and has contributed to *The South Asian Times,* a New York-based publication.

She is from Ahmedabad and resides in Los Angeles, where she works as Director, Business Intelligence and Analytics, for a music and sports promotions firm. She holds a Master's in Computer Science and an MBA in Marketing.

A national-level chess player, Parinda has won many accolades, including the Gujarat State Women's Chess Champion award at the age of sixteen. In her free time, she indulges in professional and recreational photography, shooting small-scale weddings and events.

She is married with a daughter.

---

## Favourites:

**Movie:** Based on the number of times I've watched them, it'd have to be a tie between *You've Got Mail* (please don't judge me) and *Silsila*

**Drink:** Coffee (regularly) and Mimosas (occasionally, to detox)

**Fictional character:** Dilbert

# In Conversation

**What was the first book you ever read? Who introduced you to it?**

The earliest recollection I have is of a few *Nancy Drew*, *Famous Five*, and *Trixie Belden* books. My mom used to get them from the next-door book/movie rental shop that doubled up as a beauty parlour.

**Is there a book which you wish you had written?**

*Up in the Air*. That way I could be the brilliant author of the book whose movie adaptation George Clooney acted in!

**Is there a book that instantly put you to sleep?**

Yes, several. I have the attention span of a gnat, so if the book loses me in the first chapter, I somehow end up losing it, unintentionally, of course. I still haven't managed to finish reading *Unaccustomed Earth* and *The Inscrutable Americans*.

---

**Author:** One for each day of the week—John Grisham, Chuck Palahniuk, Upamanyu Chatterjee, Murakami, Sophie Kinsella, Anurag Mathur, and Stephen McCauley

**Book:** *The Accidental Tourist*

**Quote:** 'A body of clay, a mind full of play, a moment's life; that is me'

**Have you ever read or seen yourself as character in a book or a movie?**

Yes, I'd kill to be a Woody Allen heroine.

**Are the names of the characters in your book important to you?**

Definitely, in the ones I read and write. For instance, when a novel starts with a protagonist by the name of Tattamagouche, you know you're in for an entertaining ride. When I am writing, I continue to look for names until it feels right and fits. I prowl through the Internet and/or rack my brain to recall unusual names of people I have met. *Powerplay* has some interesting character names, as well. There's Kourosh, Khumalo, and Keya. My previous novel had an Indo-Canadian character called Nick Navjot Chapman.

**What is the most blatant lie you have ever told?**

I once told a kid on my flight that Robert Pattinson is actually half-Indian and my first cousin. I think he bought it.

**What's the oddest place where inspiration has struck you?**

Inspiration for me is that elusive friend who only calls you when you can't answer. Like when I'm going through security check at the airport, in a swimming pool, or out on a bike ride with my kid. It has the worst timing as far as I'm concerned, since most times I can't recall it later.

**How did you come up with the idea for writing *Powerplay*?**

I believe it was at a Dodgers game (major league baseball team). The team had been undergoing a period of turmoil in management and had just filed for bankruptcy.

**What was the most challenging part in this book for you as a writer?**

To keep those alluring detours that hit me in the form of sub-plots at bay and focus on the central story line.

**What would the last line of your autobiography be?**

Perhaps something like, 'It was time to start over. Again.' If this is a trick question, let me add that I do not intend to pen an autobiography ever.

**What are you working on next?**

It's a thriller that involves chasing the bad guys, endlessly. Shocker, right?

# Acknowledgments

I'm immensely grateful to my writers' group, 16 eyes, for the kindness and criticism I received while writing this book. It has significantly enriched my perception of creative writing.

Special thanks to:

Varun, for all the good times, for always being there, and for the guidance and pointers;

Siah, for being the perpetual joy in my heart;

Brig HC Joshi, for sharing his passion for cricket with me;

Bruce Shigeura, for his unwavering confidence in me (even when mine was shaky) and for the brilliant insights;

Kusha Shukla, for all the backing, earnestness, laughter, and for always showing me a silver lining;

Pramit Ghosh, for the invaluable feedback.

I'm especially appreciative of my near and extended family and friends for their eternal love and support. To them, I remain forever indebted.

This book wouldn't exist without the vision of my commissioning editor, Arcopol Chaudhuri, who told me to start over and then guided me till the end. My sincere gratitude to him.

I'm very grateful to my terrific editor, Pooja Dadwal, for her belief in this book and for her scrutiny and expert editing. The gruelling process wouldn't have been half as much gratifying if not for her.

Finally, I'd like to thank Fingerprint! Publishing for adding this book to its catalogue, and to its entire team for all their hard work and effort.